THE L

The Fantasy League

MEG READING

Edit and Proofread by My Brother's Editor

Cover Design by Cover Ever After

To Natalie,
If soulmates are real, you are unequivocally mine.

ONE

SCARLETT

I'D BEEN CAUGHT RED-HANDED.

The pool house door creaked open and closed in the distance, and heels clanked against the hardwood floor, making their way toward where I was standing in the kitchen.

Click-clack.

Click-clack.

"Have you ever been so in love you couldn't breathe?" the male narrator's voice boomed from my computer speakers.

"Scarlett, I swear to fucking God! If you're listening to those cheesy romance novels again, I'm going to throw you *and* your computer into the pool," Mae called down the hall to me. The sound of her heels quickening their pace drowned out the sound of the latest audiobook I was listening to.

No, no, no. Not again.

There was absolutely no way that I was going to be able to set down the pan in my hands, take off my oven mitts, *and* dive for my computer before she made it to me.

Shit.

In my peripheral vision, I saw Mae turn the corner and charge her way past me, swiping my laptop off the island and dramatically slamming it shut. "You've got to be kidding me." Her lips pressed together in a tight line and her eyebrows raised an inch on her forehead. I didn't tell her that though. If I had, I had no doubt she would've booked an emergency Botox appointment with her dermatologist. "You're already on what, your fourth book boyfriend this month?"

She said that like it was a bad thing.

And... it was the fifth, but who was counting?

I didn't know there was a problem with having *too many* book boyfriends. So what if I coped with my lack of a love life by living vicariously through fictional characters?

There were worse crimes.

"Put it down!" I shouted, setting down the pan in my hands onto a trivet before attempting to grab my laptop, which was now raised over Mae's head, with oven-mitt-covered hands. I refused to let the fact that she stood well over six feet in her red-bottom stilettos stop me.

"Fine." I ignored her eye roll as she reluctantly handed over my beloved laptop. Walking over to the opposite side of the kitchen, she opened the utensil drawer and pulled out two forks. "Scarlett, babe. I say this with love, but we need to get you laid." The disappointed look she threw my way while she plopped down onto the barstool directly across from me didn't go unnoticed.

Over the last twenty-four years, I'd mastered the art of deciphering Mae's microexpressions. The look she was giving me right now might've fazed those who didn't know her well, but I'd gotten this look precisely once a day for... well, twenty-four years.

That had given me plenty of time to master the nasty

habit of purposely zoning out of the conversation when she gave me that look which annoyed her even more. Much like I was doing now.

Mae and I had been sisters since diapers. And while we *technically* had different parents, they purposely raised us together like we were siblings, so it was really just a matter of semantics.

My mom and Mae's dads had been roommates in college their freshman year. Throughout the years, they'd grown to be inseparable. So, as good friends do, they made a pact that they would continue to do life together no matter where life took them.

And they did just that.

After Desmond and James got married and my mom got settled into her career, they bought two houses right across the street from each other in a quiet neighborhood in Sarasota.

A year later, when Mom was considering getting a sperm donor and starting a family, Mae's dads decided they would begin the adoption process. Just over a year and a half later, Mae and I lay side by side in our cribs, attempting to squirm our way out of our matching swaddles.

To the outside eye, our family might not have been conventional, but our lives were filled with unwavering love from three parents who would have moved heaven and earth for us.

And that was all either of us could've ever asked for.

But two years ago, our family was rocked when Mom passed from cancer and Mae's dads decided that they were retiring to the Keys. The four of us video called and visited as often as our schedules allowed, but an overwhelming sense of loss lingered among us now that Mom wasn't around.

Although our family looked different now, Mae and I had stuck to the promise that we made as kids, to keep up the tradition that our parents had and to never stray too far from one another in life.

We went from school night sleepovers to college roommates. And even as we grew into grown adults with bills and careers, we still held tightly to the vow we made as children. Mae had stuck by my side as Mom's cancer peeled her away from me and she helped pick up the pieces when I thought that all was lost.

While we *might* have been forced into friendship by our parents—okay, fine, we were definitely forced—I knew that Mae and I were meant to find each other. Call it soul mates if you want, but despite all of our differences, there was no one in the world that would stand by my side the way she had.

The only thing that made her somewhat unbearable was the fact that she was a five-ten blonde supermodel. Seriously? *Come on.* Would it have killed Mom to have picked a better-looking sperm donor? Sure, sperm donor eleven thousand twenty-three did a pretty decent job if I said so myself, but I *definitely* wasn't supermodel material by any means.

Nine times out of ten, whenever we told people we were sisters, we were immediately met with tilted heads and squinted eyes.

Assholes. All of them.

"Hello, earth to Scarlett?" Mae waved a hand in front of my zoned-out expression.

"Cut it out." I swatted her hand away from me.

So maybe I was guilty of having a book boyfriend or twenty, but I refused to be shamed for them. "I am getting laid. Mentally laid... by fictional men," I said smugly,

4

waggling my brows at her. "And none of my book boyfriends have failed me yet, if you know what I mean."

"Gross!" Mae squealed loudly, scrunching her face as she stuck her fork right into the center of the cake that I'd just pulled out of the oven. She shoveled a large bite into her mouth, not giving it the chance to cool down first. "I do *not* need to know the details of the mental orgasms you've received from fictional men. It sounds unsanitary." Her whole body cringed as she scooped out another giant bite of cake onto her fork and shoveled it into her mouth, barely finished with her first bite.

"Don't knock it until you try it." I shot her an overexaggerated wink. "Plus, you know I've never been good at dating anyway." I sighed, twisting the small emerald ring on my middle finger round and round.

Mom had found the ring in a small pawnshop on one of her work trips years ago and brought it back as a gift for my birthday. These days, when I wore it, it felt like a piece of her was there to comfort me when I needed it. "I wouldn't know where to begin if I tried."

Growing up, I'd never been the kind of girl who got asked out in high school—or college, for that matter. I had my first real relationship just out of college, if you could even call it that.

We were together for a little less than a year, but it was a long-distance relationship and I could count on one hand the number of times that we saw each other in person.

Since that "relationship" ended almost two years ago, I'd been *a bit* skeptical of dating. Most people who are nearly a quarter of a century old have an elaborate dating history. I, on the other hand, felt so inexperienced in the realm of dating that the rare dates that I did go on were practically over before they started.

"I know, Scar." Mae's voice was more tender than usual as her fork made another dive into the red velvet cake.

"You know…" Mae smirked, perking up from her chair and pointing the cake-filled fork toward me. "You could always ask out Mr. Tight End." She waggled her eyebrows.

Abel Abbott, the best tight end in the league, lived across the street from Mae and me. And to my dismay, he also happened to be my boss. I didn't exactly hate the guy, but in the eight months that I'd worked for him, we'd maybe said a hundred words to each other… and that was pushing it.

We had met through a mutual friend of ours, Lea. And I knew it was probably too good to be true when I found out he was looking for a chef *and* lived right across the street from us, but I was desperate for a job and took it anyway.

Turned out I was right… it was too good to be true.

Because Abel Abbott was the biggest asshole I'd ever met.

My only saving grace was that I only worked for him part time and our paths didn't cross often. If I had to work for him full time the last few months, I would have quit by week four.

Over the past few months, Abel and I had mastered the art of avoiding each other at all costs on the rare chance we were in the house at the same time. I couldn't thank God enough that his mornings were spent doing team work-outs while I prepped his meals for the day.

"You could offer me a million dollars *and* a slice of pizza, and I still wouldn't go on a date with the guy," I grumbled, shoveling a large bite of cake into my mouth.

"Come on, Scarlett! He's gorgeous. Have you seen his thighs? They're huge!" She made a motion with her hands to show me the size like I hadn't seen them every day for nearly a year. Not to mention the guy is six foot five and two hundred and sixty pounds. I'd venture to say everything about him was huge. "You can't possibly tell me that you don't want a slice of him."

Was it possible to roll your eyes so hard that they fell out of their sockets?

"First of all, he's my boss," I started, holding up my pointer finger. Although there weren't enough fingers and toes in the world to count the reasons I would never date Abel. "Second, he hates my cooking. And third, he hates me. I can assure you that I don't want a *'slice of him.'"* My fingers formed mocking air quotes.

Mae walked across the counter and stood in front of me, placing her hands on my shoulders with a softened expression. "Scarlett, he doesn't hate you or your cooking. If he did, he would have fired you by now."

"Then explain the first two weeks I worked for him, huh?" My eyebrows rose an inch higher as I slumped my shoulders.

The first few days that I worked for Abel were a nightmare to end all nightmares. On my first day, he took one bite of the breakfast that I made for him before running off to "practice." Unbeknownst to him, I saw Coach Sterling, our friend Lea's dad, driving down the street two hours later. He stopped to chat and told me that the Matrix never practiced on Tuesdays.

I wouldn't have thought much of it had I not found his breakfast sitting on the top of the trash the next morning while I was peeling vegetables. If that was a one-time event it would have been understandable, but I found his breakfast in the garbage for the next two weeks straight.

The food sat there in the trash can, mocking me.

Every. Single. Morning.

The real kicker came on day ten when the idiot kicked

me out of his house right as I was in the middle of prepping his salmon for lunch later that day.

A lanky Korean girl, maybe a year younger than Mae and I, stood on his doorstep with two giant suitcases.

When he saw her standing on the porch as he peered through the window, he whispered that I needed to sneak out the side door as quickly as possible and come back in a week.

What a freaking asshole.

Mae said she recognized the girl from the modeling network. Apparently, she was a fashion designer from Los Angeles who'd been in town because her fall line was being featured at Miami Week of Fashion.

But that still didn't explain why Abel frantically shooed me out of his house like some dirty little secret. The guy hadn't dated in years according to my internet research, so why did he feel the need to hide his chef from some girl he was hooking up with for the week?

"He didn't want his side chick seeing his hot chef; can you blame the guy?" She jokingly smacked my butt as she passed me on her way to the living room. Plopping her long legs on the coffee table, she settled into the fluffy white sofa. I let out a small laugh as I sat next to her on the couch.

"Doubtful. Can we change the subject, please?" I begged, laying my head lightly on her shoulder.

"Sure… are you going to tell me why you've been stress baking all day?" she said gently as she placed her head on top of mine.

My heart fell into the pit of my stomach. I was hoping she hadn't noticed. But then again, it was hard to miss the two loaves of banana bread and three pizzas sitting on the counter.

Fresh out of culinary school, I started a food blog that

had gained a steady following over the years. I started posting new recipes every week as a way to keep a digital cookbook. Now nearly a million people viewed my recipes every month.

When an agent reached out to me a few months ago to see if I had interest in turning my blog posts into a cookbook, I jumped at the idea. The only problem was that I *might* have kept it a secret from Mae.

I didn't know if a book deal would actually come of it and I didn't want to get my hopes up by telling her.

"So, a cookbook deal, huh?"

My head shot straight up, forgetting hers was right on top of mine. Both of our heads bang together, followed by searing pain. *Jesus Christ.* I cupped my forehead in my hands, attempting to ease some of the stinging underneath my skin.

"How did you know?" I shouted, shocked at her admission.

How could she have known that I got a cookbook deal? I haven't told a single soul. Not even Dads knew yet.

"Scarlett, you can't hide anything from me." She cocked a brow at me as if I shouldn't have been shocked by her profession of omniscience. "And when I asked to borrow your computer yesterday… I *might* have looked through the emails between you and your editor."

"You snoop!" A laugh jumped out of me. Of course, she was going through my emails. "So, you're not mad I didn't tell you?" I questioned a bit uneasily as I leaned back against the couch cushions.

"Are you kidding me, Scar? I'm so proud of you!" she exclaimed. "I'm just disappointed you didn't share this big life event with me. We're supposed to do these things together, you know?" Her voice grew tender as she opened her arms to embrace me.

"I knew you would be happy for me... but I didn't want to get my hopes up until it was set in stone. Even now, it still doesn't seem real."

"Yeah, I'm sure it doesn't. I saw the number of zeros on that contract." She said that like she wasn't one of the highest-paid models in the world. Although, I did appreciate her attempt to make me feel special. "You could put a down payment on a house if you wanted!"

Yeah, a one-bedroom shack in the worst part of town.

Mae made more money in two days than I made in two years. So, she was more than a *little* out of touch.

When Mom was sick, Mae was kind enough to cover her medical bills, but paying for the funeral and the business costs for starting my blog wiped me clean, and until recently I'd spent every spare dollar I made paying off my crippling six-figure culinary school debt.

Last summer, Mae decided to buy a house in the neighborhood where most of Miami's elite lived. Hence why our neighbor was the best tight end in the league. I knew that I could *never* afford to live in this neighborhood, even now with no debt and a fairly decent income for a twenty-four-year-old; it would take me seven hundred years to afford a house in this neck of the woods.

Trust me, I did the math.

Growing up, we had always dreamed of having houses next to each other and raising our kids together, the same way our parents raised us. But now, that dream was looking less and less like it would become a reality. Unless I wanted to live in Mae's backyard forever.

Granted, the pool house was more of a mother-in-law suite than a room used to hold beach floats and cleaning solutions. It had a bedroom and bathroom with an expansive living room and kitchen area with modern appliances.

Aside from the stupid bird that sang outside my

window at six sharp every morning, it was the perfect space for just one person.

Mae and I had never lived apart from each other, let alone spent more than a week away from each other at a time. And the idea of that changing in the next few years utterly terrified me.

I was happy that Mae was able to buy such a beautiful house, but I hated knowing that our dreams meant more to me than they did to her.

"We'll see." I rolled my eyes and sagged my body into the couch cushions.

"Hey. You could always convince Mr. Tight End to fall in love with you and then move in with him," she said with an arched brow.

If only it was that simple.

TWO

ABEL

"YOU NEED A GIRLFRIEND, SON."

Coach Sterling leaned back in his chair, eyeing me intently. This is what he called me at eight thirty in the morning demanding me to meet him in his office for?

On a normal day, I might have been a bit more concerned, but since we just won the League Bowl two months ago, I wasn't sure what to expect. This conversation had to be a fucking joke.

Slouching back in my chair, I raised an eyebrow at him pensively. "Did you sign me up for one of those shitty reality dating shows or something?"

Wilson, our defensive end, nominated me for one of those shows last year as a joke. I still got calls weekly, begging me to fly to Los Angeles to audition for the lead role.

I played games professionally; didn't they know I could see right through their bullshit "reality" TV show?

"Don't play with me, son. You know I'm more of a traditionalist when it comes to dating." Coach rolled his eyes like *I* was the one letting ludicrous words slip from my mouth.

"Then tell me exactly… why do I need a girlfriend?" I argued while keeping my features deceptively composed.

"Well, I'm sure by now you've heard that the public relations team has been working on rebranding the Matrix as a more family-friendly team."

I hadn't noticed, but it would be wrong to incriminate myself in front of Coach. "Sure," I managed, casually trying to cover my lie with a shrug.

"Right." Coach glared at me, obviously seeing through my bullshit. "Well, after winning the League Bowl, the PR team noticed that most players had wives, girlfriends, or family to celebrate with…" He nodded at me to see if I was getting where he was going.

Unfortunately for me, I knew what he was getting at. So what if I didn't have anyone to celebrate with after we won the League Bowl?

Mom and Steve had spent the month in Iceland and were planning on coming to the game, but their flight got canceled due to inclement weather.

If they had made their flight, I could assure you that I wouldn't be sitting in Coach Sterling's office having this conversation right now. Who knew it was such a fucking crime to go straight to the locker room after interviews?

When I was growing up, Mom sacrificed a lot when she was left to raise me by herself after my dad left us. And no amount of championship wins compared to paying off Mom's debt, so she could travel full-time with my stepdad.

As sad as I was that they couldn't make it to the biggest game of my career, I knew it wasn't intentional. If they could've been there, they would've and Coach knew that.

I nodded back to Coach curtly, trying to cool the heat

that was rising in my bloodstream. "So, they think that I need a girlfriend?"

"The PR team thinks that it would be best for the team's image. We can't have our star player branded with the 'unattainable bachelor' image that the tabloids keep posting." He even used fucking air quotes.

Coach wasn't wrong about my reputation though. Since entering the league five years ago, I hadn't so much as gone on a date with a girl. The headlines only got worse after the League Bowl win.

Abel Abbott, football's forever bachelor. Abel Abbott Mr. Tight End can't even catch himself a tight end.

Fucking idiots.

If the press got wind that I had a girlfriend, they would all jump at their shot for a front-page cover. Not happening.

"I—"

"No, son. It's not up for discussion," Coach abruptly cut off my attempt to protest. "I'm not asking you to get married. Just find someone to keep around for the next few months until we can get your image in line."

Fuck. He was being serious.

"Just make sure it's not my daughter. Got it?" Coach said sternly, his fists clenched on his desk.

Lea Sterling.

Fiery redhead who not only ran public relations for the Miami Matrix but also happened to be Coach Sterling's only daughter. I wouldn't be surprised if she was the mastermind behind the rebranding charade Coach just pitched my way.

Phil Sterling was one of the best quarterbacks in the league when I was growing up. Turned out the guy was an even better coach than he was a player. Getting the call that I would be playing for him on Draft Night? Fucking surreal.

But before putting pen to paper on my first contract with the Matrix five years ago, he made one thing clear. He didn't give a damn what was written in the contract; if I so much as looked at his daughter with longing eyes, he would cut me from the team before I finished blinking.

I wasn't shocked to find out all the other players got a speech to the same tune on signing day too.

Don't get me wrong. Lea Sterling was a gorgeous girl, but I had my sights set on the five-two brunette who'd been making me breakfast every morning for the past eight months.

"You know who isn't off-limits though?" Coach leaned back in his chair with a smug smile. "Lea's friend… chef girl, what's her name again?"

"Scarlett?" I asked, sitting up straighter in my chair at the mention of her.

"Yeah, her. Makes a mean banana bread, that girl." Coach propped his feet up on his desk as he turned his gaze to look out the floor-to-ceiling windows that over-looked the practice field. "Lord knows you've had eyes on the girl since the day she came barreling through that door with that basket full of baked goods."

Coach was making a lot of good points, and I wasn't a fan of it.

I was the first to admit I had a crush on Scarlett the moment I laid eyes on her. How could a guy not when she looked that good and baked like a *fucking god*?

The deal only got sweeter when Lea introduced us and informed me that Scarlett was my newest neighbor.

I knew I had to see her more frequently than just a wave across the street, so I took a chance and asked if she was looking for a job. I mean, she showed up at a sports facility full of two-hundred-fifty-pound men with multiple baskets full of food. The girl was either a saint or looking for a job.

Thank fuck to whatever gods were out there that I was the first to meet her and offer her the position. I doubted she would've taken another player's offer anyway since the commute to my front door was only a couple hundred yards, but still.

Somehow after our initial five-minute meeting together, I fucked up everything and completely obliterated any chance that I had with her.

Her first day working for me, my brain short-circuited and I couldn't form a coherent thought. To save myself from sounding like an idiot whenever I decided to open my mouth, I decided it best to not say anything at all.

She probably thought I was an asshole and for that, I wouldn't blame her.

I knew I had fucked up immensely, but the thought of trying to convince her otherwise without sounding like an even bigger asshole didn't seem like a possibility for me.

Every time I went to say something to her, my mouth would open, but the words I wanted to say would get caught in the back of my throat.

So, to save myself from internal turmoil, I laid low around the house whenever she was around and kept our conversations short, so I wouldn't spend hours lying in bed replaying the entire conversation, trying to figure out what I could have done differently.

I looked over at Coach to find a sheepish grin still plastered on his face as he pressed his coffee mug to his lips and took a swig. *"Traditionalist when it comes to dating,"* my ass.

"I'll think about it." I pushed off the uncomfortable

accent chair that was too small for someone my size and gave Coach a nod before walking out of his office.

Walking down the hallway of the training facility, I spotted Lea talking to two of the team's biggest sponsors. "Sterling," I muttered, walking up to the group. "And how are you fine men doing? I hope Miss Sterling has been on her best behavior." I winked at the guys, slinging my arm around Lea's shoulders.

She was going to murder me for this.

Fuck it.

"Mr. Abbott." Mark flashed his biggest sponsor smile at me as we exchanged handshakes. "Congrats on the big win last season, man! How has the off-season been treating you?"

"Doing well. Working hard. We've got to put in the work now if we're going to be back-to-back League Bowl champs, don't we?" Both men chuckled loudly as they shared their agreements. "You men mind if I steal Miss Sterling from you for a moment?"

"By all means," they both replied in unison, and we exchanged parting handshakes paired with empty promises to stay in touch.

"I thought we were friends, Lea," I huffed, turning to face her as we stopped in our tracks once we were out of earshot of Mark and whatever the other guy's name was. "Yet, the conversation I just had with your dad tells me otherwise. You told him I need a fucking *girlfriend*?"

"Abel, you haven't gone on a single date since I met you... almost six years ago." She let out an exasperated sigh as she began walking down the corridor, her heels clanking loudly against the marble floor with each step. Clearly not giving me a choice but to follow, I caught up and walked alongside her down the hallway. "Look, you follow three women on your social media accounts. One is your mother, and the other is your personal chef's blog account. Not to mention the fact that the tabloids are having a field day with this 'unattainable bachelor' headline again after that video of you walking off the field alone after the League Bowl win went viral."

"I'm not seeing your point here."

She paused to look at me, keeping a firm gaze that made my skin crawl. "It doesn't look good for you, Abel. Just like you need the players on the field in sync to win games, I need this team's reputation in sync to win sponsors." Picking up the pace again, she kept her head positioned forward, looking away from me as the next words slipped from her lips with the traitorous ease of a serpent. "If I read the fine print correctly, which I always do, I'm pretty sure that hundred-million-dollar extension only matters if you're on the active roster. It would be difficult to play with a broken leg, wouldn't it?"

"What the—"

She tripped me. She fucking tripped me.

I stumbled at her attempt to humble me but made a smooth recovery as I regained my balance. The conniving smirk on Lea's face unnerved me.

"Listen, Abel. I don't care if you get a real girlfriend or a fake one. Honestly, as long as you look like you're in love and keep your reputation intact, I couldn't care less how you go about it. Any questions, comments, or concerns?" she said sternly, cocking an eyebrow at me.

"Someone is feisty this morning, damn." I poked my elbow at her side and gave her a sly smile to try and win my way back to her good side. Though knowing Lea, she could probably see right through my ploy.

One thing about Lea Sterling was that she was a master manipulator. If anyone was born to be a publicist, it was her. The only person that could possibly scare her in this world was her father, and even that was questionable.

She might have put the fear of God in me a handful of times, but she'd become a damn good friend over the last six years. And she'd saved my ass on more than one occasion.

"Fake girlfriend, huh?" I squinted. "Might not be a half-bad idea, Miss Sterling." I shot her a wink that she didn't appear to be amused by.

"Call me Miss Sterling again and I'll rip your dick off and feed it to you whole. Don't try me, Abbott." Her tone was dark and serious which only made me wince more at the mental image.

"Noted."

I brought two fingers to my forehead and gave her a farewell salute as we reached the exit of the training facility that led to the player's parking lot. How I hadn't noticed that she was walking us—or should I say me—to the exit was beyond me.

I could've spent an eternity racking my brain around how subtly she could control a situation, but I had more important things to worry about. Like appeasing Coach and the PR team by finding a fucking girlfriend.

Brushing off the thought for a moment, I reached for the door handle of my SUV and slid into the leather driver's seat. I turned the key in the ignition and the engine roared as I backed out of my spot and made my way out of the lot.

My track record with previous girlfriends wasn't great and Lea's idea of finding a pretend one wouldn't be a bad idea… if I knew where to find one.

My phone pinged from the passenger seat with a new text as I reached the first stoplight. Picking it up, I took a quick glance at it.

Aera: We need to talk. Call me when you get this.

Immediately dismissing her notification, I tossed my phone into the back seat, where it would stay for the rest of the car ride. I started to make a mental note to text her back later, but she and I both knew that I wouldn't.

I didn't have time for Aera's shit right now. I needed to focus on how I was going to convince Scarlett to go out with me. And more importantly, how I was going to cope if she rejected me.

When Scarlett first started working for me eight months ago, I wouldn't have hesitated to ask her on a date. If I was being honest, that was most of the reason I'd asked her to come work with me. But with how I've acted toward her, I doubt she would be up for it.

Her first two weeks working for me, I fucked up... royally.

It all started when she arrived for her first day of work and I gave her the most awkward kitchen tour in the history of kitchen tours. Had a camera crew from one of those home renovation channels been around, they would have fucking laughed in my face.

I blamed those big brown eyes of hers for incapacitating my brain.

To save some of the looming discomfort, I told her that I needed to take breakfast to go because the team had early practice that week, which was a fat lie. Not only did we never have practice on Tuesdays, we also never got called in early because half the guys struggled to show up on time as it was.

However, it was on day thirteen that I realized that my biggest fuckup of all was throwing whatever breakfast Scarlett made that I was too nervous to eat in the trash.

Because the first person to use the trash can in the kitchen each morning… would be my chef.

My blood boiled thinking about how much of an idiot I was.

Between that and me barely saying a word to the girl, I wouldn't be surprised if she thought I hated her guts. Granted, the last seven months hadn't been as awkward as those first few weeks were, but then again, she only communicated to me through blueish-green sticky notes these days, most of which I didn't bother responding to.

Maybe if I finally grew the balls to ask her on a date, I could clear the air between us? Give us a fresh start?

Stumped at the thought, I brought the car to a stop in the driveway and softly banged my forehead on the steering wheel as I let out an exhausted groan.

I looked up to find Scarlett standing in front of the hood sporting a shy grin and an uncomfortable wave.

Fuck.

Opening the driver's door, I let out a giant sigh. "Sorry, rough morning."

"Oh, sorry." Her eyes dart to her sneakers. "Is there anything I can do?"

"Not right now." I blinked. Her big brown eyes peeked up at me through her lashes. "Thanks though," I offered, trying to ease the tension.

Her eyes jumped down to her sneakers again. "Okay, well, your second breakfast is on the counter. And I put a new batch of overnight oats in the fridge if you get hungry again later," she replied, twirling the ring on her middle finger the same way she always did whenever she was nervous. "If you don't need anything else, then I guess I'll see you tomorrow morning?"

I shifted on my feet uncomfortably. "Alright." She nodded back to me. I watched as she made her way down the long driveway and across the street until she disappeared behind the large white gate.

That conversation was probably the longest we'd had since her first day working for me. It couldn't have been more than what, fifty words?

Scarlett and I had this unspoken rule for the past eight months. She came over to cook in the mornings, I grunted thanks if I was around, and she left immediately after. There was no chitchat… just silence. And that conversation solidified the fact that there could never be anything more than silence between us.

Walking into the house, I grabbed a clean set of utensils from the dishwasher and the second breakfast that Scarlett left for me. Plopping down on the couch, I sank into the cushions and slowly worked my fork into the delicious protein waffles that were waiting for me.

How was it possible that I could talk to reporters or do countless postgame interviews and not get flustered? Yet, when it came to having a conversation with *my employee*, my brain and my mouth seemed to sever their connection.

Taking a deep breath, I closed my eyes and let out a sigh.

Scarlett was pretty much my fucking dream girl and now Coach was all but forcing me to ask her out because we both knew I wasn't going to ask anyone else.

Sly motherfucker, that man.

At least if she flat out rejected me, then I could always use the partial truth—that the team was making me get a fake girlfriend—as backup.

What was the worst that could happen anyway? She'd quit?

THREE
SCARLETT

"I'M QUITTING!"

I flung myself onto Mae's couch dramatically and sank into the cushions while fully embracing the frustrated groan that expelled from my mouth. How was it that every encounter with Abel got even worse than the last? I didn't even know that was possible.

More importantly, I didn't have to put up with his shit anymore. Now that I had this book deal under my belt, I didn't necessarily *need* to continue working for him.

I was planning to stay purely out of convenience. With him living across the street and paying me a full-time salary for part-time hours, I didn't think it would hurt too much if I stuck around a while longer.

Plus, unbeknownst to him, I'd been testing out new recipes on him for months without him knowing. There was no sense in posting a recipe for the world to try if a guy who shoveled in six thousand calories a day like it was nothing didn't like it.

At best, he was free and easy quality control.

I didn't mind the routine that we had going on lately

anyway. You know, the one where we didn't say a damn word to each other or acknowledge each other's existence.

On rare occasions, he'd throw out an impassive "Thanks," but those were few and far between. These days they'd become so nonexistent that I was starting to think I'd made them up in the first place.

As far as work environments went, it was an introvert's wet dream. I didn't mind spending my mornings in silence or throwing on my headphones and listening to an audiobook while I prepped his meals.

But after I watched him *bang his head* against the steering wheel all because he saw me in the driveway?

Nope. Nada. Not happening.

There was no way I could recover from that, right? Anyone could notice that he didn't enjoy my presence, but I didn't think I was *so* insufferable that he was willing to give himself a concussion at the sight of me.

With that, I decided I would wallow. Because when I walked into work tomorrow, I was left with no choice but to quit. I wasn't sure when Abel was planning on firing me, but the head-bashing gave me reason to believe that it would be happening sooner rather than later. I knew my pride couldn't bear the blow of him firing me, so I had to beat him to it.

In the midst of my depressive episode over the loss of a job that I didn't even like, Mae walked out of her office with a huff holding out two different headshots of the same girl toward me. My eyes scanned over the photos for a long moment. "Left," I answered honestly, pointing to the photo where the girl looked more relaxed, yet still striking.

Around the same time I started my cooking blog, Mae started her own modeling agency after her former employer was caught in a scandal that showcased the disgusting antics some of the scouts and photographers got up to while on the job. She decided that if other agencies weren't going to advocate and support their models, she would take it upon herself to create one that did so.

Between Mae's company expansion, my book deal, and my impending loss of a job, tensions were high in the house. What the two of us needed was a night of good clean fun to unwind and relax from the stress of our work lives.

"I knew that was the better one," she mumbled, biting her lip as she walked back into her office.

"Did you hear me? I said that I'm quitting my job working with Abel," I grumbled, slightly annoyed that Mae wasn't feeding into my momentary display of dramatics. Didn't she notice that I was *obviously* in crisis mode?

"I heard you." Mae's face remained neutral as she walked back into the living room. "And frankly, I'm thrilled! Now you can come work for me." She flashed me a mischievous dimpled smile as she sat on the edge of the couch where my feet lay. Her long legs extended outward and two new headshots faced downward in her lap. "Whatever he's paying you… I'll double it. Free room and board included," she said with waggled eyebrows.

I couldn't help but roll my eyes. "I already get free room and board," I fired back at her with a scowl.

When Mae offered to let me move into the pool house, I told her that I would be paying her rent every month. Although she was the one to offer, I didn't want her to think that I was taking advantage of her.

We never discussed a set amount, so I scrounged up what I could manage and wrote her a check on the first of every month. Nearly nine months later, and none of the checks that I had given to her had been cashed.

Not a single one.

"Your checks got lost in the mail." She attempted to lie right to my face. Though both of us knew, I handed each of the checks directly to her.

"Last time I asked, you told me they fell into a puddle on your way into the bank…"

"Same difference." She shrugged before holding up the two headshots from her lap for me to review. I let out a groan as I pointed to the one on the right, which was the obvious choice even at first glance.

Mae might've thrown on a tough exterior and admittedly been a *wee bit* selfish at times—as her best friend, I was the only one allowed to say that. But when she finally let her guard down with someone, she exposed her heart of gold. It just happened to be buried deep, deep, *deep* down there.

"I'm being serious, Mae! I have no choice but to quit," I huffed. "The guy was banging his head on the steering wheel when he saw me leaving his house this morning." I mimicked the head-banging motion for her as I recounted the memory that I so desperately wished to forget.

"That bad, huh?" Her eyes softened and her lips turned down into a pout. "Scar, you know I'm always on your side. But do you think that… maybe you're only seeing what you want to see when it comes to Abel?" she questioned, gently placing her hand on top of mine, which lay folded on top of my stomach.

I paused and took her question into consideration, but all possibilities of her being right came up short. Nope, not freaking possible.

Someone didn't blatantly ignore their employee every day for nearly a year if they were a nice person. Or throw out the food their chef spent hours making for them. Or concuss themself at the sight of said chef.

"Hmm… doubtful," I replied, shaking my head side to side.

"C'mon, Scar, the guy has been nothing but nice to me anytime that I've interacted with him. Remember when he saw me struggling with that giant package last summer and he ran across the street and carried it up the stairs for me?" She paused, waiting for my answer, but I refused to feed into her persuasion tactics. "And you know Lea has told us countless stories about how he pays for his parents to travel full-time and how he beats all his other team-mates' charity hours by a long shot every year."

Hmm, I must have tuned those stories out because they didn't ring a bell. Not to mention the fact that I'd spent thirty hours a week with him whereas Mae had spent all of half an hour with him… if that!

His good looks could easily catch someone's attention, so *of course* she would give him a pass so easily. But unfortunately for him, good looks wouldn't cancel out his dickish personality.

What a shame that someone so good-looking was such a terrible human. Hopefully Hell would be hot.

Desperate to change the subject, I leaned up on my elbows. Only *one thing* could fix my dreadful mood. "I was thinking…" I trailed off, looking down at the headshots in Mae's hands, hoping to bring her attention back to her work stress just long enough for her to give in to my request. "Maybe we could have a girls' night?"

Since Mae and I have always lived together, most nights could technically be considered girls' night. But we only *officially* called a girls' night when the situation was bad enough that major reinforcements were needed. And by major reinforcements, I meant wine. *Copious amounts of wine.* And the occasional bad decision.

"I'll call Lea," Mae concluded. Hopping up from the

edge of the couch, she darted into her office without another question. I made no attempt to hide my smirk, knowing that Lea's skills had begun to rub off on me.

A BOTTLE OF WINE LATER, we had done our standard prank calls to all of the people who had recently wronged us. And sang tone-deaf karaoke renditions so horribly that the neighborhood patrol guard, who came to warn us of a noise complaint, told us it would be better for humanity if we lost our voices.

I would place bets that the complaint came from our eighty-six-year-old hag of a neighbor, Miss Rita.

Assholes. Both of them.

Before we got too plastered, I filled Lea in on the dramatics of my morning encounter with Abel. She told me that he was probably just stressed about some new regulation that had been issued to players and not to take it too personally.

An hour of raunchy girl talk and another bottle of wine down the hatch after that, I found myself sitting on the toilet in Mae's guest bathroom, eager to break the seal. My head spun in circles incessantly as I tried my best to remain still.

When did I grow two new legs?

Everything immediately began to spin in circles, making it hard to rip the toilet paper off the roll. Jesus, Mae. Didn't she know that the toilet paper was supposed to hang over the roll, not under it?

In a fit of drunken rage, I ripped the entire roll off the holder in protest as I finished my business.

What I wouldn't give to throw a roll of toilet paper at Abel Abbott's perfectly symmetrical head.

All of a sudden, my mouth curved into an unconscious smile as I stared at the roll of toilet paper in my hand. I might not have been able to throw it at his head, but I *could* throw one at his house.

I was a genius. A complete and utter genius. And I wasn't just saying that because I was drunk. Okay fine, it was definitely because I was drunk.

Eagerly pulling up my leggings, I dove to open the cabinet underneath the sink and plucked out all of the rolls of toilet paper that I could fit into my arms. Though I hit a bit of an obstacle when I remembered that I needed a free hand to turn the knob in order to get out of the bathroom.

After a few minutes of wrestling with the door handle, I successfully escaped with an overflowing armful of toilet paper. I barged out of the bathroom and into the living area where I found Mae and Lea doubled over on the carpet in hysterics over a video of a dancing squirrel playing on the flat-screen TV.

"Ahem!" I cleared my throat, casually announcing my presence as I moseyed into the living room, making my best attempt to stay upright. The slight wobble in my walk and toilet paper rolls that fell from my arms had been a dead giveaway to my state of being.

Tilting their heads toward me with furrowed eyebrows, Mae and Lea slowly simmered their fit of laughter.

"Toilet paper." A smile of defiance tugged at my lips while I nodded in the direction of the front door while giving little elaboration on the plan that was brewing in my mind. Even if I wanted to elaborate, I wasn't sure my words would've been coherent anyway, given my current state.

"There's more upstairs. I'll grab it," Mae chimed in,

nodding profusely. There wasn't a second of hesitation before she popped up from the couch and trotted up the stairs. Thank God our telepathy always came in handy when it mattered most.

"I've got the pool house!" Lea shouted back to us as she slipped out the back door. I watched through the window as she stumbled across the backyard, nearly falling into the pool, but with arms winding in circles she worked her way upright at the last possible second.

Ten minutes later, our trio convened in the entryway with three bulk-size packs of toilet paper ready for war. We came to a mutual agreement that it would be best to use all available toilet paper due to the gargantuan size of Abel's house. One measly pack of toilet paper was *not* going to cut it for the job we had in mind.

Lea took lead in devising the charade that we had given the name "Operation Toilet Paper Payback." Was it cheesy? Yes. Were we also drunk as hell and thought it was hilarious? Also, yes.

"What about neighborhood patrol?" I questioned as I pulled my hand away from the handle of the front door. We had already gotten a warning from them earlier after our noise complaint and we would get fined if we got another.

"Lea," Mae and I both deadpanned in unison after a moment of weighing our thoughts.

If anyone would be able to pull one over on the nightly security guard, it would be Lea Sterling. The girl had the mastermind of a freaking criminal. Honestly, I probably should've been more concerned about that than I actually was, but that was a problem for another time.

After regrouping the plan, Lea set out down the street toward the security hut in the tightest little black dress she could find in Mae's closet. It might have been two sizes too small, but her boobs looked fantastic which was exactly what we needed.

Mae and I watched from behind a trash can as Lea slipped through the door of the security hut and the guard stood to greet her.

Game on, Abbott.

The late-night hour paired with a dreary, desolate street made our operation feel as though we were criminals. And while it might not have been explicitly written in the law, toilet papering someone's house definitely balled the line somewhere between littering, trespassing, and vandalism.

We waited for a few minutes until we were sure there were no stray patrol guards in sight, and we snagged our packages of toilet paper from the ground and crept across the street.

Throwing caution to the wind, I picked up the pace and started strong with stringing toilet paper across the tree limbs as Mae took over wrapping the mailbox until it was covered in white squares so thoroughly that no black paint from the mailbox showed through.

We did our best to stifle our triumphant laughter—well —until one of the rolls that I'd thrown over a palm tree smacked mercilessly against Mae's head and knocked her to the ground.

Feeling liberated, I headed for the house next. I chucked a roll as hard as I could and watched as it landed perfectly on the highest point of the roof.

Bull's-eye.

"Hope you have fun with that one, asshole," I mumbled to myself as I made another throw toward the roof again. I was exhausted and running out of toilet paper. But I still didn't feel satisfied.

I wanted to have the last word and by God, I was going to have it.

"Abel, if you're watching this from your window right now, just know that no matter how sexy your gray sweatpants might be, I will *not* be tempted by them!" I whisper-yelled at his front door so as not to wake the neighbors.

Okay, so those weren't exactly the last words that I had planned in my head. But at this point, the wine had gone straight to my vagina, so I couldn't blame myself.

After using the last of our rolls to wrap his SUV, which conveniently sat in the driveway, we stalked down the front yard at the same time Lea came walking up the street with an amused smirk.

The girls and I stood at the curb and stared up at our masterpiece. "What a beauty," Mae marveled at our creativity.

People had always said that revenge tasted sweet. And now that I had gotten some of my own, I couldn't help but love the taste.

"Sorry, Mr. Abbott," I muttered smugly under my breath before the three of us turned around and swiftly snuck back across the street and into the safety of Mae's home.

Oh, what I would've given to be a fly on Abel's wall when he woke in the morning.

Sleep tight, asshole.

FOUR

ABEL

GROANING, I sat up in bed after being woken by a loud noise that came from downstairs.

Rolling out of bed, I threw on a pair of gray sweatpants and rummaged through my dresser drawer for a black T-shirt. I tugged one out and pulled it over my head and down my torso as I walked across the cold tile into the en suite.

I paused to look back at the clock that sat on top of the nightstand — 7:02 a.m.

Great.

It had been just shy of twenty-four hours since Coach had given me orders to get a girlfriend, and so far, I'd made no effort toward achieving that.

Brushing it off for the moment, I picked up my tooth-brush out of the holder and slathered on a healthy amount of toothpaste. Meeting my eyes in the mirror, self-mockery invaded my stare, making me feel like a fucking moron.

What other twenty-eight-year-old professional athlete was struggling to find a girl? None.

Placing a hand on either side of the sink, I spat my

toothpaste into the basin and watched as the water washed the contents down the drain before looking up again and shaking my head.

Restless and irritable, I tread back into the bedroom to swipe my phone from the charger on the nightstand. Only forty-seven emails since yesterday afternoon.

Fan—fucking—tastic.

Opening the latest thread from my agent, I didn't pause to read what he'd sent before shooting him back a reply telling him to stop sending me so many damn emails.

Stomping my way into the kitchen, I found a busy brunette chopping up the last of a green bell pepper and throwing it into the pan.

"Sorry if I woke you." Scarlett's face was as red as her name suggested. "I couldn't reach the pan on the top shelf."

"No worries," I responded back as I took in the way she looked in her sundress. "So, uhh, how have you been?" I questioned, trying my best to keep a casual tone despite the sense of inadequacy that swept over me.

Fuck if I didn't feel like a middle schooler trying to talk to his crush for the first time.

Shaking my head, I dropped down onto the barstool at the island and admired Scarlett as she flipped a giant breakfast omelet with ease.

"How have *I* been?" she repeated the question back to me, glancing uneasily over her shoulder with the spatula still in her hand.

I nodded, giving her another awkward shrug. "Yeah. How have you been?"

Scarlett whipped her body around and stared at me, open mouthed and speechless. "…Are you feeling okay?"

she questioned skeptically after a beat, clearly avoiding my question.

"I feel fine... why?"

"Just curious..." Her eyebrows curled upward as she walked a few feet to grab a plate from the cabinet. "I was actually wanting to talk to you about something..."

"So, do you have a boyfriend?" I cut her off, the words spilled from my mouth before I could catch them.

Fuck. I closed my eyes, hoping to erase the last five minutes. Internally chastising myself, I let out a deep sigh and ran my palms down my stubble-covered cheeks. How was I fucking this up already?

"No..." Scarlett trailed off while removing the omelet from the pan, moving it over to the plate. I let out a relaxed breath, feeling a chunk of tension I didn't know I had released from my shoulders at her answer. "Abel, are you sure you're feeling alright?" She tilted her head to the side as she held out the plate toward me.

I wouldn't tell her, but my appetite dissipated the second I started this conversation, and it wouldn't be coming back anytime soon.

"I feel fine," I scrounged out under my breath while digging my fork into my breakfast and cutting it into bite-sized pieces. "So I was thinking that... maybe, uhhh... we could go out sometime?" I muttered.

There was no going back now.

Clearly, I hadn't thought this through.

I was her *boss* and she was my *employee*. I couldn't go around asking her on a date out of the blue like that. How fucking unprofessional. If I were a betting man, I would've put big money on a retelling of this encounter making the headline of Page Six first thing in the morning.

Scarlett sucked in a sharp breath, frozen in place. "What'd you just say?"

"I—" *Fuck.* "Was wondering if you wanted to go on a date with me?"

She stared back at me blank and tongue-tied, blinking those midnight-black lashes at me for an extended moment before wandering over to the spice cabinet.

What the fuck? Was she... pulling the spices out of the cabinet?

Locking my gaze on her, I analyzed her while she opened each lid, sniffed, and before moving on to the next. Oddly spending more time on the oregano compared to the others.

"What are you... why are you smelling my spices right now?" My brows grew together and concern coated my voice as I inched over to where she was rummaging through the bottles.

She swiveled around, holding the oregano clutched tight against her chest. The blood drained from her face and she looked like she was going to vomit.

For fuck's sake, what was going on?

Scarlett slowly raked her eyes over my face and body. On a normal day, I probably would've gotten a hard-on from her checking me out, but I wasn't the slightest bit turned on with how weird she was acting.

"I-I don't know how to tell you this... but I think I might have accidentally drugged you." Her voice shook like a leaf in the wind.

"What do you mean, you might've *accidentally* drugged me?" I tried my best to hide the shock in my voice so as not to scare her, but if she slipped me drugs and league officials found out, I would be royally fucked.

"You asked me to go on a date with you..."

"I know that."

"Exactly! You never would've done that if you weren't on drugs. And well, you see, Mae has been known to participate in… recreational activities from time to time and I thought she might've been playing a joke on me."

Fuuuuuuck.

"How did this happen?" Scarlett muttered to herself as she paced back and forth in the kitchen and I asked myself the same question.

I hadn't toyed with drugs since sophomore year of high school, but I didn't remember feeling *normal* after hitting a joint.

There's no way that she—*wait*—I chuckled to myself.

I hadn't touched my omelet.

My appetite had been shot from trying to grow the balls to ask Scarlett out, so I only toyed it around the plate with the hopes that she wouldn't notice that I wasn't eating anything.

Scarlett's stride came to a halt. "Okay. Here's the plan. You stay right here and don't talk to anyone." She nodded frantically while she laid out the details of her plan. "First, I'm going to go to the store and buy a drug test for you to take. Then, while we wait for the results, I'll take the test and the 'oregano'"—what was up with everyone using finger quotes lately?—"to the pool house and hide it in my trash bin so no one sees it in yours and tips off *Page Six*."

She gathered her phone and the bottle of oregano from the counter and shoved them in her tote bag. I managed to swipe her keys off the counter before she could grab them and positioned myself in front of her, trapping her between my body and the counter.

I caught her by the waist in her attempt to break free. "Scarlett," I sighed with a small chuckle, dangling the keys above my head and out of her reach.

I had to admit her effort in trying to snag them from me was admirable. But I questioned whether or not she forgot the fact that I was a professional athlete *and* twice her fucking size.

"Scarlett, come on. I'm not on drugs." I pushed down an amused smile as she continued to climb me like a tree, hooking her leg around mine for leverage and stretching her arms as high as they'd go.

She peeled herself off me and desire barreled through me at the loss of contact. "Abel, yes, you are." Her eyes grew wide as she made a final leap for the keys only to fall short.

Again, had she forgotten I was twice her size? How tall did she think she was?

"This is the drugs talking." She leveled those big brown eyes with mine. "You know, it's like when you're six shots of tequila deep and you keep convincing yourself that you're fine so you take two more?" she rambled. "And the next morning you wake up and slowly piece together all of the embarrassing things that you did the night before..." Her voice grew quiet as her eyes darted to the floorboards.

"Speaking from experience, huh?" I squinted though my eyes lit with a glimmer of mischief.

"What, me? Never. Nope." She looked cute with rose-colored cheeks and a lie written all over her face.

"Convincing." My lips twitched trying to swallow back a laugh. "I'm completely sober, Red. I promise. Although I do appreciate your willingness to commit a felony for me. It's quite endearing." Tilting her head, she threw a questioning look my way. "I know exactly what I asked you earlier, but I don't mind asking again if you need me to."

"No," she said without hesitation. "My answer is no."
Ouch.
"Why?"

"We've never had a full conversation, Abel. Why would you ask me on a date?"

Taking a step back, I quickly ran through scenarios in my head to see if I could come up with something that might be convincing enough to explain why I asked her on a date out of left field.

Sighing in defeat, I settled for a half-truth.

"Coach told me I had to get a girlfriend. The team's pissed about the 'unattainable bachelor' image"—fuck, now I was the one using air quotes—"that the tabloids have been clinging to recently. These reporters are dying to get their hands on *something*, even if that means tearing me down, and they want me to redirect their attention."

Scarlett nodded to herself and resumed her pacing. "I see... so you don't want to go on a date with me... you want me to be your girlfriend?"

"No. Well, yes. I don't know." What the fuck was I saying? It was like my mouth had severed its connection with my brain. I made a mental note to get a grip before the season started. "What if we fake it?" I suggested.

"Fake it?" She paused in her tracks and scrunched her brows. I could almost hear the thoughts swirling in her brain as she debated the idea.

After a beat, she lifted her chin in defiance and nailed me with an unamused stare. "I don't think so, thanks for the offer though."

"Why? Lea told me about the book deal. This would get you more exposure. Free marketing."

"Hmm." She made a taut face, pretending like she was considering my offer. "Still no."

"There has to be a reason, so tell me."

"No, just no."

Fuck. She wasn't going to budge.

Was the idea of going on a date with me that bad? I

knew I didn't deserve a "World's Greatest Boss" mug, but damn.

I racked my brain trying to figure out something that I could leverage to get her to agree to this. There wasn't anyone else I could picture myself in a relationship with.

"I'll give you the house," I deadpanned after a moment of contemplating my options.

"What?"

"I— I'll give you the house." I sighed, slumping back against the counter. "If you pretend to be my girlfriend, I'll give you the house. No strings attached aside from the obvious."

I hated myself for using that as a means to sway her, but I was desperate.

When Lea told me in passing about Scarlett's blog, I looked it up and perused all of her posts. And I've checked back every week since to see what new recipes she came out with. Most of which she'd tested on me before posting. I'd be lying if I said it didn't bring a smile to my face.

I liked the little stories that she wrote about each recipe telling people where the food originated from or the story that inspired it. My favorite ones, though, were the stories about her and Mae growing up together.

On more than one occasion, Scarlett has dropped hints in her posts that she dreamed of living across the street from her sister one day, so they could raise their families together.

Sure, I could've kept the house and found someone who would've done the job for free. But giving her the house didn't feel like much of a loss if it meant making her childhood dream come true.

"You would give me the house... this house? The one we are standing in right now?" she questions with her index fingers pointed toward the floorboards. "Why?"

"You can't live in that pool house forever, Red." I shrug, refraining from elaborating further. It was probably best not to incriminate myself for stalking my employee's blog.

Walking over to the island, she slumped down onto a barstool, huffing out a breath and sinking her face into her palms.

Someone must have had a rough night.

At least she finally stopped pacing. I was about to go fucking nauseous from watching her speed walk back and forth across the kitchen.

"I know I can't live in a pool house forever." I swore I heard her whisper out an "*Asshole*," but I could have been imagining it. A strangled cry of frustration escaped her lips.

Part of me wanted to remain hopeful that she would accept, but based on that sound she probably wouldn't.

If she rejected me, would she quit? Would I have to let her go? I'd have to move neighborhoods too, wouldn't I? Yup. I wouldn't be able to recover from that.

I ran my hands down my cheeks as I pondered all of the possibilities. I hadn't dated anyone in half a decade for this reason exactly.

It was too much stress, too much drama. Two things that I didn't have time or energy to deal with.

I knew early on that I wanted to be the best in the league and that didn't leave much time for dating or relationships. I sacrificed my time and worked my fucking ass off to be the best. And the Bowl ring sitting in my office upstairs was proof that I was on the path to achieving that.

Fuck, no one had even caught my eye until Scarlett caught me off guard in Coach's office. And I was fucking sold the moment I saw those big brown eyes peer up at me for the first time.

Scarlett lifted her head from her hands and we stared into each other's eyes for a long moment. No words. Just vulnerability visibly coursing through our gazes.

Sighing, I kept her gaze as I asked the fateful question that lingered between us. "What do you say?"

I knew what I wanted, but this was her choice to make.

FIVE
SCARLETT

CRAZY.

I was crazy for even slightly considering taking up Abel on the offer of being his girlfriend.

I practically stormed out of his house mumbling that I needed to sleep on it before I could give him an answer. He yelled back at me as I walked out to take as long as I needed, but I ignored him and kept walking.

Ugh, I knew I couldn't dwell on this forever though. I needed to give him an answer sooner rather than later, that way he could look for someone else if I wasn't going to go through with it.

Hmm, I wondered if he would offer the house to someone else if I didn't accept.

The entire situation felt like a fever dream. One minute I was trying to work up the nerve to quit my job and the next I was being offered a fourteen-million-dollar house—scratch that—mansion.

What. The. Holy. Hell.

What I couldn't wrap my head around though, was

why he asked me, of all people, to go along with his little fake girlfriend charade.

I'd seen the comments on his Socialgram posts before— not that I stalked him often or anything—and there were hundreds if not thousands of women who would divorce their husbands or give up their firstborn for the chance at one date with the guy.

I shook my head side to side while I made my way through the pool house and settled onto the couch. My brain pounded while I replayed Abel's and my conversation over and over in my head, trying to make sense of it.

Of all the days he could have shocked me by asking me to be his girlfriend, why did it have to be the day that I had a massive hangover?

I sank deeper into the couch, trying to ward off the bile that was rising in my throat. After a few minutes my stomach settled, but my brain still swirled with the idea of accepting Abel's offer.

Jesus Christ, I was obviously still drunk if I was seriously considering this. There was no way I would if I was sober. I angrily pulled up the hunter-green blanket that sat at my feet and threw it over my body.

I needed a freaking nap.

The blanket was fuzzy and smelled like the lavender soap I used on laundry day which soothed my worriment. I curled up into its warmth and my eyes quickly fluttered closed, sending me off into a deep sleep.

Four hours later, I peeled an eyelid open and gasped as I was met with a face hovering four inches over mine. Shrieking, I scrambled out from underneath the blanket and headbutted Mae in the forehead before realizing it was her.

We both moaned, falling back onto the couch. I slapped a hand to my forehead and applied pressure to help ease the pain, though I'm sure it was more of a placebo than anything.

"You have to stop headbutting me every time I surprise you or we're both going to end up in the hospital with traumatic brain injuries before long." A bright-red circle, the size of a golf ball, began to form on her forehead and I was confident that I had one to match.

"You were asking for it being that close to my face while I was sleeping. You know I hate surprises!" I flailed my arms at her, exasperated. "What were you doing anyway?"

"Oh, Scar, don't be mad. I like watching you sleep sometimes. You look so cute and peaceful. Much different from when you're awake..." she snarled at me. "When you're sleeping, I just want to squeeze your little cheeks."

Mae pinched her pointer finger and thumb together and I let her have at it with pinching my face. Somewhere between being hungover, half-asleep, and borderline concussed, all of my cares had been thrown out the window.

"Plus, I came over to hear the details of your rage quit with Mr. Tight End and to offer you a job as my new head chef." Mae gave me a cocky smile.

"One, I'm not taking a job from you. Two, I didn't quit." Her eyes grew wide at my second statement, but her jaw dropped when I spit out the third. "Three, Abel asked me to be his girlfriend."

The two of us stared at each other in silence for a long moment. Our twin telepathy sparked telling me she was trying to figure out whether or not I was telling the truth, so I shook my head up and down to signal the answer to her unspoken question.

Mae gasped before jumping up from the couch and pumping a fist in the air. "I have to call Lea and tell her that I won! She owes me a hundred bucks!" She let out a loud holler and ran a victory lap around the living room.

They placed a bet on me? Bitches, both of them.

"Lea told me about the new PR rule for the Matrix and we placed a bet on whether or not Abel would grow some balls and finally ask you out. And I won!" She did another victory lap around the room for good measure before tackling me on the couch.

"What do you mean 'finally'?" I scoffed, arching a brow at her.

"Scarlett. The guy has a crush on you. It's painfully obvious."

"You're delusional."

"If you say so." Mae grinned from one corner of her mouth like she knew something that I didn't.

This conversation was pointless. There was no way that my boss had a crush on me, and on the off chance he did, how would Mae know? She'd seen us interact together, what, four times? And that was pushing it.

Brushing her off of me, I waddled toward the bathroom, barely making it before liquid threatened to run down my thighs. When I reached over to grab some toilet paper from the holder, realization hit me.

I didn't have any toilet paper.

Neither did Mae.

Goddammit.

I picked up one of my stray tote bags that conveniently lay on the ground and sifted through it, hoping and praying to find a napkin or something.

Anything.

Aha! I pulled out half a Chipotle napkin from the bottom of my bag. Thank God I hadn't cleaned this place since Sunday and had shit laid around everywhere. It might not have been one of the finer moments in my life, but I'd work with what I was given.

Memories from the night before flooded to the forefront of my brain once again. A noise complaint. Wine. Karaoke. More wine. Toilet papering Abel's house.

Yikes.

This morning was still a blur, but what I hadn't pieced together was why there were no remnants of our toilet paper destruction on Abel's house when I walked over this morning.

How was he able to get it cleaned up so quickly? And why didn't he say anything about it?

If I was him and my house got vandalized in a gated neighborhood, the first people I would interrogate would be my neighbors. Specifically the girls who lived across the street.

Ehh, I guessed the security team took care of it before he woke up. Surely one of the guards saw it during their hourly patrol and didn't want to risk losing his job.

Smart guy.

After washing my hands, I shuffled out of the bathroom and down the hall to pick up the packages I left in the entryway yesterday afternoon.

Struggling to carry them down the hall, I huffed and puffed before I managed to set the box on the island.

I took my time unboxing the new set of cookware that I had absolutely no space for. I'd been guilty of falling down the rabbit hole of a fifty percent off flash sale at two in the morning a few weeks ago.

But my regrets were minimal as I unwrapped the perfectly crafted pots and pans that I'd had my eye on for the last year. I wasn't one to splurge often, but I knew these ceramic pans would look great in the photos for the cookbook, so it was worth every penny. Which was still steep, even at half off.

"You never told me if you said yes to him or not," Mae piped up from the couch where she had been immersed in her phone for the last few minutes.

"I told him I needed to think about it. I don't think I'm going to say yes though." I turned on the faucet to the sink, hoping to drown out the conversation as I washed my picture-perfect cookware.

"I think you should do it. Just one date. That's it. You were planning on quitting anyway, so if it's horrible you can go back to the original plan and come work for me," Mae shouted, loud enough for me to hear her over the running water.

"Did you just make another bet with Lea about whether or not I was going to say yes to him?"

"No…" The evident lie coated her voice.

"You're a horrible liar. You know that, don't you?" I shouted back to her and laughter rose from my throat while I placed the clean pans on the drying rack.

"Please, Scar. Humor me. It'll be fun!" Mae slapped on the same giant puppy-dog eyes that she used to coerce men into buying her drinks at the bar.

"If you give me the hundred bucks for winning the first bet, I'll think about it," I bargained. I was already thinking about it, so the least I could do was turn a profit from it. "No promises though."

A few seconds later, my phone pinged with a notification that Mae had sent me a hundred dollars. Dismissing it, I opened up my text thread with Lea instead. A pleased smile passed my lips while I thumbed out a message to her.

Scarlett: I heard about your bets with Mae. Remind me to never go to Vegas with you.

Scarlett: P.S. I've heard food poisoning is a bitch.

"I NEED MORE TIME."

I spent all weekend wrestling with myself on whether or not to accept Abel's offer while simultaneously trying to make progress toward my cookbook and plan out blog posts for the next few days.

I barely made it out of bed with the cloud of exhaustion that loomed over me. Maybe, just maybe, I'd bit off more than I could chew. And adding Abel's "situation" to the mix would only spread my already overextended time even thinner.

If I was being honest, I didn't want to accept his offer. In fact, I hadn't so much as hesitated to shoot him down until he brought the house into the equation.

How in the world could he have known that would be my only weakness?

Don't get me wrong, Abel was a good-looking guy. Dark hair that was curly on top and shaved on the sides. A short beard that he always kept trimmed to perfection. And there was the fact that he was six foot five which instantly made any guy two points hotter.

If we were just going off looks, he was exactly my type. But the cold, aloof personality that he only seemed to have around me and no one else annihilated that teeny tiny crush I had before working for him.

There was no way that we'd be able to easily convince people that we were madly in love with his usual demeanor. Plus, I wasn't exactly inclined to helping out an asshole, no matter how hot he might've been.

Fourteen-million-dollar house. Fourteen-million-dollar house.

Ugh, why couldn't it have been Henry Cavill asking me to be his girlfriend and offering me a mansion?

"Take as long as you need," Abel said, grabbing his gym bag off the counter and slinging it over his shoulder.

I hadn't said anything yet—mostly because I didn't know what to say—but when I came into work earlier, I noticed that Abel had moved all of the pots and pans to a lower shelf so that I could reach them more easily.

I couldn't figure out if I was more baffled at him remembering what I said the other morning about struggling to reach the pans or the fact that he had actually done something nice for a change.

And I didn't have to ask him to do it. Probably because he knew I never would've flat out asked him to rearrange his kitchen set up for me though.

It was kind of like when you're dating someone and they got you flowers, not because you asked for them, but because they wanted to get them for you.

Abel wanted to do something nice for me.

What. The. Hell. That was a first.

I couldn't lie, it did spark curiosity to find out what other sides of Abel I didn't know about yet. I couldn't help but wonder what lay beyond those solid brick walls he'd built up against me.

Was he funny? What kind of movies did he watch? Had he ever committed any crimes? I had so many questions and so few answers.

"Will you, uhh, tell me about yourself? I feel like we don't really know each other and it might make it easier for me if I knew whether or not you're a horrible person."

"Sure. What do you want to know?" he replied, flashing the tiniest of grins at me.

Abel smiled at me.

For the first time in eight months, Abel Abbott smiled at me.

What the hell was going on?

"I guess whatever you're willing to give up. Committed any crimes recently?" In my head, the question sounded more like an interrogation, but the words that slipped from my lips betrayed me by sounding singsong and flirtatious.

"No crimes. No jail time. Never gotten into a fight. I had one job in high school working at a grocery store, and I made sure to put in two weeks' notice before leaving for college. I did get a speeding ticket a few years ago, the cop was a fucking asshole, but I paid it early." He paused, expelling a pent-up breath. "And I know I haven't always been the most appreciative boss…."

I held back a scoff. At least he was self-aware.

"But I like that you show up on time every day. And that you've never once complained—to my face at least. I wish I would've told you that sooner."

My breath hitched.

I never knew that he noticed those things about me. Well, aside from the complaining. More often than not, I was complaining about him in my head; I just tried not to let the words slip from my mouth whenever he was around.

"Th-Thank you." I gulped, trying to rationalize the words that came out of his mouth.

"I've gotta go to practice, but take your time with making your decision, got it? I don't want you to feel like you're being forced into this." Abel grabbed his keys from the island and rattled them in his hand.

"I don't feel like I'm being forced. It's just… it's a lot to think about."

And it was.

I was one of the few straight women in the country that refused to drop my panties at his beck and call, so why did it have to be me?

"I know." He let out a rugged sigh. "And if you decide to say no, I won't question you about it. I'll respect whatever decision you make."

"Okay." I twisted the ring on my middle finger behind my back. "I'll give you an answer on Friday."

I stood in his kitchen, baffled, as I heard the engine of his SUV roar to life from the driveway. Slumping down into a barstool, I placed my elbows on the counter and dropped my head into my hands.

I still wasn't quite convinced that I hadn't accidentally slipped him drugs. Abel was never nice to me. He wasn't ever blatantly mean, but he definitely wasn't nice either. And now he was being nice to me twice in one day?

Something wasn't adding up with him.

I couldn't put my finger on it, but I also wasn't going to dig around for something and stop his nice streak either.

Oh well, time would tell.

SIX

ABEL

"ABBOTT, you made any progress on finding a girlfriend yet?" Coach tipped his head, motioning for me to join as the rest of the guys headed toward the locker room.

Even in the off-season when workouts weren't required by league officials, Coach made sure players knew practices were mandatory for anyone who stayed in town during the off-season.

My sweat-covered T-shirt clung tightly against my torso which made me want to avoid this conversation more than usual. All I wanted was to feel the hot water from the shower scalding my back. Not have a fucking conversation about my girlfriend problems with Coach Sterling.

"Tons," I deadpanned. "Last I checked, I had four hundred private messages from girls begging to take the title of 'Abel Abbott's girlfriend' after I announced I was in the market on my Socialgram story yesterday." My lips fought a smile as the lie spilled from my mouth.

Practice was off for the next two days and if Coach was going to be pissed at me for playing around, so be it. By the time we came back on Monday, he wouldn't remember this conversation or the punishment drills he planned to give me anyway.

Coach placed a hand on his hip and narrowed his eyes at me begrudgingly. "You better be busting my nut, kid."

"Fuck, Coach. Please don't use that phrase again." I cringed.

He lifted up a brow, clearly not understanding what "busting a nut" meant, which almost made it worse. I tried not to think about how many people he'd unknowingly used that phrase on before me, which made another cringe ripple through my body.

I made a mental note to tell Lea about that one before Coach decided to slip that phrase into one of our press conferences. What a fucking headline that would be.

"Why?" he started to ask before cutting himself off with a shake of his head. "Whatever. I don't have time for this. Seriously, you made any progress with chef girl?"

"Her name is Scarlett," I corrected him. "And yeah, I've made some progress."

"What do you mean... some?" he questioned with knotted brows that made the crow's-feet around his eyes more prominent.

"I asked her to, uhh... be my girlfriend," I bit out, not giving him the whole truth.

What Coach didn't know wouldn't hurt him.

His daughter was the one who gave me the idea for the fake relationship in the first place, so he couldn't give me too much shit if he ever found out.

"She's supposed to give me an answer this morning." I tilted my head toward the locker room to give Coach the nonverbal that he was holding me up from finding out the answer to his prodding question.

"Get on with it then, son. You best pray that girl says

yes." He shook his head and gave me a pat on the back as I started to walk away. A bleak look covered his face like he wasn't confident she was going to say yes.

I couldn't blame him. Fuck, even I wasn't sure she would accept.

A week had passed since I had asked her, and while I wanted to respect Scarlett's wishes and give her time to think on it before making a decision, I was running out of time. With practices picking back up and team events scattered over the next few weeks, I needed to get this girlfriend situation squared away.

Walking into the locker room showers, I turned the nozzle to the hottest setting before peeling off my sweat-covered clothes and stepping into the scorching water. I spent the next fifteen minutes practically burning off the first layer of skin while internally debating whether or not Scarlett was going to agree to this.

Part of me was starting to regret offering Scarlett the house. Not because I wanted it. I didn't need the damn house. But after seeing how embarrassed she got when I offered it to her, I felt like a dick for feeding into one of her insecurities.

I wasn't planning on bringing it up again unless she mentioned it first.

Stepping out of the shower, I pulled the towel off the hook and wrapped it securely across my waist. Fortune, our wide receiver, slapped my ass with his towel as he passed me in the locker room on his way to the showers and I let out a low chuckle.

I threw on a clean black shirt and a pair of gray joggers before slipping on the latest tennis shoes that were given to me by one of my brand partners, Nagem. I'd been working with them for a few years and they paid me a fuckton of money to wear their clothes during team interviews or in the pictures I posted on Socialgram.

Occasionally I'd fly out to Los Angeles to do an advertising campaign photo shoot or to film a commercial for them.

Aside from playing, this brand deal was my favorite perk of being a big name in the league because it meant that I hadn't gone shopping for clothes at a regular department store in years. I had another connection to the fashion industry, but I would rather go naked than wear some of the high fashion bullshit she designed.

A new message lit up on the home screen of my phone as I finished lacing up my tennis shoes. Picking it up off the bench, I keyed in the password. "Speak of the devil," I whispered under my breath as a new text popped up from none other than Aera Chase herself.

Aera: If you keep ignoring my texts, I'm going to show up on your doorstep again, but this time it will be to murder you.
Aera: With a chainsaw.
Aera: While you're sleeping.
Aera: I wouldn't doubt me if I was you.
Abel: We both know you wouldn't go through with it. Orange isn't your color, Aer.

Smirking, I thumbed out my response, knowing that it would keep her occupied for a while. I turned my phone on do not disturb mode after her fourth notification came through. Picking up my gym bag from my locker, I threw it over my shoulder and shouted goodbyes to the boys before leaving the locker room and heading out toward the team parking lot.

I slid into the driver's seat with a sigh and turned the

key in the ignition. A momentary panic consumed me thinking about going home to hear Scarlett's answer, so I prolonged the situation and unnerved myself even more by driving ten under the speed limit and taking the longest route back to my place.

I had a hunch that I would eventually get over it if she ended up turning me down, but I wanted her to say yes. More than that, I wanted her to *want* to say yes.

My grip on the steering wheel tightened remembering how she flat out said no four times before agreeing to consider my proposition. And that was only after I'd thrown in the house as collateral.

Fuck.

My stomach churned and I started regretting taking the longest route back to the house. I needed to get this over with before I went mad.

Turning the wheel on a dime, I took a shortcut, speeding through the familiar side streets before making it to the neighborhood's back gates.

The only productive thing I'd come to terms with on my ride was the fact that I had been an asshole to her.

And it was no one's fault but my own.

But beating myself up for it wasn't going to get me anywhere though.

Growing up, Mom always said that the cards would always play out in my favor if I played long enough. Then again, she was the town poker champion six years in a row though, so I'm not sure whether she was spitting out life advice or poker advice.

Regardless, I was hopeful that Scarlett would give me a shot to show her my true self. Not the asshole of a boss she probably thought I was. I knew that if she gave me a chance, she wouldn't fucking regret it.

I'd make damn sure of that.

I pulled the SUV into the driveway and the tires slowed to a halt. Grabbing my bag from the passenger seat, I made my way into the house, silently hoping that Mom was right and that the cards would play out in my favor.

"IF, and that is a very big if," Scarlett started. "I agree to do this, we need to set some ground rules." She waved her giant spatula at my face before swiveling around to turn back to the stove where she was making breakfast.

The jeans she wore hugged the curve of her ass tightly and my mind drifted to all the positions I wanted to put her in. Doggy. Reverse cowgirl. Missionary, so I could see her face. Every fucking position in the *Kama Sutra*.

I shook my head and pulled myself back into our discussion. "What kind of ground rules?" I arched a brow in question.

I wasn't exactly sure what stipulations were involved in a fake relationship, so I didn't account for "ground rules" in the scenarios I had played out on my car ride earlier.

Fuck, if I was being honest, I hadn't exactly accounted for anything. It's not every day that you get tasked with finding a fake girlfriend. I silently cursed Coach and the Matrix for putting me in this situation to begin with.

Scarlett glanced at me over her shoulder. "Yeah. If we're going to pretend that we are a couple we need to have boundaries. If we're both on the same page with whatever this"—she waved her spatula between the two of us—"is, it will make people less likely to question us."

The girl had a point. "Okay… what do you have in mind?"

Scarlett turned back to face the stove and worked her spatula around the pan. The delicious smell of cinnamon pancakes filled the kitchen. Her gaze dropped down to the pan once again.

"If we're going to be in a fake relationship, I'm not going to date anyone else. I don't expect you to stop seeing other people, but if you're going to hook up with other women, just um… be discreet about it. You know?" She sucked in a breath after her words tumbled out faster than I could comprehend them.

Her eyes met mine timidly as she peered over her shoulder once again to gauge my reaction.

"No," I said firmly, my jaw clenched. My fingers wrapped tightly around the fork in my right hand.

"No?" Her eyes shot up to meet mine as she finally turned her body toward me. Her cheeks reddened to the color of her name.

"No, Red. I'm not going to see anyone else." I blew out a long, slow sigh, letting out a heavy breath, releasing some of the tension that had been building in my shoulders. Though the grip on my fork remained secure. "I would *never* do that to you," I mumbled under my breath as she handed my plate to me.

Not that I was sleeping around anyway. Fuck, I couldn't even remember the last time I got laid. But even if I was fucking around, I still wouldn't do that to her. I wouldn't risk embarrassing her with a scandal like that, especially when her career was taking off.

I liked this rule though. I hadn't seen any men over at her pool house before, but I didn't want any other guys touching her. Especially if she was going to be mine.

Well, pretending to be mine.

Fuck, I hated that.

"Oh, um, okay then. If that's what you want." She expelled a breath before turning back to face the stove yet again. "So, we're not seeing other people. Yup, got it…" She trailed off, moving her spatula around the empty pan. She must have forgotten that she'd already handed me the plate with my food on it.

"That's what I want. Any other rules?" I said firmly, scooping a giant bite of fluffy cinnamon pancake into my mouth.

"Yes," she replied curtly, although she appeared to be struggling to come up with another ground rule. I watched as she twirled the small emerald-green ring on her middle finger around and around. "No kissing," she blurted out as I took another massive heap of pancake into my mouth.

Seemed a bit juvenile being that I was two years shy of thirty, but whatever made her comfortable. Or so I thought until she added an addendum, "Oh, and no sex."

My eyes grew wide and I pressed a fist to my mouth to suppress the cough that expelled from my lungs. A giant bite of pancake stuck in my windpipe, making it hard to breathe.

She thought I wanted to fuck her? Okay. Fine. I wanted to fuck her, but not under these circumstances.

Holy fuck.

"What did you just say?" I managed to croak out my words between coughs.

"Uhh, no kissing… and no sex," she confirmed, shrinking back into herself a bit.

I nodded. Which was all I could manage with my brain full of images of Scarlett and I fucking. If she asked me to take her right here on the kitchen island, I'd bend her over in an instant.

My dick twitched realizing that she'd thought about us

having sex too. Well, probably not in the same way I had since she was banning us from doing it, but still, the thought had crossed her mind.

Either way, it was a step in the right direction.

"Anything else?"

"Hmmm, I don't think so. Do you have anything to add?"

Did I have anything to add? Yeah, that I wanted to ditch rules two and three. But I wasn't going to out my desires by negotiating with her. I'd take whatever she was willing to give me, even if it meant not being able to kiss her.

"Nope, nothing." I shook my head as I recovered from my near death by pancake.

"In that case, I guess I'm in." She stuck her hand out toward me.

Huh. That had gone along smoother than envisioned. I expected her to have more resistance like last week or make an attempt to bargain for more than just the house.

If I had known it would've been that easy, I might have grown some balls sooner and asked her out months ago.

"Deal." I slipped my hand into hers and we shook on it, sealing our fate.

"Now grab your phone and take a picture of me handing you your breakfast, but don't get my face in it." For the first time in months, she smiled at me, a genuine smile, and it knocked the breath from my lungs.

Her smile was like a drug and I instantly craved more of it.

She could've broken my fucking heart the next second and I wouldn't have cared. I'd let her break me a million times if it meant seeing her smile like that again.

SEVEN
SCARLETT

IT HAD BEEN a week since Abel and I came to an agreement on the terms of our fake relationship. We had each initiated soft launch photos on our respective Socialgram accounts to generate buzz among fans about a potential relationship.

Neither of us had named the other or shown the other's face in our posts, but it didn't take long for people to put the details together. Granted, my ring in the photo he posted was a dead giveaway since my hands are in the majority of the cooking photos on the blog.

I made a mental note to remove any obvious personal identifiers should I find myself in another relationship publicity stunt.

With our covers all but officially broken, our first public appearance together as a couple was impending any day now.

Abel and I had been talking more than usual the last week, but our conversations were surface level at best. I couldn't *imagine* sitting across from him on a dinner date making small talk for two hours with people and cameras watching, but for a fourteen-million-dollar house, I would force myself through it with a smile.

I was still baffled by the entire situation. The guy was a professional freaking athlete, for Christ's sake. I wouldn't put it past him to have a handful of girls on speed dial at any given moment.

I hadn't wrapped my mind around why he had chosen me, of all people, but at this point, it wasn't like we could change it. So I guessed whatever reasoning he had must've been a good one.

After parking my car in Mae's driveway, I rounded the corner toward the pool house. Pausing in front of the pool house doors, I attempted to fish my house key out of the never-ending tote bag that hung from my shoulder.

It was only when I looked down to search through the bag that I found a box with an envelope taped to the top sitting in front of the French doors.

That was odd…

I crouched down and peeled the light-green envelope off of the box and opened it to find an invitation to a charity gala for later that night. Thank God it wasn't a dinner date and Lea would be around in case I needed an escape. I continued reading the card to see it was for the… National Cervical Cancer Coalition.

My breath caught in my lungs.

That was the kind of cancer that my mom had passed from two years ago. Did Abel know about that? If so, who the heck told him? I turned over the back of the invitation and found a handwritten note from Abel.

Be my date?
I'll pick you up at seven.
- A

I wasn't sure whether I was more shocked at our first official outing happening sooner than I had anticipated or the fact that Abel had better handwriting than I did.

Shoving the invitation back in the envelope, I picked up the box that was sitting at my feet before pulling my house key from my bag.

I opened the doors and walked down the hallway heading toward the kitchen where I sat the gorgeous golden box down on the island. My stomach turned thinking about what might lay inside the handcrafted box staring back at me.

What could Abel possibly have given me? The wrapping alone was probably more expensive than my monthly car payment.

The box taunted me as I paced back and forth across the kitchen a few times before perching myself on the barstool and timidly pulling the box across the counter so it sat in front of me.

My heart thumped loudly in my ears while I mustered up the courage to slowly, slowly open the box. Peeling away the tissue paper, my lungs tightened as I took in the most beautiful emerald-green dress I had ever laid eyes on. It was probably the most gorgeous piece of clothing I had *ever* laid eyes on.

Tears pricked the back of my eyes when I noticed it was the exact shade of my beloved ring that Mom had given me.

Oh. My. God.

I couldn't fight my heart from swelling at the gesture of Abel picking out a dress for me to wear to tonight's charity event. Specifically one that matched my ring.

Sure, I could have borrowed a gown from one of Mae's closets, but him going out of his way to do this for me made it feel like an actual date.

But why?

I pulled my phone from my bag that rested on the barstool next to me and quickly shot a text to Mae.

Scarlett: Pool house. Immediately.
Mae: Aye, Aye, Captain!

My fingertips were hot as I removed the soft crepe material from the box and carried the dress to my bedroom. I hung it on the doorframe of the closet, marveling up at the floor-length gown with my jaw agape when I heard the front doors open.

I called for Mae to meet me in my bedroom and moments later she peered into the room from the doorway and her mouth formed a perfect *O* as she came and stood next to me. I handed her the invitation and turned it over so she could read Abel's note too.

"So he did this all by himself? You didn't ask him for this?" She picked up after a beat of silence.

"Never said a word," I replied, still plagued with shock.

"I think I'm in love with him."

"Mae!"

"Kidding, kidding! So, I take it you said yes to being his girlfriend?"

"Yeah…" I trailed off.

I still hadn't told Mae that this whole thing with Abel was a ruse or that he would be giving me his house at the end of it. When she asked about our Socialgram posts, I told her that we were still feeling things out.

Pretty sure she thought I meant we were hooking up based on the smug grin she gave me when I told her. I probably should've shut down the idea, but at least this would stop her from trying to help me get laid.

"I can't wear it. It's got to cost my entire salary if not more."

"Mine too."

"Don't say that! I'm already nervous enough. What if I spill something on it? What if I break the zipper?"

Mae took the dress off the door to look at the tag on the inside. Her face paled and her eyes grew wide as she looked up at me. "Um... do you remember that designer that stayed at Abel's house the time he kicked you out...?" she questioned, waiting for my response.

How could I forget? That was humiliating. I felt like I was a one-night stand being shuffled out the door before the guy's roommates woke up. I nodded my head up and down in response.

"Aera Chase, she's the designer of the dress. 'Inamra' is the name of her fashion house."

"You're lying."

Mae handed me over the tag to show me the label of the dress with tiny letters that read, *"An Inamra exclusive."*

He gave me a dress that was designed by one of his flings.

I knew I shouldn't have gotten my hopes up thinking that he had thought of this by himself. She had probably left it at his house when she visited last fall and he was trying to get the dress out of his closet.

"Burn it."

I wanted to stuff it in the fireplace and watch it go up in flames. The blood underneath my skin turned hot and my body went rigid as I gave the dress another once-over.

"No. We're not going to burn the dress." Mae drew back her shoulders and a curl played at her lips as she held up the dress in front of me. "Because when he sees you in it, it'll bring him to his knees. And it will be more satisfying to watch him suffer."

A conniving grin took over my face.

Watching him suffer was something I could get behind.

I'D ALMOST CONSIDERED WEARING one of Mae's dresses out of pure rage, but decided against it after trying on the dress Abel had given me. Mae was right, I looked damn good in it.

Like forget your ex was the one who made the dress good.

At seven sharp, a knock sounded on the front door and my pulse began to race. My heart beat recklessly against the walls of my chest. Why was I so nervous all of a sudden? It wasn't like this was a real date. I took a calming breath before opening the front door.

Holy hell.

Abel looked hot.

The "we're no longer going to this party because I'd rather practice making babies with you instead" kind of hot.

Was it appropriate to think those thoughts about your boss? Probably not, but I couldn't help it. The three-piece black suit he wore was tailored to perfection, showing off every handcrafted muscle on his body. I raked my eyes over him another time for good measure.

I'd never seen him out of workout clothes before, but this was just… wow.

"You look gorgeous." Abel smiled, looking me up and down with a heated gaze that made my thighs clench together as he stepped through the door. Unsure if I should go for a hug, I settled for a small wave and what

I'm sure was a stupid grin. "The dress is… wow. You're beautiful, Red."

"Thank you," I bit out with a curt tone. I didn't want to talk about the stupid freaking dress anymore, especially with him.

Although it was gorgeous, this dress would find its new home in my trash can after tonight's event. Exactly where it belonged.

"Should we get go—" I started before Mae's holler from the living room cut me off.

"Scarlett, wait!"

Mae waltzed into the entryway with her laptop held out in front of her so the screen was facing Abel and me. She tried to hide the stupid grin on her face while the video call connected and the screen expanded, showing us two old dudes lying on the beach.

Oh no. No no no.

"Hi Dads." I waved sheepishly at the screen; I could see my face flushed with embarrassment in the small box in the upper corner with our faces in it.

I should've *known* they'd do something like this.

Dads and Mae played a "fun" game where they tried to ruin my dates before they even started. This game was part of the reason I could count on one hand the number of dates I'd been on in this lifetime.

I hoped that they had forgotten about our little tradition, seeing as I hadn't gone on a date in two years, but I was wrong. Oh so freaking wrong.

"Hi, Scar. We heard you're going on a date tonight?" Desmond quirked a brow at me. James sat next to him, noticeably holding back a chuckle.

Bitches. All of them.

"Yeah, Dads, this is Abel. Abel, these are our dads,

Desmond and James." I gestured a hand to them respectively.

"Hey guys, it's nice to meet you. You have good weather down in the Keys?"

Wait, how did he know that Dads lived in the Keys? Abel and I had never talked about our families before.

Weird.

Maybe Lea told him in passing?

"Fantastic. You'll have to come down sometime. That is if you're going to keep our daughter safe tonight. You will, won't you?" Desmond's brows pinched together.

Hearing his voice was like a knife to the heart. I didn't realize how deeply I missed having them around until now.

"Yes sirs. I won't let anything happen to her. I'll make sure of it."

"Good, good. And you're not going to try any funny business?" James questioned in an attempt to be stern.

He failed. Miserably.

Poor guy didn't have a stern bone in his body. Mom and Desmond took turns laying down the law when needed.

"Oh my god." A groan slipped from under my breath and I could feel the heat spreading throughout my face and neck.

"I'll be an absolute gentleman. You have my word," Abel responded, with that gorgeous smile that made my stomach flip upside down. At least he was taking this better than the others who had come before him.

"And you're going to have her home by midnight?" Mae chimed in for good measure. I couldn't know for sure, but I'm pretty sure this was comparable to being emasculated.

Stupid bitch. I was going to have to cut her for that later.

"Yes ma'am."

"Very well. Bye, Scar. Make good choices and don't forget to use protection," James quipped with a wave before the screen went black. Mae laughed as she walked back to the living room with the laptop in hand.

"I'm so sorry. I didn't know that they would..." I slapped a hand to my forehead, silently hoping that I could erase the last ten minutes from my memory.

Abel peeled my hand away from my face and tilted my chin upward so that our eyes met. "Don't be embarrassed. They just want to make sure that I'm going to treat you right." He stared into my eyes, briefly glancing down at my lips. For a sliver of a moment I thought he was going to kiss me, but what was worse was my heart shrinking when he didn't. "Can't say I wouldn't do the same if I were them."

Abel's hand left the underside of my chin and I felt empty at the loss of warmth from his hand.

I shook my head in frustration, trying to snap out of it when he turned to grab my coat from the entry table.

What was going on with me?

"You ready?" He turned back to me and gently took my hand in his while he led me out toward his car.

"Ready as I'll ever be."

THE ENERGY in the ballroom was daunting.

There were beautiful women in gorgeous gowns with hair and makeup done by professional artists. And the men were all dressed to the nines in their designer suits.

It was easy to distinguish the players from the sponsors simply based on height and stature. Not to mention most of the players were crowded around the table that was filled to the brim with appetizers.

One might've thought that the night would've gotten off to a slow start before picking up.

Wrong.

It was absolute madness from the moment we walked through the doors two hours ago. Abel had hardly handed over my coat to the attendant before we began getting bombarded with questions about our "relationship."

How did you all meet?

When did you know he was the one?

Would you like to join us on our couples vacation next off-season?

How soon did you all say I love you?

I would've enjoyed lunch with wolves more than answering these questions, but I was having more than enough fun replying with the most obnoxious answers I could come up with on the fly.

I couldn't wrap my head around how oblivious these people could be to the lies I came up with. If I told them we met on a skydiving trip on the moon, they probably would've believed me and asked where they could buy tickets.

For people who were supposedly super successful, they weren't all that great at detecting a couple of frauds among them and that seemed like a liability on their part.

In their defense, Abel had done a great job playing the part of attentive boyfriend. His hand rested on the small of my lower back all night. He would occasionally place a kiss on my forehead during moments when we were really trying to sell our "love."

If I didn't know any better, I would have thought that he was being sincere with how believable he was.

"Oh we're neighbors. I saw him taking out the trash shirtless one morning while I was taking my morning run and just knew I had to 'bump' into him with a fresh batch of cupcakes in hand. He invited me inside and well…" I winked at the latest couple—Sharron and Paul, mid-fifties, two kids from previous marriages—that bombarded us with overbearing questions.

"The rest is history," Abel added in with a wink like he'd done all night whenever ridiculous retellings of our fake love story left my lips.

He didn't seem the least bit annoyed at my responses, although most of them were meant to embarrass him. I told the team owner of the Matrix that Abel still swam with arm floaties because he was scared of the deep end and he didn't even flinch. In fact, he seemed more amused than anything.

We said our goodbyes to Sharron and Paul and moved toward one of the outer corners of the ballroom to take a snack break from the madness. I plopped down at one of the tables and Abel plated appetizers for us.

"You're a charmer, Red. Everyone loves you." Abel smirked, handing me over a plate of crab Rangoon. "Color me impressed."

"Who knew I would finally be able to put those improv classes from college to good use?"

"It's not every day you get the chance to lie to the face of multi-millionaires, huh?"

"Even creepy Bob has *multiple* millions?" I questioned. "What am I doing wrong?" I muttered under my breath while stuffing my face with the appetizer plate Abel handed over to me.

How could a guy who looked like a walking gargoyle have that much money?

"You ready to get back out there?"

"No. Please don't make me," I pleaded, pressing my hands together in front of my chest. "Those people are awful."

"I know. I fucking hate these events with a burning passion, and it's usually worse when I'm alone because people are trying to set me up with their daughters and nieces."

"What a travesty to have options." I rolled my eyes playfully.

Between middle-aged women trying to set him up with their daughters and the flood of women thirsting over him on Socialgram the better question was who *didn't* want to be with Abel Abbott?

Other than myself, of course.

"You don't think you have options?" Abel bounced back at me. "I've been giving guys the death glare all night because they won't take their eyes off of you." I picked up on the hint of annoyance laced in his tone before he knocked back a glass of scotch.

"What? No, they haven't."

"You're oblivious, Red." Abel shook his head with an elongated breath. After clearing my plate in record time, he held out his hand to pull me out of my seat.

My feet were *dying* in these heels, but I tossed back another swig of wine to help ease the pain and let him pull me back into the swarm of people.

Mere feet away from the safety of Abel's teammates, one of the biggest sponsors, Mr. Kirk, intercepted us and dragged us into a dreadful conversation about stocks and investments.

God, these textbook schmoozing conversations were exhausting.

"Oh, no," I gasped, looking at a giant clock on one of the walls. "It's really getting late. We should probably head out." I turned to Abel and stared into his soul, hoping he would pick up on yet another one of my lies, but he didn't say a word.

Instead, his gaze flickered down to my mouth for a small moment before he met my eyes.

"Isn't that right, *my love*?" I asked, gazing up at him with my best puppy-dog eyes.

EIGHT

ABEL

FUCK.

Scarlett knocked the breath out of my lungs with two words. Two words, that was it.

How was that fucking possible? She gave me one look and I could hardly catch my breath.

God. What I would give to have her look at me like that every day, every hour, every second. Fuck.

And don't get me started on the way that little "my love" made my dick twitch against the seam of my pants.

Was she trying to fucking kill me? If she kept up this act, I would have to take her to the coat closet and fuck her senseless before the night ended.

"Right?" she asked again, this time with a concerned look on her face.

I'd been too startled at how she looked at me to respond. Clearing my throat, I pulled myself back into reality. "Mhmm, yes," I hummed.

It was the best I could manage, given the lack of oxygen flowing to my brain and the overabundance of blood rushing to my cock.

Scarlett pinched my forearm and pinned me with a glare that could scare the devil. She must not have noticed that Mr. Kirk had checked out of the conversation five minutes earlier, so she had nothing to worry about.

The guy was too busy taking an interest in our defensive end's wife to pick up on our ruse. The guy didn't make the slightest attempt at subtlety, locking his eyes on Tommy's wife's chest.

It was like he was in a trance. Fucking pervert.

Fearing Scarlett's warning, I snaked my arm gently around her waist and tugged her back against my chest.

People weren't going to believe we were madly in love if we stood shoulder to shoulder all night, would they?

Scarlett's back flushed against my chest and she sank into my touch like being in my arms was the most natural thing in the world. To the naked eye, anyone would have thought that we had done this a thousand times before.

Fuck, did I wish we had.

If only she knew about all of the nights that I'd lain awake imagining this reality. All of the hours that I'd watched her flow around the kitchen with ease as she cooked, wishing I could have wrapped my hands around her waist and pulled her closer to me.

Witnessing her effortlessly mold to my touch soothed me until the thought of another guy touching her like this made my muscles grow stiff against her back. At that moment, she tilted her head upward and the big grin and those brown fucking eyes dissolved any tension in my body.

Fuck me. This girl.

Our eyes stayed sealed to one another's for a brief moment, only silence passing between us. I gripped her tighter at the waist and pressed my lips to the side of her forehead.

"Look at you two lovebirds," Mr. Kirk chimed in with the corners of his mouth turned upward. "I'll leave you to it. Miss Sawyer, don't wear our star player out, alright? He will need some energy come time for training camp."

Fucking sleaze bag with his obnoxious wink. I could kill him for standing there thinking about my girl in a sexual manner.

Scarlett's infectious laughter vibrated against my chest. "Don't you worry, Mr. Kirk. This guy here can't seem to keep up these days." Her mouth quirked with humor as she tried to hold back another laugh from passing between her lips.

If the night's events had taught me anything, it was that Scarlett's shy girl act around me was exactly that, an act. And only around me.

Scarlett was damn good at playing games. She'd been trying to get a rise out of me all night and I hadn't let her. She seemed to forget that I played games for a living and competition was ingrained in my nature. She could try to knock me off-kilter, but in that case... game on.

Squinting my eyes at her, a small smile curled up the corners of my lips. "You're funny...but I can assure you that wouldn't be the case," I whispered low enough for only her to hear.

Her breath hitched and a flash of red rose to her cheeks. Mr. Kirk chuckled and waved goodbye, aiming his stride toward Tommy and his wife.

Disgusting.

Scarlett's head landed backward on my chest as the laugh she was holding in came barreling out of her. "You're a better actor than I thought you'd be, Abbott."

My hands stayed firm around her waist and I held her steadily against me, desperate to have her close for as long as she'd let me.

Sweeping her hair to one side, I dipped my head low enough that my lips lightly brushed her ear. "Two can play this game, Red."

Pulling my head back slightly, our faces sat inches apart from each other. I drank in the comfort of her nearness, knowing that if I moved my head two inches closer I could have her the way I'd wanted her all along.

Did she feel the desire that swarmed between us as deeply as I did?

Slow and unwavering, my gaze slid down from her eyes to her lips. Her bottom lip was faintly fuller than the top and I could smell a faint scent of the cupcake-flavored ChapStick she was wearing.

Which wasn't much of a surprise, given the fact that she'd gone through at least half a dozen tubes of that fucking cupcake ChapStick since I met her. I'd bet good money her lips tasted like cupcakes too.

Fuck, I wanted to taste her lips.

Snapping out of my trance, I raked my gaze back up to those big brown eyes, realizing I'd been staring directly at her lips for God knows how long.

Scarlett narrowed her eyes at me and shook her head, letting me know I'd been caught. She gave me a faint laugh and continued to lock those big brown doe eyes with mine in retaliation.

What was a semi earlier had turned into a full fucking hard-on and she could probably feel my cock growing as it pressed up against her ass.

Fuck. This girl was going to be the death of me.

The moment between the two of us faded as a familiar male voice boomed above the chatter of the crowd, heading in our direction.

"Scarlett Sawyer as I live and breathe. To whom do I owe such an honor?"

"October!" Scarlett squealed as she flailed her hands in the air and wrapped her arms around the neck of my teammate, October Calhoun.

He got traded here last season after spending a few years with the Nashville Knights. The two of us had enough chemistry on the field to win a League Bowl, but off the field October not so much. I couldn't be bothered with whatever bullshit he got up to in his free time.

That didn't answer the question of how the fuck did Red know October though.

Could they have… nope.

Wasn't even going to entertain that possibility.

Scarlett grabbed my forearm and dragged me in to join their conversation.

"Abbott, how do you know my girl Scar?" October raised an inquiring brow and rested a tattooed arm across Scarlett's shoulders.

His girl?

What the fuck right did he have calling her "his girl"?

My jaw clenched and my fists turned to stone at my sides. It was a miracle I didn't break my own damn hand.

Scarlett wiggled herself out from under his arm and plucked a glass of scotch off of one of the server's trays as they whirled by us and held it out to me.

I knocked back the glass and set it on another server's tray who whizzed by. Scarlett gave me a faint smile and willingly drifted back into the comfort of my arms.

I'd be lying if I said it didn't fuel my fucking god complex when she did that. All night, I had been the one to initiate contact between the two of us. She didn't shy away from it, but she'd never been the one to initiate until now.

"Scarlett's my girlfriend." I looked October dead in the

fucking eyes. I could feel my jaw clench as we stared at each other for an extended moment.

Not a single word passed between us.

Scarlett must have sensed the building tension, because she interlocked her fingers with mine before clearing her throat to speak. "Uh, October grew up on the same street as Mae and I."

My shoulders relaxed at her words.

Childhood friends, huh?

How had I not put it together that October and Red were from the same small town a few hours west of here?

"How's Hallie?" Scarlett asked, looking in October's direction.

Apparently, his mom had an unhealthy obsession with Halloween. So much so that she named her kids October and Halloween. At least his sister had the brains to go by a nickname.

"She's good, getting ready for her freshman year of college," he replied to Scarlett's question but kept his gaze on me with eyes narrowed to slits.

I don't know what pissed me off more, the fact that I was jealous over a girl who wasn't mine or that he had picked up on my jealousy.

"Don't worry, Abbott. I'll tell you all the embarrassing stories you want to know about little Scarlett here." October flashed a sly wink in my direction, nudging Scarlett with his elbow.

I wanted nothing more than to punch that smug grin off the fucker's face, but it wasn't worth unleashing the wrath of Coach and Lea. Or putting my contract in jeopardy before training camp started.

Scarlett slapped him playfully on the chest with the back of her hand. "You wouldn't!"

"Looking forward to it," I replied in a neutral tone, trying to settle the war that was raging in my mind.

"I take it you've been taking care of my girl?"

His girl.

He really needed to stop fucking calling her that before I smashed his face into the wall.

"He is," Scarlett whispered, her eyes locked with mine and her cheeks flushed a light shade of pink.

October's eyes followed a blonde in a black dress who walked past us and she gave him a knowing wink as she strode out of the ballroom.

"Unfortunately, I'm going to have to cut our reunion short. I've got a lanky blonde waiting for me in the bathroom. Scar, let's catch up soon, yeah?" Scarlett smiled at him and nodded. "Abbott, take care of our girl." October winked, clapping a hand on my back.

Scarlett and I watched as he picked up another woman and slung his arm around her shoulder before heading out of the ballroom and in the direction of the blonde.

Just as I was about to suggest we head out and grab a bite to eat, I spotted Lea making her way through the crowd toward us.

Could this night get any longer?

She wore a bright-red dress that matched her hair, and Fortune, the team's wide receiver, had his eyes glued to her all night. Thank fuck Coach was too engulfed with talking to sponsors to notice or he would have had Fortune's ass kicked off the team by morning.

Fortune and I played ball together in college at Wadecrest and, aside from my buddy Carlo, he was arguably the closest thing I had to a best friend. Which wasn't saying much considering we only hung out once a month... if that.

Who would've guessed that the forbidden Lea Sterling was his type? Huh, interesting.

"Lovely couple!" Lea's voice rose an octave while she strutted up to us with a taunting smile. She poked me playfully in the side and I made a mental note to get back at her for that later.

It wasn't that I'd be mad if Scarlett found out how I felt about her, but when the time came, I wanted her to hear the words from me. Not someone else.

"You know, Scar. Your date here left the biggest donation of the night." Lea turned to Scarlett with a raised brow.

"You what?" She looked up at me with tears forming in her eyes.

I read about her mom passing away from cervical cancer on her blog a few months ago when she shared a post about how she made her mom's favorite lasagna dish on her mom's birthday every year.

Lea had mentioned it in conversation a time or two as well, so Scarlett probably wouldn't think anything of it.

I debated on whether or not to bring her to the gala tonight when I saw the charity—I didn't know if it would be too difficult for her—but I wanted to make a donation in her mom's honor. And in order to do that, I needed to have a date on my arm to adhere to the team's new protocol.

She wasn't supposed to find out about the donation though. I never planned on telling her about it. "Yeah. It wasn't that much. Don't worry about it." I shrugged, trying to brush it off.

Scarlett whipped her head to Lea. "How much?"

"A quarter of a million dollars," Lea piped in.

Fuck. Okay, I lied, it was a lot.

Scarlett threw her hands around my neck and

squeezed me so hard I could barely breathe. I wasn't complaining though. She didn't let go for a long while and Lea stood there looking at me with a mischievous smile.

I couldn't be mad at Lea for telling her though, because this moment was worth every single fucking penny.

AFTER A HALF HOUR of chatting with teammates, Scarlett and I made a final round across the room, saying goodbyes and promising other couples to stay in touch, even though both of us and the other couples knew we wouldn't so much as wave at each other if we ran into each other at the grocery store.

It was just one of those courtesies that all couples had to do to play their part and pretend like they enjoyed getting to know each other.

Scarlett had done better than I had expected tonight. I didn't realize that she was such a natural at this kind of thing. If I'd known sooner, I wouldn't have subjected myself to the torture of going to these events alone.

"You're good at this," I said matter-of-factly, leading us out of the ballroom.

"I've been Mae's date to plenty of her modeling events and after-parties over the years and it's always the same song and dance with these kinds of people. Over the years, I've just mastered the art of obligatory small talk, I guess." She shrugged.

We walked toward the coat closet and with no one around but the attendant, I could already feel Scarlett beginning to shy away from me.

"Why are you only shy around me?" I questioned

abruptly, grabbing Scarlett's coat from the attendant and holding it up for her to slip her arms through.

All night she had been a social butterfly and as much as she could chalk it up to her being experienced in small talk, I knew that version of her was the truest version of herself.

It was only after seeing her effortlessly start conversations with people, cracking jokes, and talking to people like she had known them for years that I picked up on it.

Yet, the second we were alone together, a switch flipped inside her and she retreated back into herself.

"You make me nervous," Scarlett replied timidly after a beat.

My stomach took a nosedive as I processed her words. I made her nervous? That was the last fucking thing that I wanted her to feel around me. She was the one that made me nervous. When did those roles reverse?

"Why?" Deep down I knew why, but I needed to hear the words from her mouth for it to be real. I'd spend hours overanalyzing her statement if she left me without an explanation.

Scarlett smoothed her hands across her dress, keeping her eyes peeled to her shoes as we walked out of the building.

"I mean, we didn't exactly get off to the best start, and I never really knew how to act around you after that. And until recently, every time you were around me, you hardly spoke and what little conversations we did have were always so formal. Like a boss and an employee. And now that we're doing this—" She waved a hand between us. "I guess I don't know how to act whenever we're not pretending. Even our current arrangement is a business transaction if you think about it."

Her honesty felt like a blow to the stomach, but I didn't

respond, only furthering her point. I understood where she was coming from, but fuck, it hurt to hear those words said out loud.

Scarlett winced with every step as she made her way through the parking lot. I noticed her feet had been hurting her all night, although she tried to cover her pain when others were watching.

"Here, let me carry you," I said, scooping her up swiftly before she could decline my offer.

I should've loved having her close to me, but right then, I hated it.

So fucking much.

I wanted her to wrap herself around me because she wanted to. Not because we were trying to impress a bunch of sixty-year-old men with money or attempting to sell our relationship to my teammates.

I hated knowing that tomorrow she'd go back to being detached and aloof with me. I knew it was a lot to expect her to act how she did tonight with me all the time, but I wanted her to.

A lot more than I was willing to admit out loud.

NINE

SCARLETT

I WISHED I could've said that my first public outing with Abel was awful, but that would make me a stone-cold liar.

Schmoozing creepy old men? My forte. Poking fun at Abel's stamina in bed? Absolutely comical. And pretending that we were a couple that was *super massively major* in love? A lot easier than I'd envisioned.

If Abel were asking, I would never admit it, but he was actually a pretty great date.

I tried to hide my blush when he picked me up bridal style and carried me to the car like I weighed nothing. Though, I realized I'd failed miserably when he opened the passenger door for me. My face must have been the color of a firetruck based on the way he tried to hide his grin by wiping his thumb across his lips.

It definitely wasn't hot either.

My boss? Hot?

Nope. Not here. Absolutely not.

Abel steered the car through the desolate streets and the two of us sat in uncomfortable silence. We lived away from the buzz of the city, but it was an unusually quiet night which made it feel like time was slowed down.

He wore a solemn expression on his face for the last twenty minutes and hadn't once glanced over at me despite my frequent peeks over at him.

Truthfully, I hadn't meant to respond as bluntly as I did earlier when I told him I didn't know how to act around him when we weren't playing pretend. But now that it was out in the open, I didn't regret saying what I said.

I peered over at Abel, enamored with watching him possessively grip the steering wheel. Jesus Christ, why did he have to look like that while driving? Add on the way his perfect three-piece suit accentuated every one of his hard-earned muscles and my thighs were clenched together for the second time tonight because of him.

Pretty sure it was illegal to think about your boss like that. And if it wasn't… it should be. This was probably a repercussion of the one too many drinks I snagged off of serving trays throughout the night.

"You good over there?" Abel *finally* looked over at me with a coy smile.

"Huh? Um. Yup." I cleared my throat, bringing myself back to reality where I was absolutely not allowed to think about what my boss looked like naked. "Doing fantastic. You?"

Cursing myself, I bounced my gaze toward the window. My words had betrayed me nearly as much as my thighs did. I might have been a *little* drunk but not enough to act like the freaking idiot I was being.

I needed to get it the hell together.

Immediately.

I didn't allow myself to look over at him, but I had an *overwhelming* feeling that if I were to glance in his direction that I'd find one side of his lips curved up into a grin.

He hadn't said a word in almost an hour and now he wanted to make jokes?

What an asshole.

I gulped down a steadying breath, trying to gather my bearings. Given my state of mind, I didn't trust that the next time I opened my mouth I wouldn't start oversharing.

"I had a good time tonight," Abel said softly, finally breaking the suffocating silence between us.

Praise freaking God.

Another second longer and I would have internally combusted.

"Same, surprisingly," I replied, although I couldn't believe I was admitting it out loud. "Who knows, maybe if you had asked me on a date instead of me coming to work for you, we could've made a good couple."

Shit shit shit.

I didn't mean to say that out loud either.

Goddammit, Scarlett.

I knew I should've kept my mouth shut.

"You think so?" A frown line creased at the corner of Abel's lips when he craned his neck to look at me as we pulled up to a red light. His eyebrows pulled together, but those burning eyes were directed right at me.

Analyzing. Watching.

Heat stormed through my veins under the weight of his stare. "Maybe… who knows." I looked over and gave him a sheepish smile.

Stupid, stupid, stupid.

"Who knows…" He repeated my words back to himself and a muscle in his jaw flexed.

Abel parted his lips like he was going to say something else, but instead of saying what was on his mind, he flattened his lips into a straight line at the last second.

Our silence commenced once again.

I kept trying to sneak glances at him for the rest of the car ride, but his face remained unchanged. His dark brows stayed permanently knotted, and a pained expression told me he was either constipated or wrestling with a troubling thought.

My guess was the former.

"Thank you, by the way," I whispered softly, deciding to segue from our earlier conversation as we pulled up to the neighborhood gates.

Just thinking about the donation that Abel made to the cervical cancer research foundation made tears prick the back of my throat.

How was it possible that the biggest asshole I'd ever met was also the person single-handedly responsible for the nicest thing anyone had ever done for me?

"You're welcome, Red," Abel spoke lowly, grabbing my hand from my lap and intertwining it with his. Only this time, when we touched, it wasn't laced with the pretend affection that we used hours earlier to display our "relationship."

It was just for us.

A silent olive branch that things weren't going to go back to how they used to be between us which I was happy to accept.

Our hands stayed connected as he drove through the quiet neighborhood illuminated by streetlights.

It was right then that I felt a *teeny tiny* bit of the resistance I had built up toward him begin to crack.

Maybe it was the wine or maybe it was because I was feeling a bit emotional about my mom, but I was starting to get the inkling that maybe, *just maybe*, Abel wasn't an asshole after all.

ABEL PULLED his SUV into Mae's driveway, cut the engine, and rounded the hood before I could gather my shoes from the floorboard.

"You don't have to—" I started as he opened the passenger door for me.

"I want to," he cut me off while slipping a hand under the thickest part of my thighs and the other under my back and tugging me against his chest.

He *really* needed to stop pulling me into a bridal cradle before I gave myself any ideas.

I blamed it on the suit. Not the man wearing it.

He slammed the door shut with his foot and I tightened my grip on his neck while he carried me across the backyard and through the pool house until he placed me ever so gently on top of my bed.

Like he'd been here a thousand times before, Abel walked over to my closet and riffled through the hangers before pulling off a sleep shirt and picking out a pair of shorts from the dresser drawer. "These good?" he asked, holding them up in his hands.

I nodded.

"Up," he demanded, placing the sleepwear in front of me and grabbing my arms to lift me upright. "May I?" he asked as he positioned himself behind my back and swept my hair over my shoulder so it wouldn't get caught in the zipper.

I nodded, holding the front of my dress in place so as not to flash him.

What a story that would've been.

Abel's fingers lingered for a moment, leisurely grazing

the exposed skin on my back. A shiver shot down my spine at his touch.

My heart pounded recklessly inside my chest while every nerve ending in my body stirred and danced.

I cleared my throat, and Abel jerked his hand away. A beat passed, and relief flooded over me when I finally heard the undoing of the zipper.

Abel stopped the zipper when he reached my hips and stepped away abruptly into my en suite bathroom. "Change. I'll be right back," he called from the other room, though the faintest scent of his sandalwood cologne lingered around me, making it feel like he was still here.

I quickly slipped off my dress and threw on the T-shirt that Abel had picked out for me. A few moments after slipping on my shorts, he walked back into my bedroom with a package of makeup wipes, mouthwash tablets, and a hair tie in his hands.

He placed the toiletries on the nightstand and peered down at me with an earnest look in his eyes. "I want us to be friends… if you're up for it." He spoke as if he was uncertain about the words passing from his lips.

Abel wanted to be my friend?

Earlier in the car, when he hadn't responded to my confession about not knowing how to act whenever we weren't pretending, I'd assumed he didn't want to be friends with me.

Well, he hadn't exactly said *anything*, so I had no reason to believe otherwise until now.

I would've understood if he wanted to keep our relationship strictly professional, but deep down, I wanted him to be friendly with me.

If I was honest with myself, I think that's what I'd wanted from the beginning.

So, whenever he treated me like I didn't exist or threw out the meals I'd worked so hard to make for him, it hurt.

A lot.

And I might've taken it more personally than I should have. But now he was offering us a chance to start fresh.

Friends.

I could do that.

"I'd like that." I smiled up at him.

But to my surprise, he didn't smile back. Instead he just locked his eyes on me intently for a long while until his breaths grew shallow and uneven.

I couldn't help but feel like there was more that he'd wanted to say, but much like earlier, no words passed his lips.

"Would you mind grabbing me some water from the kitchen? The cups are in the cabinet above the dishwasher," I asked, trying to break the tension.

Abel nodded curtly and made a left out of the room toward the kitchen.

Okay, so *maybe* my eyes lingered on his perfectly toned butt as he walked away, but I didn't get to enjoy it because the second I was alone I let out a giant breath that had been trapped in my lungs since the moment we pulled in the driveway.

So few words had been spoken between the two of us since we left the gala, but the ones that had coiled tightly in my chest.

Hell, Abel was in my house. *In my house.* And not only that, he was picking out my pajamas and getting me water.

What the hell was happening?

A week ago, I never would've let this happen. Ever.

"I saw the bottle sitting on the counter. Thought you might need some." He held out a bottle as he walked through the doorway. "How bad do they hurt?" He tipped his head toward my swollen feet while he dropped four of the red painkillers into my palm.

They hurt like a freaking bitch.

I hadn't looked down, but I was sure that when I did, they'd be swollen twice their regular size. I could feel the blisters throb along the bottoms of my feet, and a fresh cut from where the back of the shoe dug into my achilleas all night.

They hurt almost as bad as the time Mae stomped on them to stop me from talking so we didn't get caught by the cops for underage drinking while we hid behind a tree.

"I'll survive."

"I hope so." Abel's lips curled upward, and he bent down to place a quick kiss on my cheek. "Good night, Red."

THE NEXT MORNING, I dove headfirst into fixing the suggestions that my editor had sent over to me earlier that week. It was my first go-around implementing suggestions, and I'd be lying if I said that some of them didn't hurt.

Having someone completely rip apart your life's work was... humbling, to say the least.

I'd always felt especially attached to the little blurbs and stories that paired along with each recipe, so seeing a few of them ripped to shreds by my sweet, extremely pregnant editor put a damper on my mood.

After spending two hours in bed rewording sentences and scrapping paragraph after paragraph, I was *finally* content with the edits that I'd made so far. I could only cross my fingers and hope that Gina felt the same.

A lightness filled my chest when I heard the front door open. "Knock, knock," Mae's voice echoed down the hallway.

"In here!" I yelled to her, unwilling to move from my position on the couch. Not because I was lazy, but because my feet had never ached so badly in my life.

At nearly twenty-five, one would've thought that I'd learn by now to break in heels before wearing them to an event where I'd be standing all night. Admittedly, I should've known better, but now I was reaping the agonizing consequences.

Not to mention the borderline hangover headache that squeezed my skull so tightly I thought it would explode.

This was nothing compared to the hangovers I'd endured in college, but these days I didn't drink as often and when I did I was *done* after two glasses of wine.

As if reading my mind, Mae waltzed into the bedroom holding up a take-out bag that smelled exactly like my holy grail hangover meal. A chicken tender tray with double onion rings, three barbecue sauces, and a large sweet tea, to be exact.

"I had a feeling you might need this after I watched Abel carry you into the house last night." She tossed me the bag and I ripped it open, digging into grease-filled hangover heaven.

She got my order perfect too, even down to the three sauces. Praise God, she knew me so well.

"You're the best," I moaned, taking the first bite of chicken into my mouth. "But he didn't carry me in because I was drunk… well, sort of. My shoes murdered my feet last night. Why didn't you tell me to break them in more?"

"I tried telling you… twice! You're the one who

insisted you'd be fine." She flailed her hands as she took a seat on the corner of the bed. "Now tell me everything. Don't leave out a single detail. Did you see his dick?"

"Oh my god, no. I didn't see his dick." My mind reeled back to how Abel took care of me last night. How intimate the entire encounter had been. Like something a boyfriend would do for their girlfriend. "We did decide that we're going to be friends though."

"Oh my god, you like him! You fucking like him, don't you?"

"Like is a strong word…"

"Please tell me there is a 'but,'" she pleaded with her palms pressed together.

"*But* I don't hate him." I lifted my shoulders nonchalantly while scarfing down onion rings.

Mae jumped up from her seat and squealed in excitement. "I have to call Lea!"

"I swear to God if you guys are placing bets on me again, I'm going to lose it."

Those stupid bitches wouldn't stop placing bets on me. The week before they'd placed a bet to see which one of them I'd respond to first when they both texted me at the same time with 911 emergencies.

Obviously, Mae won. She was my sister after all.

"It's not much of a bet if we both want the same outcome."

"Calm down. It's not like I'm going to fall in love with him. We're just friends."

"If you say so…" Her words dropped off at the end and her lips turned up into an obnoxious grin that made me narrow my eyes at her. "It's just that everyone who claims they're '*just friends*' are never actually just friends."

Okay, in any other circumstances I probably would've agreed with her, but that wasn't the case with Abel and me. Even if I maybe, *sort of kinda just a little*, formed a tiny crush on him last night.

Damn him for being such a freaking gentleman.

"You'll never guess who I saw last night... your *best* friend in the entire world." I not so subtly changed the subject in an attempt to get her off my case.

"You looked in a mirror? I'm so proud of you, sweetie."

"You're an idiot." I rolled my eyes and passed her my tray so she could eat my leftover onion rings. "Abel and I ran into October at the party."

"Revolting." Mae pretended to retch.

Maybe it was the newfound crush talking, but I could've *sworn* I picked up on a spark of jealousy between Abel and October last night too.

Not that Abel would ever have anything to worry about since we both agreed we wouldn't see other people while we were "dating" each other. Plus, October was more like a brother; just the thought of the two of us going on a date sent chills across my skin.

Mae and October had hated each other since we were kids, and apparently, some things would never change.

Anytime I mentioned I was going to hang out with him now that he was back in town, she'd pretend to vomit, immediately followed by some lame excuse about how she couldn't join us.

Once she even lied and told me that her dog was sick... she didn't even have a freaking dog. If anyone would know if she had a dog, it was me, the person who lived in her *backyard*.

"What'd you do with the dress?" she questioned, quickly changing the subject like I knew she would.

I nodded toward the fireplace with a wicked smile playing at my lips.

TEN
SCARLETT

ABEL and I had officially been friends for one whole week and I hadn't resorted back to hating him yet. According to my therapist, I was making progress with extending grace toward Abel and actively participating in our friendship.

We talked every morning for approximately twenty minutes while he ate his breakfast before leaving for practice. It was nothing more than basic chitchat, but weirdly enough, I started looking forward to it every day.

I was ashamed to admit that when coming down the stairs this morning, I had to conceal a smile on my face.

I confessed to my therapist about the ruse and gave her all the nitty-gritty details—given that whole doctor-patient confidentiality rule, it felt like a safe space.

Plus, she'd heard me whine on and on about my disdain toward him for months, and she'd probably ask me a list of inquisitive questions if she found out from a news source before hearing it from my lips.

Although I was proud of the progress I felt I was making when it came to forgiving Abel, I was a *little* upset when my therapist gave me homework—which was to initiate hanging out with Abel. She said it would show him that I was making a *mutual* effort toward our newfound friendship.

And that's how I found myself sitting on one of Abel's barstools, patiently waiting for him to get home from midmorning practice. I'd finished his turkey burger and mixed vegetable meal preps for the weekend half an hour ago and in the meantime, I had a lengthy panic-induced pace and started a batch of cupcakes that I was now watching bake in the oven.

The door handle jiggled, signaling his arrival. I turned to look over my shoulder to greet him. "Hi." I smiled, taking in his sweat-stained shirt and the heap of disheveled curls on top of his head. He usually showered at the training facility before coming home, but today must have been an exception.

I'd be lying if I said I didn't enjoy seeing his rock-hard abs clinging tightly to his shirt.

"You making cupcakes?" he inquired with a grin that matched my own.

"Yeah, they'll be done in a few minutes."

I could do this.

I could ask Abel to hang out with me.

The worst he could say was no, right?

"Soooo, I was wondering if you wanted to, I don't know… hang out this weekend? Maybe we could go to dinner or watch a movie or something." The grin on his face rose higher as my senseless babbling continued. "But only if you're free! If you're not free, we can do it another time. Or, um, if you don't want to, that's cool… no pressure."

"I'll make time for you, Red," he said, leaning back against the countertop across from me and crossing his arms over his chest. "My buddy Carlo owns an Italian restaurant downtown, Mafiosa's, best in the city. They're closed on Sundays, but we could do dinner together tomorrow." A cocky smirk pulled at his lips as he spoke his next words with eyes locked to mine. "That is, only if you're free. Or, *um*, if you don't want to that's cool... no pressure."

He was mocking me.

Abel Abbott was mocking me.

And holy shit, that snarky emphasis on the "um" was sexy as hell.

My cheeks flooded with embarrassment and I did my best to pretend I was scratching the back of my head to hide the reality that I was twirling my ring with my thumb.

"O-okay, sounds good. Does seven work?"

He nodded with a devilish grin while I couldn't grab my purse fast enough. Scurrying toward the door, I gave a wave and threw a sheepish smile back at him. I was too frazzled to know for certain, but I could've sworn I heard him say, "It's a date," just before the front door closed behind me.

I didn't know what was worse, the fact that I'd bolted out of Abel's house, leaving him to deal with the burning cupcakes in the oven or the fact that a spark lit in my chest at the idea of him thinking it was a date.

I FINALLY BROUGHT out the little black dress that had been sitting untouched in my closet for months on end. I didn't know if there would be cameras around or not, but either way, I wanted to wow the public for my debut in the tabloids.

If I was going to be forced into the spotlight, the least I could do was look devastating.

A knock on the door startled me. I peered over at the clock... seven sharp, just like last time. I opened the door and Abel's eyes widened. I thought I heard him vaguely mutter, "Fuck," under his breath, but it's possible I was just trying to fuel my own ego.

"No green today?"

I liked that he picked up on the fact that I wore something green every single day. It had been my mom's favorite color and wearing it was always a little reminder that she was with me.

I stuck out one of my stilettos to show him my shoes. "They look darker in this light, but the website said they were green." He unashamedly raked his eyes from my shoes and up my body until our eyes met. "Is it okay? Should I change?"

I hated that I felt so self-aware whenever he was around.

Every time he entered a room, I suddenly felt how tight my clothes were or how short a dress was. He never said anything about my appearance to make me feel that way, but no matter how hard I tried, I couldn't curb the uncomfortable feeling. Especially now that he was openly giving me a once-over.

"It's more than okay."

"You clean up nice," I said in a silky voice, turning the attention away from myself.

He looked better than nice.

I didn't say that out loud though.

Well, at least I hoped I hadn't.

Abel was draped head to toe in black and was the epitome of sex appeal and sophistication, which was so unlike his usual post-workout sweatpants and T-shirt ensemble.

"No interrogation this time?" he asked with a trace of laughter in his voice.

"Ha. Ha. Hilarious."

With a coy smile on his lips, Abel placed a hand on the small of my back as he led me out the door. His touch was so hot I was surprised my dress didn't singe.

Our car ride to the restaurant was significantly easier than the last car ride together. This time, the conversation flowed easily and before I knew it, we were handing off his keys to the valet.

"Hi Abel, long time no see." The woman at the hostess stand beamed up at him when we walked through the door. Abel immediately let go of my hand so he could engulf her in a giant bear hug.

"Gianna, how are the twins?"

"They're getting so big. Want to see?" she asked and Abel nodded, moving back over to my side and slipping his hand into mine once again. Gianna pulled out her phone from her back pocket and scrolled for a few seconds before turning her phone to show us a picture of two adorable twin boys.

"They're huge!" Abel exclaimed, and the two of them chatted comfortably as she walked us to our table and the two of us got settled into the booth.

"Carlo will be with you in a minute." She smiled at me with a genuine smile before patting Abel on the shoulder and making her way back to the hostess stand.

"Mio fratello!" a long-haired Italian man bellowed from across the restaurant, no doubt notifying all of the restaurant-goers of Abel and I's presence here. "You've finally decided to come see me?"

Abel rose from his seat and embraced the man, patting him on the back before returning to his seat.

Okay, seriously. What was going on with all the hugging?

"Dio mio! Who is this?" The man nudged Abel's side and I gave him a smile, still a little shell-shocked at all of the eyes on us.

"This is my girlfriend, Scarlett." Abel's lips broke into a full smile and the corners of his eyes softened. "Isn't that right, *my love*?" He shot me a subtle wink, making no attempt to hide the smug expression on his face.

He was mocking me. *Again.* This was the second time in twenty-four hours he mocked me.

What a freaking asshole.

I gently kicked his shin from underneath the table, but his smile only grew wider as he ignored it and continued chatting with Carlo.

Okay fine, I had to admit the irony was *a little bit* funny.

Who would've guessed that underneath all of our awkward encounters together that *Abel Abbott* actually had a sense of humor?

Not me.

That was for sure.

My mind wandered back to the car ride after the charity gala. Somewhere in the recesses of my brain, I still wondered if he'd been like this, *himself,* from the beginning, if we would have become more than friends.

I wondered whether he'd brought any other girls here before… and that thought instantly pulled me away from the possibility.

Of course we couldn't be more than friends.

The thought was a momentary lapse in judgment on my part. There was no way he would ever see me as more than a friend. And I kept conveniently forgetting the fact that he was still the one who signed my paychecks every two weeks.

The condensation on my glass chilled my fingertips as I picked it up off the table and brought it to my lips. Sitting back in my chair, I sipped on my water leisurely as I studied Abel interacting with his longtime friend.

He looked happy, relaxed even.

Confident. Definitely confident.

And hot. God, he looked so hot.

The corners of my mouth turned up as I watched him. I liked seeing him with his guard down, giving me a glimpse into his normally closed-off world.

My eyes swept over to his giant arms, remembering how warm they felt wrapped around my body when he pulled me closer to him at the gala. How natural it felt to sink into his touch. How, for a few minutes, I forgot we were even pretending at all.

"Right, Red?" Abel tapped my hand with his fingers and a jolt of electricity rattled through my bones at the contact.

"Mhmm, yup."

"You do realize you just agreed to eat cow tail?" He narrowed his gaze at me.

"What?" Dammit, I must have zoned out harder than I thought.

"I'm kidding," he joked. "I'll have my usual, and she'll have the risotto." He grabbed the menus from the table and handed them to Carlo who then walked back to the kitchen.

"You know I'm capable of ordering for myself, don't you?"

"I'm aware." He relaxed his shoulders, keeping the same permanent grin he'd had all night plastered on his face. "But I've tried everything at least a dozen times, so I know you'll like what I picked." Abel's face softened. "Trust me, Red."

"Fine," I grumbled, unrolling my silverware from the napkin. "So this is the place you come when I skimp you on leftovers?" I asked, looking around the dimly lit restaurant.

"You could say that." He smirked. "Carlo and I have been buddies since I moved here after being drafted. His family's been good to me, especially when I first got to town and didn't know anyone. It was nice to be a part of a big family for the first time, you know?"

My heart sank at his words.

I didn't know.

I'd grown up surrounded by four overbearing family members and an extended family with a nasty habit of showing up on our doorstep uninvited.

I didn't know the last thing about what he experienced.

"So, have you brought any of your other girls here?" I arched a brow. Nearly every table in here was filled with couples aside from the group in the back, which I presumed—based on their slicked-back hair and pristinely ironed suits—were here for a business dinner. "I'm sure Carlo has met them all, so I'll be sure to ask for pointers so we can make this thing more believable before we leave."

Shit. He'd just opened up to me about his childhood trauma and lack of friendships in his life and I turned it back on myself.

Who was the asshole now?

"I'm so sorry. I didn't mean to turn that around and make it about—"

"None," he cut me off.

"*None?*" I questioned with widened eyes, not entirely sure I understood what he was saying.

"You're the first girl I've ever brought here." He lowered his voice low enough that I almost missed it. "And probably the last."

"Wha— why?"

"This place. These people." He nudged his head toward Carlo whose arm was slung over Gianna's shoulders. "They're special to me, so I don't bring many people here. Especially not people who have the potential to be temporary in my life."

Wait, wasn't this entire situation between the two of us temporary? Which meant his statement didn't exactly make sense, but I wasn't going to ruin the conversation again by questioning him on it.

I hated to admit it, but a large part of me was starting to like whatever dynamic was going on between us though. Mornings at his place were easier. And the conversations weren't as painful as a root canal anymore. And it was kind of nice to spend time with someone other than Mae and Lea for once.

What if I didn't want to be temporary in his life after all of this was over?

Our conversation was interrupted by Carlo bringing our meals to the table.

Saved by the bell.

I wasn't ready to have whatever conversation Abel was trying to have. Especially since he made it clear that there was an impending expiration date when we signed up for this little charade.

Abel and I scarfed down our plates in record time, and I even asked for seconds of the risotto. I hated to admit that Abel was right, but everything he ordered was absolutely mouthwatering.

How had I never heard of this place before?

"I'm pretty sure this is the best food in Miami."

"Aside from yours." Abel winked.

"Don't be smug."

Excusing myself, I wandered off to the lavish restroom down the hall. And just as I was about to slink down into my seat, Abel pulled me into his lap.

A gasp escaped my lips as he cradled me sideways against his chest. One of his hands snaked around to hold me by my waist and the other gripped the back of my neck and pulled me closer to him.

Holy. Freaking. Hell.

He really, really, *really* needed to stop holding me like this.

"Don't freak out. There's a few paparazzi outside the window behind you and they've been eyeing me since you got up from the table," Abel whispered, his lips brushing gently against the shell of my ear, sending a shiver down my spine.

My whole body turned to stone, yet every nerve ending in my body ignited at the way his faint touch overwhelmed me.

Testing out my improv skills on old couples at a charity event was one thing, but making sure our relationship looked realistic through the eyes of the paparazzi?

Not so simple.

"Relax, Red. You're doing great." Abel pressed his forehead against mine. "I know we said no kissing, but I assumed that only meant on the lips." His voice was low and husky which made goose bumps flare across my skin. "Am I allowed to kiss your cheek?"

I nodded wordlessly, ignoring the fact that I could feel my cheeks turning pink before he planted a kiss against my skin. When he pulled his head back our faces were inches apart and my stomach lurched thinking about what it would be like for him to kiss me. Really kiss me.

"I like it here," I whispered after a beat. Though I was unsure whether I meant the restaurant or sitting on his lap.

"I had a feeling you would." His lips curled and he stroked his hand across my outer thigh as he held my body against his. I watched while his hazel eyes fervently roamed across my face and a hint of dizziness whirled through me.

He didn't know it, but a wet spot began to form in my panties as heat soared between us. I desperately needed to scoot off of his leg before I soaked through the fabric of my dress.

Oh god, what if he could feel my heat through his jeans?

Just at the thought, Abel broke the gaze he had on my lower lip and nudged my leg, indicating that it was time for us to go.

Thank God.

My stomach dipped as I peeled myself off of his lap and stood on two wobbly feet. As much as I tried to ignore it, I liked it when Abel pulled me close to him. If I could, I would've stayed curled in the warmth of his chest for the rest of the night.

Despite my urge to push him back down into the booth, I smoothed down my dress with my palms and made my way toward the exit. My stomach erupted with nerves as Abel caught up with me and grabbed my hand before leading the way to the front door.

"Wait, wait." I stopped, turning on my heels to head back to the table. "I have to go back and pay." Abel wrapped his hand around my wrist to stop me. "Abel, seriously, I have to go back," I stammered.

"I paid while you were in the bathroom." Abel shifted himself behind me, placing a possessive hand on my hip as he walked us out of the restaurant doors, giving Carlo and Gianna a wave before we passed them. "And for the record, whenever you're with me, you won't be paying for a damn thing. Got it?" he whispered, his breath hot against my ear.

Oh god, was it *that* obvious I was broke?

Obviously he knew how much money I made, but surely that was pocket change when you factored in his league contract, the brand deals, and his real estate investments.

According to the league's official website, my annual salary was equivalent to two of his games when I looked up a few months back. Still, it was beyond embarrassing when the hottest guy you'd ever gone out with—even if it was fake—knew that you were broke.

"O-okay, if you insist," I muttered hastily, not entirely sure how to respond to him, but also not stupid enough to fight him on it.

The moment the giant wooden doors to the restaurant opened, we were assaulted with bright camera flashes and demanding questions from the paparazzi who'd been stationed outside the restaurant.

My hands trembled, but Abel gave my hip a tight squeeze reassuring me that he wouldn't let anything bad happen.

I didn't know much, but I did know one thing for sure.

Abel and I made a great couple.

Even if it was just for shits and giggles.

ELEVEN
SCARLETT

"GREAT WORK." Abel flashed me a sly wink as he slid a brand-new edition of Page Six across the kitchen island where I was sitting.

"Oh my god!" I gasped, picking up the magazine that's front cover featured me sitting on his lap in a restaurant booth, our faces inches apart, his eyes locked on my lips.

Holy hell, that picture was hot.

Abel peeked over my shoulder, caging me between his arms and the island, as I read the article in front of me.

Mr. Tight End, Abel Abbott, spotted on a romantic dinner date with new girlfriend and food blogger, Scarlett Sawyer. The couple first hinted at their relationship together last month with subtle Socialgram posts, but close sources said the pair have been together for four months.

I couldn't believe I was photographed on the *cover* of a magazine looking like I was seconds away from having a public make-out session.

"These tabloids always tell such half-truths. Like what 'inside source' told them we had been together for four months? Only a handful of people knew that I even worked for you before we made it 'official.'"

"It's all a bunch of bullshit," he complained. "They'll do anything to get their money, even if that means making up lies and twisting stories."

It was one thing to read articles as a bystander and assume some of the contents were made up, but it was another to be the one being written about and *know* that what was posted was a complete and utter lie.

Granted, we were *trying* to convince the paparazzi that we were in a fake relationship, so I'd give them some grace. But coming up with fake "sources" and inaccurate time lines was a bit baffling.

Oh, if only they'd known how much I hated Abel's guts four months ago, then their story would be entirely different.

"I don't have anything planned, but we could go out again tonight if you want," Abel suggested with a shrug.

"Sorry, can't." I was a lot more disappointed at turning him down than I should've been. "Mae called a girls' night tonight and I'm not allowed to say no."

"Girls' night?" Abel questioned from over my shoulder. "What exactly happens at a *girls' night*?"

"Calling our old boyfriends, celebrity gossip... naked pillow fights. You know, the usual," I deadpanned, swinging my head around to meet his eyes.

"Naked pillow fights, huh?" A lopsided smile nudged the corner of his lip upward. "Tell me more."

"I'm kidding, you idiot." I rolled my eyes and slapped the back of my hand playfully against his chest. "It's mostly me cooking a bunch of food while we sit around the kitchen, drink wine, and talk about our problems."

"You're having problems?" He furrowed his brows at me. "Why didn't you tell me?"

"I'm not having any problems… well, at least not right now. Mae's going through it because her old modeling agent blasted her on Socialgram recently for starting her own company to spite him, so it's more for her than anything," I explained, trying not to get too riled up over my anger at the idiot who kept trying to ruin Mae's career.

"You know if you're ever having any problems, you can talk to me, yeah?" he volunteered.

All I could do was smile up at him.

I hadn't known… but now I did.

MAE and I were holed up on the lilac purple accent couch in her home office, studying headshots when a knock at the front door startled us.

Lea had called an hour earlier saying she had an emergency at work and would be late joining us. She said something about having to clean up a PR disaster after one of the Matrix players punched a sponsor for flirting with his wife.

Couldn't blame the guy.

Mae and I shared a concerned glance just as another round of knocks rapped against the door. The two of us slowly, slowly inched up from the love seat, careful not to make too much noise.

We couldn't risk being heard on the off chance that the Jehovah's Witnesses had snuck into the neighborhood again.

Ruthless. All of them.

Mae slid across the hardwood floors with her fuzzy

socks and dipped into the library across the hall so she could peer out of the blinds at our guest, and I quickly trailed behind her. Both of our heads cocked to the side at what we saw—or should I say *who* we saw—standing on the front porch.

A middle-aged man dressed in culinary attire with a few large bags that sat on the ground next to him.

Who the hell was this guy?

"Should we answer it?" I whispered.

Mae looked at me and gave me a shrug as she waltzed over to the door and turned the knob.

"Good evening, ladies!" the strange man exclaimed as we opened the door. "My name's Larry and I'll be your private chef for the evening," he said proudly, sticking his hand out between us.

"Hi, Larry, great to meet you!" I piped in over Mae's shoulder, taking his hand in mine and giving it a shake. "I think you might have the wrong address though, we didn't hire a chef."

We spent the next few minutes playing that song and dance where we reassured him that neither of us had hired a personal chef for the evening, and he *insisted* that he was at the right place.

He pulled out his phone from his front pocket and read off Mae's address and ours, including Lea's, from the booking request. Scrolling some more, his eyes perked up. "Aha! Courtesy of Abel Abbott."

"What?" Mae and I said in unison, shooting each other glances out of the corner of our eyes.

He reached down to grab one of the bags that rested at his feet. "Ahh, Miss Sawyer. I have a note for you that might help clear things up, my dear." The crow's-feet around the outer corners of his eyes turned upward as he handed me a note typed on a crisp green stationery card.

"I don't know why I didn't think to show you sooner. Must be my age showing."

I smiled at Larry before squinting down at the familiar handwriting on the card in front of me.

Thought you could use a break. Enjoy your girls night, Red.
- A

I blinked, reading the note again. And again. And again a third time just to be certain I read it right the first two times. My heart swelled and I let a small laugh pour out of me as I handed the note over to Mae whose eyes flashed widely after reading what Abel had written.

I'd told her earlier about the joke he made thinking girls actually got naked and slung pillows at each other in their free time.

After our doorstep mishap, we happily waved Larry into the kitchen and let girls' night commence. Including Larry, of course; he told us that he wanted to be an honorary girl for the night, so we let him join our clan.

We laughed with him as he told us stories from his younger years and he gave us wise advice for our trivial life problems.

I watched as he chopped vegetables, the exact way all culinary students had been conditioned to do, and added them to the primavera. My stomach rumbled at the delicious smells as they blended together with the garlic and lemon juice.

The kitchen had been my favorite place since I was a kid. I used to spend hours watching my mom glide effortlessly around with hot pans while double-checking to make sure she was following recipes correctly. Although she'd almost always forfeit the recipe halfway through and added her own twist because it was "just better" the way she did it.

Her words, not mine.

It was days like this that I missed her most. I know she would've loved laughing with us while Larry cooked. Or how she would've shot silent glares across the room to let me know that whatever he was doing to the dish, she could do a thousand times better.

Life felt empty without her here, but it was moments like this that reminded me how much I loved and cherished the short time that I had had with her.

It's the most beautiful curse to have someone you love so much pass on, leaving their impact deeply rooted in your being. In a way, all of us were simply mangled tessellations of the habits and mannerisms of the people we loved most. And something about that comforted me.

I threw my arm around Mae's shoulders where she was sitting next to me at the table and gave her a squeeze. She must have sensed I'd been thinking about Mom because she reciprocated with a knowing hug. "Love you," she whispered before pulling back with a sorrow-filled expression.

Two hours and one of the best meals I'd ever eaten later, Mae and I waved Larry off as he pulled his pickup truck out of the driveway.

Just as he drove out of sight, Lea's white sports car sped down the street and whipped into the driveway with music blaring so loudly her car shook.

Cutting the engine, she stepped out of the car with perfectly blown-out hair and makeup that appeared untouched. For someone who'd just spent twelve hours working to spin the narrative of a player punching a multimillion-dollar sponsor, she looked regal.

"I didn't know if you had wine so I brought my own,"

she shouted over to us, opening the door to the back seat of her car and pulling out an entire crate of wine.

"Bad day?" Mae questioned with a faint laugh.

"Don't even get me started." Lea rolled her eyes and breezed past us, inviting herself into the house.

She set the crate of wine down on the kitchen island and I grabbed the wine opener and three clear glasses from the cabinet.

Grabbing one of the bottles of cabernet sauvignon from the crate, I opened it and began pouring the bloodred liquid into one of the glasses. Just as I finished pouring, Lea grabbed the glass by the stem and knocked it back like she was taking a shot.

Mae and I looked over at each other with widened eyes. "*Soooo,* Scar was just about to tell me all about her *love* for Abel," she deflected with an evil smile as I handed a glass over to her.

She was lucky I didn't spill it on the front of her shirt.

"Ooh, do tell." Lea waggled her eyebrows while pouring herself another glass of wine and filling it to the brim.

"Not much to tell." I shrugged. "We just started seeing each other so it's not that serious yet."

"Your picture on Page Six said otherwise…" Lea shot Mae a knowing wink.

I lifted my shoulders again.

What they didn't know wouldn't hurt them.

AFTER A FEW HOURS of comparing meaningless celebrity gossip, Mae and Lea both fell asleep on the couch.

Once I knew they were both thoroughly knocked out, I

slipped into the kitchen and plated some of the leftovers before tiptoeing down the hall and sneaking quietly out the front door.

With two plates in hand, I jogged across the street, heading straight for Abel's front door.

It wasn't until I was standing on his porch that I realized that what I was doing was pathetic.

Completely utterly abysmally pathetic.

Making a desperate attempt to see Abel outside of work and our "arrangements"? Pathetic. Pathetic. Pathetic.

Sure, I could've brought him leftovers in the morning to say thanks like any rational person would do. But no. I was standing on his doorstep because I *wanted* to see him. Granted, a large part of me wanting to see him after "business hours" was because I'd always been curious to find out what he did whenever I wasn't around.

The guy hardly ever left his house if it wasn't work related and I'd only seen one of his buddies over at his house before—that one guy who eyed Lea all night at the charity gala. What was his name again... Fashion? Forbes? Something with an *F*.

Stopping on his front porch, I released a steadying breath before rapping my knuckles against the black door. I silently prayed that it was loud enough for him to hear from wherever he was in his house. In retrospect, I probably should've used the doorbell, but I was too busy internally reprimanding myself to realize my error.

A few seconds of waiting felt like an eternity when nerves were pooling in the pit of your stomach. A sigh of relief left me when the door finally swung open and my eyes were met with Abel wearing gray sweatpants and a black T-shirt that molded against his every muscle.

My mouth watered at the sight of him looking sleepy and relaxed.

I couldn't even deny my attraction toward him anymore. It was becoming too exhausting to fight it.

"Sorry, did I wake you?" I asked, biting the inside of my cheek.

"No, I was just watching a movie. Want to come in?"

"Sure. I brought you pasta primavera and key lime pie." I held up the plates as I stepped through the threshold to his home like I had hundreds of times before, but this time it felt different.

Because this was the first time that either of us willingly came to see each other. Although, I was *simply* giving my thanks like any good person would do.

At least that's what I kept telling myself.

"What'd I do to deserve this?" The corner of his lips twitched.

"You know what you did." I nudged his side. "Thank you, by the way. That was really sweet of you."

"Anytime, Red."

"Carlo and now Larry. Are you cheating on me with other chefs, Abbott?"

"I'd never fucking cheat on you," he said firmly, walking into the kitchen. Maybe it was just me but his tone almost sounded… defensive?

"Good, now bring me a fork so I can steal some of your pie," I shouted back to him while plopping myself onto his couch.

"Get your own," he grumbled jokingly.

Abel sat down next to me on the couch so close that our thighs brushed against each other. He handed me a fork and a small plate with a slice of key lime pie that looked like it was cut directly down the middle from the piece I'd given him.

I couldn't hide the smile that pulled at my lips. I'd totally been joking, but he gave me the pie anyway, just in case I meant it. "You know, you're a lot more thoughtful than I would have guessed."

"Hmmm."

"I guess I'd never realized that you were paying attention to me… and now every time I think I've finally got you figured out, you do something that surprises me."

"Oh really? Tell me more."

"Well, for starters, I never would have guessed that you'd watch rom-coms in your free time." I tilted my head toward the television where a movie with a couple running breathlessly into each other's arms before engulfing each other's faces was playing on the flat-screen TV.

Abel's head flew backward and his chest rumbled with the most captivating boom of laughter I'd ever heard. I was so caught off guard by it that I nearly fell out of my seat.

He laughed.

Abel laughed.

He had never laughed around me before. At least not like that.

These days he smirked or huffed out a breath of air at my horrible attempts to tell jokes.

But that laugh? It was intoxicating.

I smiled up at him and he returned the favor back down to me.

"I forgot to tell you. I'm leaving at the end of the month for Los Angeles. I'll be gone for about three weeks." His eyes flickered down to his plate.

My heart sank.

We'd *finally* become friends and now he was leaving?

"What are you going to do out there?"

"I'm filming a few commercials and doing a campaign shoot for Nagem's new athletic line, but I'll probably catch up with a few friends while I'm out there too." He shrugged.

"Oh, sounds fun." Disappointment coated my voice. Abel and I were just starting to flow together and I was nervous to see how time apart would affect our dynamic.

A small part of me feared that he would come back and realize that he didn't want to have me as a friend anymore. The thought alone made my stomach drop.

"Care to tell me what you're overthinking about over there?"

"Oh, nothing. It's silly." I brushed it off, hoping he'd change the subject.

"Tell me."

"I was just thinking about how you might go out to see your real friends and realize that you didn't want to be mine anymore," I told him honestly. I shook my head at how stupid I sounded. "It's dumb. I-I don't even know why I thought about it."

"I'd never replace you, Red." Seriousness coated his voice. "Have you ever tasted your fucking cooking? My buddies from college burned instant ramen more than a handful of times, so I'm keeping you around for as long as you'll let me."

I gave him an uneasy grin

I liked when he told me tidbits about his life before I knew him. For the longest time I'd constructed him to be such a monster in my head, and now when he told me stories about growing up with his mom or his college friends it made him seem more... human.

Comfortable silence passed between us while we ate our pie, and when I looked over at Abel, I found his eyes were already on me.

"Did I ever tell you about the one time Mae accidentally robbed a bank?" I asked, breaking our silence.

"How does one *accidentally* rob a fucking bank?"

Abel and I laughed for another hour as I told him stories of all the stupid shenanigans Mae and I got into as kids, like the one time we stole Dads' shaving cream and replaced it with hair removal serum, only for us to realize hours later that we didn't really do anything because they were going to shave off their beards anyway.

When I began yawning uncontrollably, I took it as a sign that it was time to go home for the night. I had to be back here in a few hours for work after all.

Abel stayed planted on his front steps as he watched me sneak back across the street with clean plates in hand.

I waved at him from underneath Mae's porch light and quietly, quietly opened the front door and slipped inside. Placing the dishes in the sink, I decided they'd be future Scarlett's problem, and instead I stealthily climbed back into the same spot I had lain before I left and tucked myself underneath a fuzzy throw blanket.

"Scar, where'd you go?" Mae lifted her head from her pillow across the couch.

Damn her for being such a light sleeper.

"I just went to give Abel some leftovers and say thanks, nothing serious."

"Nothing serious," she repeated back to me with a small smile before pulling a blanket over her head and rolling to face the couch cushions.

TWELVE

ABEL

"TROPICAL STORM PAULA will be hitting landfall overnight. Miami-Dade County residents, we encourage you to take precautionary measures as needed. We'll be back with more details after this commercial break," the female news reporter's voice blasted through the flat-screen speakers on the wall.

I lay spread out on the couch, bored out of my fucking mind before settling on the weather channel. Who knew you could flip through infinite channels and still find nothing worthy of watching?

It had been almost a week since I'd last seen Scarlett and I was starting to regret letting her take the week off. Especially since I was leaving in a week for Los Angeles.

But she hadn't exactly given me much of a choice.

Monday morning I found a bright-green sticky note taped to my windshield telling me that she'd stocked the fridge with prepared meals and the directions on how to reheat them were on the counter. Oh, and that she'd be back in a week.

A fucking week.

She did leave a cute fucking heart at the bottom of the note where she signed her name which eased some of my annoyance.

Apparently, she had early morning meetings with her editor all week to finalize the recipes that they would be using for her cookbook. At least that's what Lea had told me when I interrogated her at practice about it.

Now that Scarlett and I had gotten close, it was lonely not having her around in the mornings. I liked teasing her about her cooking and seeing her eyes light up with fire whenever she got offended by my taunts.

It amused me more than I liked to admit.

I silently cursed myself realizing that I could've had mornings like that with her for nearly a year had I not been such a fuckup. My thoughts reeled back to our car ride after the gala a few weeks ago when she said that we might have been something different if our relationship started off differently.

I hated when she said that, but only because I knew she was right.

Forcing myself off the couch, I walked upstairs to my office and stopped in front of the giant window that looked out across the street toward Scarlett's pool house.

A few weeks after she started working for me, I was sitting at the desk in my office on a video call, which was rare, and noticed that I had the perfect view of Scarlett's pool house. Whenever I was home in the mornings, I would watch her walk across the street to make sure she made it home safely.

We lived in a gated community but a crazy fan and a Jehovah's Witness had slipped through the gates a time or two since I'd moved in. Making sure she was safe getting home—even if it was only a couple hundred yards—was the least I could do.

I zeroed in closer on the small apartment and noticed the windows were illuminated with light and her sedan was parked in the driveway.

I needed to see her.

And I was willing to make any excuses necessary to make that happen.

I jogged across the hall to the master bedroom and pulled out a sweatshirt from the dresser to throw on while I bounced down the steps. Grabbing the remote, I turned off the news reporter's shrill voice and laced up my tennis shoes.

Stepping out the front door, I waited until I heard the lock settle into the latch before jogging down the steps and making my way across the street.

I knew there was a tropical storm, but *fuck*, the wind was ridiculous. I'd barely made it to the end of the driveway before it tried tackling me to the ground. And I was two hundred and fifty pounds of pure fucking muscle.

Why the hell was Scarlett staying in that tiny pool house in this kind of weather? Was she trying to blow the fuck away?

I rounded the corner to the backyard and quietly slipped through the gate, picking up my pace again when the pool house was in sight. Rain droplets splattered against my face as I pounded my fists on her front door. "Red, it's me. Open up." I was met with silence for a long minute and waited a few more seconds before pounding again. "Red!"

Just when I thought I was going to have to kick the door in, it swung open and I charged my way past Scarlett without being invited in. I was more than pissed off that she wasn't taking this storm seriously and my stone-cold expression was a good tell of that.

"Red, you do realize there is a fucking tropical storm outside, don't you? You can't be staying in this measly fucking pool house that could blow over any minute! What are you thinking?" I scolded, watching as she ignored me and spun around and headed toward the kitchen instead, leaving me standing all alone in the entryway.

"Cheesecake?" she shouted down the hall at me. I barreled into the kitchen to find her cutting me a slice and placing it on a small dessert plate.

"You must not have heard me. It's not safe to be in this pool house during a tropical storm. Go grab your stuff. We're going back to my place."

She looked at me with a growing smirk on her face. "One slice or two?"

"Tw— what? Red, have you not listened to anything I've said for the last five minutes?" My tone grew agitated at her lack of awareness. The pool house was maybe a thousand square feet, if that. It wasn't safe for her to stay here by herself with the howling wind and rain pouring down.

Her knife glided into the white cake before she plopped a second triangular piece down onto the plate and handed it over to me. "I'm not leaving the pool house, but you're welcome to stay over if you'd like. We can watch a movie or something," she said firmly, not daring for a second to break eye contact so she could assert her dominance.

"Scarlett, please. I can't have you being swept away in a fucking tropical storm while I'm sitting in my storm-proof house a thousand yards away." Her lips perked up for a third time before she pressed her lips together to stifle a laugh.

There was something she wasn't telling me.

"Why do you keep making that face?" I asked her frankly as I brought the first forkful of salted caramel cheesecake to my mouth.

Scarlett looked at me with a giant grin. "Repeat what you just said a few seconds ago."

"I can't have you getting hurt in the storm?" I repeated my words back to her with an arched brow.

"No, no. The next part."

"While I sit a thousand yards away in a stormproof house?"

I could tell she was holding back a laugh, but I still couldn't figure out what was so fucking funny about me worrying she was going to get hurt.

She walked over to my side and threw an arm around my shoulder and gave me a small hug. My hands were too full with the fork and plate to hug her back. If the cheesecake wasn't so damn delicious, I might've been more pissed about missing the chance to hold her.

Scarlett backed away but kept her arm resting around my shoulders. She gave me a smile so big her eyes scrunched. "I appreciate your concern. It's really, really sweet actually... but you do realize that we live in the same neighborhood, right?"

I shot her a quizzical look. My mouth was too full of caramel-laced bliss to formulate words, so the look I gave her would have to speak on my behalf.

Seriously, what did us living in the same neighborhood have to do with anything?

"So, that means we had the same home builder..." She trailed on. I still didn't get her point and my face must have shown the confusion I felt because she picked up where she left off. "And if we have the same builder that means our homes are built with the same materials, right?"

Motherfucker.

I'd been too consumed with making an excuse to come and see her that I ditched all logic and forgot the pool houses in our neighborhood were stormproof too. "Fucking idiot," I cursed under my breath.

Scarlett held a hand on my shoulder to steady herself while she hunched over in laughter.

I might have looked like the biggest fucking idiot on the planet, but I would've become the village idiot a thousand times over if it meant hearing her laugh like that again.

"If you wanted to hang out, you… could've just asked." She beamed up at me after taking a handful of deep breaths to calm herself. "We're friends. Friends hang out, right?"

Friends.

I fucking hated that word.

Flashing a smile at her, I pushed down the weight in my chest. "Do you want to hang out, *friend*?"

She didn't hide the giant smile on her face as she threw her arms around me again. The corner of my lip turned up at how affectionate she had become with me the last few weeks. She'd touch my arms sometimes when we talked and she hugged me before I left for practices in the morning.

Now whenever she was around, I craved her touch. Patiently waiting for the next time she'd offer it to me. And I fucking *reveled* in it when she did.

Scarlett grabbed my hand, pulling me from my seat and leading the way to the enormous gray sofa in her living room. I took a seat in the corner of the couch as she reached across the coffee table for the remote. My stomach clenched when she took a seat in the opposite corner, but I quickly kicked it down.

"Do you have a movie preference?"

"Whatever you want to watch," I offered, as a rumble of thunder sounded outside.

"Let's watch a rom-com since I know you love them so much." She laughed at her own joke, and it was fucking adorable.

"Whatever makes you happy, Red."

And I meant it.

Scarlett hopped up from where she was sitting on the couch and rounded the coffee table, grabbing a blanket from the accent chair in the corner and carrying it down the hall with her.

"I'll grab you one from the closet," she said, holding up the blanket as she walked out of sight.

A few seconds later, she drifted back into the room with her face scrunched. "So, there's a *small* problem…" She paused right in front of the television, blocking the view of the opening credits. "It's Sunday…" Her eyes darted across the room and her cheeks had turned that rosy color I loved.

"It is," I replied, not understanding the angle she was coming from. Was she trying to make a lame excuse for me to leave or something?

"Sunday is my laundry day. So, all of my blankets and bedding are in the washer right now. Except for this one." Scarlett held up the singular blanket she pulled from the chair a few minutes ago. "Uhh, w-we could share it if you want? It's pretty big and I promise I don't have any germs. I swear! I took a shower this morning. Scout's honor!" she exclaimed, holding up three fingers on her right hand.

Fuck, she was cute when she was nervous. Seeing her cheeks turn that light shade of pink and watching her as she tried to pretend she wasn't flustered made my cock jump.

"I don't mind sharing, Red." I nudged my head toward the couch next to me. "I don't have any germs either. Scout's honor," I snarked with a wink, and those flushed cheeks were as ripe as a cherry.

Scarlett draped the blanket over our legs and inched closer to me so we could both have an equal amount of coverage. I was an entire foot taller than her though so I'm not sure her logic was sound, but I wasn't going to fight her on it if it meant having her closer to me.

Throughout the movie, she would sneak glances at me during her favorite parts to see if I was enjoying them as much as she was. And halfway through the movie, she rested her head on my shoulder, dozing in and out of consciousness until the final credits rolled across the screen.

"Can I ask you a question?" Scarlett asked sleepily.

"Anything."

"Do you want to get married one day?"

"To you or in general?" I taunted.

"Be serious," she whispered sternly.

Oh, I was being serious.

"What do you mean?"

"I mean, when the whole football thing is over, what do you want out of life? Do you want to get married one day? Have kids? Tell me." Scarlett pulled the blanket up to her neck and curled into it.

"I guess I want the family that I didn't have growing up, you know? I've got the cars and the houses and Mom's taken care of, but I've sacrificed friendships and relationships to get here…"

When I was younger, I planned out my life exactly how I thought it would go. Join the league at twenty-two, get married at twenty-six, have a kid or two before thirty, win four League Bowls before retiring. But it didn't work out the way I'd expected.

And sometimes I felt like what I wanted would never come.

"Do you ever wish that you had siblings growing up?" She yawned.

"When I was younger, no," I answered honestly, letting out a heavy sigh. "But I do now. I just hope that one day, I can be the husband and father mine wasn't. And have good people around me who I can share life with, you know."

She nuzzled her head into my deltoid and rested it there for a moment without saying a word. I almost thought she fell asleep until she whispered in a soft voice, "You've got me."

Her words were a blow to the stomach.

I've got her.

Just not the way that I wanted to.

"I liked that answer." She yawned, tugging the blanket we shared until I had just a sliver of the corner left. "And for the record, I think you'll be a much better husband and father than your dad was one day."

"Glad you approve, Red."

"Stay for another one?" she asked, picking up the remote next to her before lazily browsing through movie titles.

Like I could ever say no to her.

Two hours later, Scarlett had wiggled closer so that we lay parallel with her head at my feet. In her sleepy state, she curled up with them pressed to her cheek and I already couldn't wait to make fun of her for it tomorrow.

"Red, do you want me to go?" I rasped, my voice grew low as the sound of raindrops pounding on the window grew louder.

"Stay." She tried covering a giant yawn as she clicked the play button for our third movie. "I'm not even tired."

Minutes later, I watched through heavy eyelids as she drifted to sleep next to me.

A good man would have picked her up and carried her to her bed, placed a kiss on her forehead, and walked back home.

But I wasn't a good man.

I was a selfish one.

So, I stayed, just like she asked, and slept through the night with my girl snuggled upside down against my side.

IT WAS HARDLY light outside when I woke to the sound of birds chirping loudly out the window.

I forced an eyelid open to see the sunlight slip through the opening in the curtains, meaning it was probably just after six.

Stupid fucking birds.

Scarlett stirred next to me and her eyelids began to flutter, fighting to stay open as she scrunched her face in contempt. She pulled my legs closer to her chest and let out a yawn as she rubbed her eyes.

She was gorgeous.

The sight of her chestnut-brown hair splayed across her pillow, paired with the bleary-eyed smile she gave me, made my heart lurch inside my chest.

"When were you planning on telling me you have a foot fetish?" I teased.

She grabbed the throw pillow next to her and attempted to throw it at my head, but it flew right past me. "I do not have a foot fetish!"

"Care to explain why you cuddled with my feet all night then?" I quirked a questioning eyebrow and the corners of my lips turned up to a smile.

"I did not cuddle with your feet!" she scoffed.

"Oh really? 'Cause I'm pretty sure righty made it to second base, didn't you, big guy?" I wiggled my toes which just so happened to be inches from her face.

Her head flew back and an infectious laugh poured from her lips. "Get your mind out of the gutter, Abbott."

She had no idea how deep my mind was in the gutter right now.

No fucking idea.

My morning wood ached like a motherfucker just by looking at her, and now talking about kinks with her? I was going to blow a load any minute if we didn't change the subject.

"Ironic coming from the one with the foot fetish," I shot back as I moved to stick my big toe up her nose. Scarlett pushed my foot away from her face with an eye roll.

"There is a penthouse suite waiting for you in hell," she muttered just loud enough for me to hear.

"Do I get a first-class ticket as well?" I bargained.

I liked that she could take the banter just as well as she could dish it out.

"If I was cuddling with your feet all night then you must not have minded since you didn't dare to move them, huh?"

"I can neither confirm nor deny, Red."

If only she knew how much I liked having her close to me. We'd grown closer over the last few weeks together but she hadn't given me a reason to believe that we were anything other than friends.

I was willing to be patient though.

"You know, pleading the fifth is for the guilty."

"Then I must be a criminal, huh?"

She tugged the blanket up around her neck and snuggled into it. "In other news, you're not a blanket hog. I'll be sure to give your next girlfriend a glowing review."

My *next* girlfriend?

I hated that I had to keep reminding myself that this thing between me and Scarlett was fake. Somewhere along the way, the lines had gotten blurred for me because these days, more than ever, my heart was having a hard time filtering between the ruse and reality.

I didn't know much, but I knew one thing for certain after waking up with her for the first time.

I wanted to wake up next to her again.

And again.

And again.

Every day for the rest of my fucking life.

THIRTEEN

ABEL

"YOU COMING to our charity game later?" I asked, sliding onto one of the barstools at the island.

"Hmmm, I don't know," Scarlett hummed while flipping my favorite cinnamon protein pancakes with her spatula.

Her hair was up in a ponytail that flowed down past her shoulders, and she wore bright little workout shorts that made her ass look... fuck. "Didn't get the invite until right now. Kind of short notice if you ask me."

It'd been almost a month since the night I told her I wanted us to try and be friends, and every day since she'd shown me more and more of her personality. These days, she didn't shy away from making playful remarks or those smart-ass comments I'd catch her laughing under her breath about.

"Come," I begged. "There'll be other fans there watching, so you can bring Mae if you want. And you know Lea will be there too. They'll have food trucks. You told me you love a good food truck." I was pulling out all the stops to try and convince her to come, but her poker-face expression wouldn't budge. "Please, Red. I want you there."

"Okay." She gave in with a giant grin that made her eyes sparkle.

Those eyes. They got me every damn time.

I fucking hated that I had to leave her for three weeks soon.

Pulling out my phone from my pocket, I thumbed out a message to Aera to see about staying in the Malibu house while I was in town. Seeing as I paid for half the house, I doubted that she'd have an issue with it, but I felt the need to ask in case she wasn't planning on staying at her condo in West Hollywood.

The last fucking thing I wanted right now was to spend three weeks trapped in a house with her.

Abel: I'll be in town in a few days and I'm staying until the end of the month. Am I good to stay at the Malibu house?
Aera: Sure. I'll let the housekeeper know you're coming.
Aera: Planning on seeing me while you're in town?
Abel: Not if I can avoid it.
Aera: Unlikely, but you're welcome to try.

Typical Aera, always making sure I knew she was in charge. I would have to see her at some point, but I wasn't fucking looking forward to it. Knowing her, she'd show up at the most inopportune time if I didn't.

I shoved my phone back into my shorts and brushed off the thought of seeing her. Instead, I focused on something more important. The girl who was standing in front of me whisking up some more pancake mix and pouring it into the hot pan.

"You gave in too easily, Red. If you would've held out a little longer, I would've considered giving you a raise."

"What! You should definitely still give me the raise," she scoffed, flipping the last pancake over.

"Done."

"I was kidding."

"I wasn't," I said honestly.

At this rate, if she wanted a hundred million dollars, I'd probably give it to her without a single hesitation.

"You really want me to come that bad?"

In more ways than one.

I nodded my response.

Primarily due to the fact that my cock was rock hard from thinking about her coming and the other part being that if she kept prodding about why I wanted her there I was going to spill my feelings for her right here over breakfast.

"I'll be there." She smiled, handing me a stack of pancakes.

MY JAW fucking dropped at the sight of Scarlett walking toward the practice field wearing a cropped jersey with *my number* on it and enticing as fuck Daisy Dukes that hugged her thighs while her hips swayed. Mae walked alongside her, but I was too enamored by Scarlett to notice she existed.

Fuck, Scarlett was going to be the death of me.

Partly because of the fact that I was going to have to sucker punch a few of my teammates in the gut for staring at her slack-jawed.

She spotted me from a couple yards away and I waved

her over while willing my dick to behave. She ran toward me and squealed as she jumped to wrap her legs around my waist.

This really wasn't helping my dick problem.

"Where'd you get my jersey from?" I questioned, pulling back so I could see her face. "You secretly one of my groupies, Red?"

"Don't flatter yourself." She rolled her eyes with a smile. "Lea dropped it off for me earlier. She said you'd have my head if I wore October's jersey instead, but that was the only one I had."

"She's not fucking wrong." My blood boiled at the mental image of Scarlett walking in with October's jersey as a little crop top. "Tell her thank you for me."

I held tight to the back of her thighs, hiking her up a bit. "I feel like I should probably tell you that I don't know a single thing about football."

"You're kidding?"

"If the people on Socialgram hadn't coined you with the nickname 'Mr. Tight End' odds are, I probably wouldn't even know what position you played."

Whatever position she wanted.

Both in and out of the bedroom.

Get your mind out of the fucking gutter, Abbott.

"So you've been stalking me on Socialgram, huh?" I eased her down my body and placed her feet on the ground, still keeping my hands gripped on her waist.

"Pshh, no…" She glanced off to one side. "Maybe… a little."

"As long as I'm the only one."

Scarlett glanced over to the sidelines where a few photographers were taking pictures of the practice for the press. "Should we kiss or something? You know, for practice… in case we ever need to."

I bent down slightly, pressing my forehead to her so our mouths sat a few inches apart. My lips ached for her touch. Ached to know if they tasted the same way that cupcake ChapStick smelled.

It was then and only then that I allowed myself to entertain the thought of breaking our rule. As much as I wanted to kiss her—and fuck, I wanted to more than anything—the first time I kissed her, it wasn't going to be "for practice."

No.

The first time I claimed her lips, it was going to be real.

And sure as fuck not while others swarmed around us vying for the chance at the next headline.

"Already trying to break the rules, huh, Red?" One side of my mouth curled upward. "Don't tell me you're seeing other people too."

"Well, I do have a date with a guy, John, next week. We met in the produce section last week while I was grabbing some groceries to make that Mediterranean dish we talked about…" Scarlett's eyes stayed unwaveringly locked to mine and her face was impassive. "Don't worry though. I promise I won't let anyone find out or anything."

"You what?" My jaw clamped tight and my grip around her waist tightened possessively.

Who the fuck was *John* and why did I feel the sudden fucking urge to murder him in cold blood?

"Jesus, I'm kidding." A smile curved her mouth, and she released a breathy laugh. "You should've seen your face. Who knew you were so possessive?"

Oh, I fucking knew.

"Only when it comes to people taking what's mine." I pressed a kiss to her forehead and locked eyes with her. "You're mine, you know that?"

She nodded and that cute little blush that made my

pulse race spread across her face. "I've gotta go, but stay for the whole game. I'll meet you outside the locker room afterward, yeah?" Scarlett gave me one last squeeze around the neck, and I gave her a quick kiss on the side of her hair before jogging back to where the other players were huddled by the benches.

Having her here in the stands wearing my jersey felt like a fucking fever dream. The only thing that would've made it better was if I could take her home and fuck her against the kitchen table with nothing but my jersey on.

I don't think Scarlett realized how badly I fucking wanted her.

The girl was oblivious.

The roar of fans in the crowd drowned out my thoughts of her and focused my mind back on the game. I was more than ready to show everyone how much work I'd put in this off-season.

I wanted four League Bowl rings before I retired, and I was determined to fucking get them.

At least I could use the pent-up sexual tension from seeing Scarlett and harness that energy into the game. It wasn't unknown for guys on teams across the league to abstain from sex during the season to keep their heads clear and maintain their energy.

Now I got why.

I AMBLED out of the locker room after a quick shower and spotted Scarlett chatting to one of the sports reporters for Network Entertainment Sports. Her gaze fell on mine as I neared them and her eyes brightened.

My fucking girl.

My heart soared out of my chest every time she looked at me like that. It was hard to believe there was a time not long ago that she wouldn't even look me in the eyes when we spoke. I hadn't so much as seen her nervously twirl her ring lately either.

"Don't tell me you've been harassing my girl, Jamison," I quipped, slinging an arm around Scarlett's shoulders. I practically had to slouch to make it work because of the height difference, but I didn't care.

"Wouldn't dream of it, Abbott." The middle-aged guy who sported a patchy gray beard shot me a wink while I slipped my hand into the one he stuck out. "So, are you going to let me run the story about how the two of you met or wait for Page Six to butcher it?" he prodded, and the three of us chuckled together.

This guy was fucking funny. As far as sleazy sports reporters went, he was one of the better ones, so I didn't mind giving him an exclusive. I'd rather it be him who got the story than some weird fuck who made up an elaborate one for clicks.

Things had been a bit dry for Scarlett and me lately on the tabloid front anyway. This was our first outing since we were spotted at Carlo's restaurant a few weeks ago.

Not that I fucking cared if we were seen out in public though.

I'd take hanging out with her at home and talking together over breakfast before this public bullshit any day. But it couldn't hurt for more buzz to circulate around us again; it was team fucking mandated after all.

"Subtle," I joked. "You mind if I tell him?" I looked down at Scarlett, and she shook her head side to side while wrapping one hand around my bicep and slipping the other into mine, intertwining our fingers.

"Well, a few weeks before the start of last season, I was

sitting in Coach Sterling's office chatting with him about blocking drills when a pretty brunette waltzed in with Coach's daughter, Lea. The pretty brunette had a basketful of banana bread in her hands and big brown eyes that paralyzed me the moment our eyes met." My mouth curved up into an unconscious smile and I leaned down to press a quick kiss against her hair—which I'd come to learn always smelled like coconut shampoo.

"All it took was one bite of her banana bread before I offered her a job as my personal chef. She didn't like me much at first, but I'd say I grew on her over time, yeah?" I threw a knowing wink at Scarlett.

"Maybe a little." She tilted her head to one side playfully and shrugged a shoulder. Her bare neck was exposed and all I could think about was planting open-mouthed kisses up and down it.

"Thanks, guys. See you next time, Abel." Jamison waved as he walked over toward some of the other players.

"You're great at embellishing stories," Scarlett whispered.

"Every word I said was the truth, Red."

I wanted this. I wanted her. I *needed* her.

Fuck if my heart didn't drop when she told me in the car a few weeks ago that we might have been something more if we had started off differently.

I hated that she said it, but only because I knew it was true.

Just then, one of the team's cheerleaders came running up to us. I'd never spoken to her, but I overheard some locker room talk about how relentless she was when it came to crawling into players' beds. Apparently, she'd already fucked a handful of my teammates, and I had no desire to be her next conquest.

"Hi, Abel. Great game!" the blonde exclaimed, batting her lashes too excitedly for my liking. She drilled her gaze on Scarlett—who was still underneath my arm—and gave her a long once-over before sending her a stink-eyed look.

"Hi, I'm Scarlett... Abel's girlfriend," Scarlett said with a lethal calmness, clutching my arm tighter to subtly claim me as hers. And fuck did it make my chest erupt with satisfaction.

My lips twitched, and the blonde scoffed, twisting around on the ball of her feet and stomping away.

"Who's the jealous one now, huh?" I murmured teasingly in her ear.

"Only when it comes to people taking what's mine," she repeated my earlier words back to me, batting those midnight-black lashes up at me, mocking cheerleader girl.

"You're cute when you're jealous." Without thought, I gave her a quick kiss on the side of her forehead as I tugged her closer to my side. "Did Mae drive you?"

I'd learned through our morning conversations that Scarlett hated driving. She got in a few accidents back to back in high school and then she and Mae went to school in New York where she didn't drive for four years. Now, she avoided it at all costs unless she was going to our local grocery store down the road.

"Yeah." She nodded, slipping out from underneath my arm. "I should probably call her and figure out where she wants me to meet her at. Pretty sure she and Lea were hiding under the bleachers taking edibles before I came to find you."

I should've been more shocked at her admission than I actually was, but after the whole "Scarlett thinking she drugged me" incident, I wasn't fazed.

"Ride back with me." It was a statement, not a question.

"But—"

"But nothing," I cut her off. "You're coming with me. You can text her from the car."

"You know I'm capable of taking care of myself, right?" She arched a brow. "I promise I won't float away into the void like a balloon if you take your eyes off of me."

"I know that you're capable of taking care of yourself, Red. But I won't apologize for wanting to do things for you or wanting to spend more time with you." Scarlett bounced her gaze between my eyes. "You can fight me on it all you want, but in case you haven't noticed, I'm not one to lose often."

She stopped in her tracks and stared at me, shell-shocked. Like the words that left my mouth were the answers to getting into heaven and I gave them to her for free.

I meant what I said.

I wanted as much time as she was willing to give me. Especially since I was leaving her at the end of the weekend.

We spotted Coach Sterling from across the parking lot and both of us waved at him. When Scarlett pulled out her phone from her back pocket to assumingly text Mae, Coach shot me a sly wink that made me shake my head.

The guy was no better than his daughter.

IT WAS HALFWAY through the drive back to the house when I realized that my hand had been on Scarlett's thigh the entire ride, my hands raking leisurely across her smooth skin.

She hadn't mentioned it or acted like I'd done something out of the ordinary. In fact, when I realized what I'd been doing, I found her trailing fingertips up and down the back of my forearm.

"You staying?" I turned the wheel to steer the car into my driveway and cut the engine once we came to a stop.

"If you want me to."

"I wouldn't ask if I didn't want you to."

"Then I'll stay." She gave me a small smile and unbuckled her seat belt.

Scarlett hopped out of the car just as my phone dinged and I fished it out from the cup holder.

Aera: Cute headline.

Attached was a link to the latest article from our interview with Jamison. *Damn, he worked fast.* I typed out a quick reply as I got out, walking a few steps behind Scarlett who was almost at the front door.

Abel: Thanks.
Aera: You're going to have to tell her about us sooner or later.
Abel: Not right now. Let me do this on my own terms, Aer.
Aera: Tick Tock.
Abel: Don't even think about fucking this up for me.
Aera: Sounds like you're already on the path to doing that yourself.

Couldn't blame her for taking a jab at me. She was tired of hiding, and fuck, so was I, but it just wasn't the right time to tell the world about our relationship. There were other things, other *people,* to think about which things more complicated than Aera let on.

"You want me to make us something for dinner?" Scarlett called back to me as she walked up the porch steps.

"Nah. Let's get takeout."

It was moments like this—coming home together and talking about dinner plans—that made it feel like we were a real fucking couple.

Sometimes our fake relationship felt so much like a real one that it was hard to decipher where the deception started and ended. Not to mention our "friendship" being thrown in complicated my thoughts even more.

Friends.

I still fucking hated that word.

FOURTEEN
SCARLETT

WHEN ABEL TOLD me he was going to get a driver to take him to the airport so he didn't have to leave his car in extended parking for nearly a month, I didn't hesitate before offering to drive his car back instead.

And there were few things I hated more in life than driving, so that was saying a lot. But I was willing to curb my fear if it meant soaking up a few extra minutes with him before he left.

I was convinced that God was playing a sick joke on me by giving Abel and me six weeks together to fall into a healthy rhythm of friendship after so much animosity, only for him to be ripped away for half that amount of time just as I was beginning to sort out my feelings for him.

Yes, I would admit it—well, to anyone but him—but I had feelings for him. Lots and lots of feelings, to be exact.

Maybe him leaving was for the best though? People have always said that "absence makes the heart grow fonder," and this time apart would test whether or not that rang true.

Abel tapped his fingers against the steering wheel along with the music. I, on the other hand, was doing my best to ignore the mocking voice inside my head that barely allowed a question or "what if" to cross my mind before another took over.

When we were a few miles from the airport, he slipped his hand into mine, which eased the wave of apprehension that coursed through me.

I silently hoped that he would call me while he was gone, but I knew it was wishful thinking. He would be busy working on his commercial and doing photo shoots and I would be the last thing on his mind.

Plus, we were just "friends" who had an agreement together. He didn't owe me anything outside of that, so I needed to lower my expectations before I hurt my own feelings from overthinking.

"You ready?" I shifted my gaze toward Abel as he turned into a spot in the short-term parking lot.

"You going to miss me, Red?" He turned his giant shoulders to face me, but instead of leaning back against the door like I expected, he inched closer to my side. I nodded my head up and down, not shying away from his touch despite the fluttery feeling that tore through my insides.

I took in the somber look that covered his face and tears instantly began to prick the back of my throat.

Why was I getting so emotional?

We were *just* friends and he was only leaving for *three* weeks.

It wasn't like I was never going to see him again. Well, unless his plane crashed. Or he drowned in the ocean. Or the boom mic came down and beheaded him while he was on set for his commercial.

Nope. Nope. Nope.

I needed to pull myself out of whatever pit I dug inside my brain before I went on a downward spiral and accidentally manifested his death.

There were so many words I wanted to say to him that were stuck in the back of my throat, begging to break free, but they couldn't.

My period was also due any day so that might have added to my dramatics, but period or not, this was all too much for me.

I moved closer to Abel and pressed my forehead against his and he instantly released a breath that visibly dropped his shoulders two inches.

I wanted him to kiss me—scratch that—*needed* him to kiss me. Need burned like a blazing inferno inside my core and he was the only one who would be able to extinguish the flame.

I averted my gaze, hoping he wouldn't pick up on the confusion that was plaguing me, but Abel, being Abel, must have sensed it because he cupped my face into his hands, forcing me to look up into his hazel eyes.

"Hey hey hey, nothing's changing between us, you know that?" Abel stroked his thumb over my cheek tenderly. "Please don't shut me out again, Scarlett. I won't be able to fucking survive it."

A pang of guilt struck me in the depths of my core.

That's what he thought? That I was going to shut him out?

My thought was immediately interrupted by the word he just used. "You called me Scarlett," I gasped.

"What?"

"You've never called me Scarlett before. It's always been Red, but right then, you called me Scarlett…"

Abel just smirked in response.

And then he inched his face closer to mine. And closer.

And closer. So close that our lips were millimeters away from touching.

A bundle of nerves swarmed into the pit of my stomach as I waited for him to finally cut the distance between us.

"Scarlett, I'm going to kiss you now." His lips brushed against mine as he spoke, sending a jolt of electricity sparking throughout my entire body. "Unless you tell me to stop."

"Don't stop," I breathed against his lips.

His lips crashed to mine and his tongue begged for entrance into my mouth, which I willingly gave to him. His hands slid from my face and into my hair, lightly tugging at the base as he urged our kiss deeper.

Abel pulled away from my lips and I stared at him, slack-jawed, breathless, and too stunned to utter a word. "You and me"—he waved his hand between the two of us —"we're not going anywhere, got it? In case you haven't picked up on it, you're fucking stuck with me, Red."

I. Was. Stuck. With. Him.

His mouth found mine again, making my brain short-circuit. His teeth tugged at my bottom lip which sent a whimper coursing out of me.

"Fuck, Red," Abel rasped out, hoarse and throaty. "As much as I want to keep kissing you, I've got to make this flight or my agent is gonna kill me."

"Do you want me to walk you inside? I can help you with your bag. Walk you to security." I suggested, desperately wanting five more minutes with him.

"You can't." He sighed and my heart sank. "If you get out of this car, I won't be able to take my hands off of you long enough to get on the plane."

So he gave me a gentle parting kiss.

And another.

And another.

ABEL WAS GONE.

It wasn't just that he was no longer physically present
—that part was obvious—but the fact was that my *entire*
routine was uprooted by his absence. I wasn't waking up
early for work anymore or staying an hour late every day
just to hang out with him.

Instead, I was sitting at home alone. Bored. Balancing
my time between catching up on my favorite trashy reality
TV shows I'd neglected the past few weeks and trying out
new recipes that all sucked.

Occasionally, I'd pop over to Mae's and annoy her with
my presence until she kicked me out because I was "distracting her from work."

Lame.

Ten days of boredom felt like ten months and I
suddenly realized why the stay-at-home wives with no
jobs or kids I envied on Socialgram took daily Pilates
classes and went to the grocery store multiple times a
week.

I hadn't heard a word from Abel since he left me
standing dazed in the airport parking lot with tingly lips.

Did he regret kissing me? Or worse… was I a bad
kisser?

I knew I was a little rusty, but I didn't think it was
that bad.

It took me a few days of mulling it over endlessly to
realize that all of the lingering touches, the thoughtful
gestures, and even that kiss—God, that kiss—didn't mean

we were actually together. Even if breaking one of our cardinal rules made my brain think otherwise.

I had been so blinded by our kiss that some part of me had forgotten the entire reason for agreeing to our ruse in the first place. It was hard to imagine Abel not living across the street anymore, let alone *me* living in his house.

Was I letting the possibility of a future with Abel cloud my judgment?

Probably.

Okay, more than probably. I most definitely was.

Abel and I were good together, so it was hard not to.

I just hoped that one day when I mustered up the courage to tell him the truth—that I *kinda sorta maybe* was falling for him—that he'd let me down easy. Because now, after that kiss, there was no way I'd be able to go back to how we used to be before.

Three months ago I would've rather met my maker than speak twenty words to him, but now, this curveball of a confession would rock whatever foundation we'd created the last few weeks.

Soon enough, the whole charade between us would be over anyway, which made a piece of my heart break off from the rest at the thought.

I stared at Abel's contact on my phone and opened up a new message. He gave me his phone number the first day that I started working for him, but I never had a reason to text him until now.

What kind of thing did you say to your boss who kissed you then didn't say a word after?

Scarlett: John says hi.
Abel: Tell him I'll beat his fucking face in.
Scarlett: Aggressive much?
Abel: I prefer the term possessive.

Abel: I miss you, Red.

Abel: I've been waiting for you to text me for ten fucking days. You never gave me your number and I even reached out to Lea and October for it, but they both refused to give it to me. They claimed "a boyfriend would have a girl-friend's phone number."

Abel: Needless to say, they might be on to us.

He tried contacting me?

Oh my god, Abel tried contacting me.

Scarlett: You could've always messaged me on Socialgram to ask.

Abel: I did… four times, Red. You don't follow me back so it probably got sent to your spam inbox.

Oh shit. He was right.

In my defense, he started following me the week that he kicked me out of his house, so I wasn't inclined to follow him back at the time. And while I might have perused his Socialgram account on more than one occasion, I guess I never got around to following him back.

Oops.

I WAS EATING dinner at the pool house by myself when a text from Abel came through as expected. We'd spent the last twenty-four hours texting nonstop, aside from the handful of hours that were spent sleeping or showering.

Abel: Why weren't we like this sooner?
Me: Honest answer?
Abel: Always.
Me: Well until recently I kind of assumed that you hated me...

A big part of me was embarrassed to admit the truth to him, yet the other part was relieved to finally get that nagging feeling off of my chest after all this time.

Seconds after I hit send, my ringtone blasted loudly as a video call from none other than Abel Abbott himself popped up on the screen.

I bit my lip, debating whether or not to answer with a thumb hovering between the green and red buttons.

I could do this.

I could tell my boss all the reasons I used to think he was an asshole, right?

This was the moment I'd been waiting for, wasn't it? So, why did my stomach churn at the thought of admitting the words out loud?

Ugh.

This conversation was bound to happen at one point or another, but at least it would be easier to do through a screen three thousand miles away from each other, right?

Deciding to bite the bullet, I huffed out a ragged breath and pressed the green button to accept the call.

"Are we really going to have this conversation right now?" I droned, rolling my eyes as his face came into view on my screen.

I thought it'd be best to skip the formalities and jump straight to the good stuff. Although, my chest felt like it was going to burst as Abel stared back at me with narrowed eyes. Not. Saying. A. Word.

"Yes, we're going to have this conversation right now," he finally replied, albeit sternly.

What did *he* have to be upset about? If anyone was going to be upset in this scenario, it was me!

"I wouldn't know what to fucking do with myself if I knew you went to sleep thinking that I hated you. Frankly, the fact that you've gone to sleep for *eleven fucking months* with the idea that I hate you pisses me off." His voice was icy as he spit his words out. My stomach filled with tiny butterflies at his confession.

"Well… this isn't exactly how I envisioned this conversation going," I muttered to myself.

"Tell me why you thought I hated you so I can prove you wrong."

It seemed like poor timing to bring up the past, especially given the progress we'd made in our "friendship."

Jesus Christ, I hated that word.

The truth was, I knew that Abel and I weren't really together and that he didn't owe me an explanation about the girls that came before me.

But that didn't mean I didn't have to keep reminding myself… often.

And it wasn't like he could take back the months of being a dick to me. As much as people liked to believe an apology could cure all things, it couldn't, especially in this case.

On the other hand, Abel continued to prove that whatever preconceived notions I'd created about him in my head were entirely wrong. I'd grown to like the true version of himself that he only allowed a select few to see. I liked being one of those select few.

Dammit, I knew I should've kept my mouth shut.

"You threw out my food and you treated me like I didn't exist for eight months and only started talking to me when you wanted something from me..." I said matter-of-factly. The silence that passed between the two of us was excruciating. "...but we're friends now, soooo it doesn't matter anymore. Problem solved."

"No, problem not solved. Look at me, Red," he barked out in a serious tone. Peering down at the screen, I could see the annoyance rising in his eyes.

I... was I getting turned on by this?

"You need to get one thing through that pretty little head of yours," he started. "I have *never* for one fucking second hated you. Not even close. Got it?"

I swallowed once. And then twice.

Okay, I was definitely turned on by this.

My mouth was so dry that all I could manage was a nod.

"Good."

ABEL and I spent the next four hours talking about everything and nothing. Our conversation flowed with ease. It was hard to believe there was a time not long ago that we could hardly speak a few words to each other.

I lay on my side in bed with my duvet cover pulled to my shoulders. My room was complete darkness aside from Abel's face illuminating my phone screen.

"I miss you," I admitted after a beat of silence passed between us.

"I miss you too, Red." His features softened. "More than you fucking know."

"I wish I could've come to visit you for a weekend while you were out there."

"Come this weekend."

"I can't. I have a meeting here on Sunday afternoon before my editor goes on maternity leave next week and it's probably too late to get a flight for tomorrow anyway."

Seeing as it was midnight on Thursday, I was doubtful that there would be any available flights to or from Miami now that summer was in full force and people were bouncing in and out of here for vacations and weekend trips.

Abel was silent on the other end for a few minutes with his screen paused while I scrolled through the latest Socialgram posts. Until an email notification sounded on my end. "You should check that," Abel dared, popping back into the screen with a smirk.

I opened up my email app to find a new email from Abel with… a freaking plane ticket to Los Angeles for tomorrow morning.

What. The. Hell.

We still hadn't addressed our kiss at the airport, but deep down, I wanted him to mention it. To tell me that it wasn't a mistake. That it wasn't for people that had—unbeknownst to me—snapped photos of us kissing in the car and posted them on Socialgram.

Now that he was inviting me to come stay with him for the weekend, I was getting the feeling that it wasn't a mistake.

I felt foolish for how much it made my heart swell, because you know what they say about assuming.

"You bought me a plane ticket?"

"Looks like you'll be coming to see me after all." The corner of Abel's lips twitched and his screen went black.

I rolled over to my other side with a giddy smile on my face.

An hour later, a text lit up the screen on my nightstand as I lay awake staring at the ceiling. No matter how hard I tried, there was no way I was going to sleep after Abel's confession.

Rolling over, I picked up my phone from the charger to see who was texting me this late. My heart rate sped up, a grin passing my lips as I read the message on the screen.

Abel: Good night, Red.

FIFTEEN
ABEL

I FUCKING MISSED HER.

So much so that I bought her a plane ticket to California without a second thought. And I didn't have a single fucking regret about it. Between our incessant texting and multi-hour-long video calls, I'd been glued to my phone for the past thirty-six hours straight.

I couldn't take it anymore.

I needed to see her in person.

Twelve days felt like a fucking eternity without her around.

I wanted to hear that laugh. I wanted to make stupid excuses to touch her just so I could watch as she leaned into me. I wanted to kiss those fucking lips again. And again. And again.

It was almost like there a silent vow that hung between the two of us, not to mention the kiss. And I was okay with that for now. Some things were just better to talk about in person.

Instead, Scarlett roped me in on the phone, telling me

tales about her childhood growing up and the crazy antics she and Mae got up to in college. I sat back and listened attentively, admiring how lovingly she spoke of her family.

I knew Mom did the best she could, raising me all by herself. I never went without meals or clothes on my back, even if it meant she had to work three jobs in order for me to do so.

No matter how many trips around the world I funded for her now, it would never be enough to repay her for everything she'd sacrificed for me over the years.

Yet, hearing Scarlett talk about her family confirmed that some part of me was still sad for the kid version of myself who missed out on having a big family growing up and instead spent most of his nights all alone practicing football drills on the field next to our apartment.

What Scarlett and her family had... that's what I wanted our future to look like.

After ending our call last night, I couldn't sit still at the thought of seeing her. The entire half hour I was supposed to spend relaxing and winding down before bed, my legs were restlessly begging for me to get up and move.

So I gave in and scrambled around the house, cleaning every surface and organizing everything down to the plates and cups in the fucking cabinets.

I wanted everything to look perfect for when she arrived. The house was half-mine after all, so I wanted her to like it.

When we'd bought the house, I'd envisioned coming back here for vacations after the season and spending a few weeks here during the summers before camp started, much like I was now.

The only thing that was missing was more people to enjoy it with.

Granted, Aera's name was on the deed too, but somehow, I'd managed to avoid her the entire time I'd been in town so far.

Or so I thought until I peeked at my phone between takes earlier this morning to see if there were any missed messages from Scarlett and instead saw that Aera was the one who had bombarded me with notifications.

I quickly unlocked my phone and skimmed through her messages before thumbing out a reluctant reply.

Aera: I have important news. Mandatory dinner Sunday night. Tequila's Restaurant @ 7pm don't be late.
Aera: And if for some reason you don't show, just know that I'll show up at the beach house. Or worse, I'll be waiting on your doorstep the second you get back to Miami.
Aera: Better yet, I might even tell the press *all* about our little secret.
Abel: Fine. I'll be there.
Aera: Wear something nice. I'd rather be caught dead than be seen sitting next to you at a five-star restaurant in sweatpants.

That was Aera for you.

I shoved my phone into my gym bag and headed back out to the practice field that the advertising company secured to shoot our commercial.

It was an unusually hot day out today and the black T-shirt and shorts they had me wearing made me sweat profusely. The breeze helped a bit, but fuck, I hoped they could edit all this sweat out of a commercial.

Ripley, the director, swore they could, but I wasn't entirely convinced.

Once the shoot ended for the day, just before lunch, I

dropped by the house to take a quick shower and change into a clean pair of Nagem athletic shorts and a matching T-shirt.

Snatching the keys to my rental car from the console table by the front door, I headed outside and revved the engine before starting the drive to the airport.

Adrenaline coursed through my veins the entire ride which made the fact that I was stuck in bumper-to-bumper traffic completely fucking excruciating.

The way I felt about seeing her felt eerily similar to every game day I'd had my entire career, which was somewhere between unbridled excitement and nauseous as fuck.

Trying to keep my mind off the desire to burst out of this tiny sedan the rental company gave me, I chuckled to myself, remembering Scarlett's messages from earlier.

Once I found a spot in the parking lot, I pulled out my phone from the cup holder and read them again while I waited for her flight to land.

Scarlett: Abel!!
Scarlett: What the hell is wrong with you!!
Scarlett: Why didn't you tell me this was a PRIVATE plane?!
Scarlett: I don't know how to act on a private plane. I've never even flown first class before!
Scarlett: I hope you don't get charged per snack because I totally took two of them.
Abel: Eat as many snacks as you want, Red.
Abel: See you soon.

I was getting her the private plane either way, but every flight out of Miami was sold out, so it wasn't like I had much of a choice.

Maybe I should've given her a heads-up, but it was kind of fucking adorable how nervous she was over it.

Most people assumed that all league players were wealthy when they heard about the millions on our contracts or some of the high-paying brand deals we got. For the most part, they were right. A lot of the guys invested well in the stock market or real estate to build their wealth, knowing that league money wouldn't last forever.

However, there were always a few guys on every team who'd continuously run themselves broke year after year trying to impress people with flashy jewelry, booze-filled parties, and luxury cars.

I wasn't one to flaunt my money often. Fuck, aside from my house, I hardly spent any money on myself at all, but the one luxury I allowed myself was flying private whenever I traveled.

Mostly because I hated people and couldn't be bothered with the normal airport bullshit. Fuck, even when I flew first class and sat in the airline lounges, people still found their way to badger me with questions or ask for autographs for their sister's best friend's cousin's third-grade math teacher.

Needless to say, after flying private one time on a whim a few years back, I was sold, and I wasn't ever planning on going back.

Scarlett would learn to get used to it.

A NOTIFICATION from the flight tracker I downloaded said Scarlett's plane had just landed. Knowing she'd be out any minute, I fumbled my way out of the tiny-ass car where I'd spent the last half an hour waiting.

When I entered through the automatic doors, I felt a cool gust from the air conditioning hit my face and I immediately spotted Scarlett wandering through the crowd down past the final security marker.

Her chestnut-brown hair was tied up in a ponytail at the crown of her head and she wore a faded green T-shirt that was so inherently her it brought a wide smile to my face.

Scarlett's eyes darted around the baggage claim area and a giant grin broke out across her face when our eyes locked from a hundred yards away. Video calls could never do justice to seeing that smile of hers in person.

Her smile grew wider as she picked up her pace, weaving through the crowd to where I'd been leaning against the wall waiting for her. Matching her eagerness, I picked up my stride to meet her halfway.

Dropping her bag onto the ground, she jumped up and flung her arms around my neck before locking her legs around my waist.

I exhaled a calming breath, locking my hands against her spine and hauling her snugly against my chest. I held her there for what felt like fucking hours, but was likely only a few seconds.

She reared her head back and smiled again, studying my face. Fuck, every time our faces were only a few inches apart —which seemed to be often these days—tension rippled throughout my veins, and now was no exception.

I had to physically stop myself from kissing her.

From forgetting that this wasn't real.

That *she* thought this wasn't real.

"Miss me?" She beamed up at me, breaking up my thoughts.

If only she knew how much.

I brushed my lips against her ear and decided there was no point in hiding the truth. "More than you know," I mumbled, squeezing her once more before sliding her down my body and placing her feet back on solid ground.

Picking up her bright-pink duffel bag off the ground, I threw it over my shoulder. There were a few paparazzi posted outside the airport doors when I came in, but I couldn't have cared less whether I got photographed with hot-pink luggage.

I was doubtful that a journalist could come up with a headline worthy of clickbait from the image anyway.

I scanned my eyes over her, taking her in, but my vision zeroed in on four white squares that were stuck to the bottom of her tennis shoes.

"Did you go to the bathroom on the plane?" I sneered at her, trying to hold back a laugh.

Scarlett looked at me quizzically with a raised brow. "I know it was a private plane and all, but I didn't take a solo trip to the mile-high club. If that's what you're asking…"

A laugh barreled out of my chest as I lowered my eyes down at the squares of toilet paper stuck to the bottom of her shoe again.

I thought this kind of thing only happened in movies, but *damn*, it was funny in real life.

Her eyes followed along with mine down to her feet. "Oh god." A current of breath carried her words and a bright shade of red I'd never seen before washed over her face.

My laugh turned into a full-on chuckle as I watched her waddle around like a madwoman trying to scrub off the last of the toilet paper remains from the bottom of her sneakers.

Once she'd successfully removed all of the toilet paper,

I slung my arm across her shoulder. Tugging her closer against me, I led us toward the exit. She tilted her head upward at me and gave me a shy look before she spoke. "Speaking of toilet paper…" She trailed off.

"You're finally ready to come clean about toilet papering my house, huh?" The smug smile I'd been holding back broke from my lips with ease.

A few months back, when I was woken in the middle of the night by a security system notification, my immediate fear was that someone was trying to rob me.

Maybe I was a bit paranoid from watching too many Mafia documentaries before bed. I knew my buddy Carlo was a distant cousin to some prominent Chicago Outfit members, but I found it unlikely that the Santini brothers would want to target me, of all people.

Much to my surprise, I opened my security app to find Scarlett and her sister drunk off their asses, vandalizing my front yard instead.

Scarlett stopped in her tracks just before we reached the automatic sliding doors. "Wh— how did you know that was us?"

"Security cameras, Red."

"But it's a gated neighborhood! And there's neighborhood patrol!"

"The neighborhood also happens to be home to the richest people in the city. Even with security patrol in place, one can never be too safe." A warm breeze hit my skin as we picked up our pace again. "And you're not helping my point either… all it took was twenty minutes of Lea distracting the patrol guard for you all to commit your crime."

"Wait, how did you know it was Lea who distracted him?" Her mouth dropped open.

"After watching you all on the security cameras in real

time…"—that shade of red on her face? Yeah, it got darker —"I downloaded a copy of the footage with the time stamp onto a flash drive and walked down to the security office in nothing but boxers to show the guard the tape. Took him one look at my house to realize that he was fucked."

"So, the next day, you knew the *entire time,* and you didn't even question me about it?"

Kind of hard to question her about it when I was already planning to ask her out that day. Might've made things weird.

And as much as I hated to admit it, I wasn't oblivious to the fact that she didn't like working for me. I knew damn well she was about to quit that morning,

I just beat her to the punch before she got the chance.

"How do you think your mess got cleaned up so quickly, huh?" A smirk pulled at my lips and I watched the horror of my confession run across her face. Granted, I paid a cleaning company quadruple their normal rate *plus* a generous tip for after-hours service to make that happen, but still.

"I've been waiting to see how long it would take for you to confess. Only took you two months and eighteen days." My arm still around her shoulder, I pulled her close and placed a quick kiss on her temple before whispering in her ear. "Correct me if I'm wrong, but the gray sweatpants are your favorite, yeah?"

Scarlett curled into my side and hid her face from me. "This is mortifying." Her voice was muffled against my shirt.

"Just wait until I tell you about all those times I heard you muttering 'asshole' under your breath when you thought I couldn't hear you…"

Yeah, I knew about those too.

"You heard those?" Scarlett exclaimed before making an attempt to flee. She didn't make it but a few inches before I circled my arms around her waist and pulled her back to me.

She seriously needed to stop trying to outrun me because she was never going to succeed.

"Yeah, Abel Asshole Abbott was a funny one though. I'll give you that."

"Oh my god, why didn't you fire me?"

"I had my reasons." I winked down at her when she popped her head up to look at me. "And you made a mean seared salmon that one time. Couldn't give you up after that."

She nuzzled into my side to hide her face abashedly once again. She had no idea how fucking cute she looked when she was embarrassed.

Fuck, it felt good having her close to me again. Being able to touch her and feel as she glued herself to me without hesitating.

Fuck, I missed her.

It was then that I knew I was done sitting on the sidelines and pretending that all I wanted was her "friendship." Because the next time I went a few days without seeing her or giving her a forehead kiss wasn't going to cut it.

I was going to need the real thing.

Right then, all my efforts to remain shy about my feelings for her completely dissolved.

Nothing that had gone on between us had been part of the agreement for me. Not even for a second. But I was done playing it off as a part of our "fake relationship." Done subjecting myself to the torture of keeping her at arm's length for the sake of our "friendship" like I had been.

She was mine.

And it was only a matter of time until she realized it too.

SIXTEEN
SCARLETT

AT WHAT POINT was someone supposed to tell their boss that they *sorta kinda maybe* wanted to be more than friends with them? And that they no longer wanted their fake relationship to be… well, fake.

Unfortunately for me, I had no freaking idea.

Last night after Abel and I drove around Malibu for a while, we grabbed dinner at a local restaurant by the pier where we caught each other up to speed on all the uneventful things we'd been doing the past two weeks without each other.

He was relieved to know that I hadn't gone on any dates with guys named John.

You're mine, you know that?

Every word I said was the truth, Red.

Please don't start shutting me out again, Scarlett.

I'm going to kiss you now… unless you tell me to stop.

You're fucking stuck with me, Red.

Abel's words had been on an endless loop inside my head for the last two weeks, and now that we were in close proximity again, I wasn't sure what to make of this *thing* between us.

I felt like I was in a constant state of limbo when it came to him. We'd taken one step forward and decided to be friends and almost as immediately as it started, we were forced two steps back with him leaving the picture for nearly a month.

Once we got home from dinner, the two of us fell asleep on the couch almost instantly after we sat down. It was similar to the way we had the first time he came over and spent the night at the pool house.

Innocently with no ulterior motive.

But this time, when I woke up in the middle of the night to go pee, I realized that at some point in my sleepy Scarlett haze, I'd crawled up and cuddled myself *directly* on top of Abel's chest.

Only God knew how long we'd lain like that. I assumed Able hadn't noticed yet, being that he hadn't shoved me off of him and instead was sleeping soundly beneath me.

I *subtly* attempted to slip out from the giant arm that was draped over my back, hoping that maybe he wouldn't notice if I tiptoed up to my room like nothing ever happened.

But my plan failed… miserably.

I must've startled him when I tried to wiggle out of the hold he had on my back because he jerked awake with wide eyes. Of course, this also happened to be the exact moment that my arm decided it was no longer sufficient to hold my upper body weight, and my elbow buckled.

Meaning my face was falling, wide eyed, in slow motion.

Right. Toward. His. Face.

Thank God the guy had years of mastering his quick

reaction time because he caught me by the shoulders before my face came crashing down onto his. Although him catching me wasn't much better when it meant that my mouth ever so gently, with a featherlight touch, met his just the *tiniest* bit.

I sucked in a gasp when I felt his length against my stomach from underneath his shorts. I was too stunned to speak. Too stunned to move, knowing that *I* did that to him.

Jesus Christ, why did things like this have to happen to me at the worst possible times?

Our eyes locked and his breath grew shallow as his heat-filled eyes drifted down to the faint connection of our lips.

I almost gave in right then. Almost moved downward and dove for his mouth without a second thought. Took the risk to see if he would reciprocate or not.

It was only once he cleared his throat that I pulled myself out of the trance that I was in and backed my head away from his.

Pretending I was still half-asleep, I yawned, moving off of him and standing on my own two feet. I stretched out my arms over my head and then grabbed the throw blanket that lay over the back of the couch. Then I tossed it over the back of my shoulders, wrapping myself inside the cocoon.

I didn't chance looking back at Abel as I pretended to groggily waddle up the steps to my bedroom.

Was I a hypocrite for acting like nothing happened? Yes.

Would I have to deal with the confrontation later? Hopefully not... but probably yes.

I peered over at the clock on the nightstand as I crawled into bed and curled up with the blanket I stole from the couch. It was only four in the morning, but I had a feeling I wouldn't be sleeping anytime soon.

A few minutes after I got settled into bed, I heard Abel's heavy footsteps pound up the stairs until his bedroom door closed quietly.

There was a wall that separated us, but I could've sworn I could still feel a tangible tension between the two of us.

My hope of catching a few more hours of sleep before starting the day was a complete and utter failure. No matter how many times I tossed and turned, switched out pillows, or moved to the opposite side of the bed... I couldn't freaking sleep.

How the hell was I supposed to anyway after Abel and I *kissed*?

Okay, maybe the subtle lip touch we shared was questionable as to whether or not it could be classified as a kiss. But if there had been the *tiniest bit* more pressure, it would've without a doubt been one, no matter what scale or scorecard system was being used.

After wrestling between the sheets for well over two hours, I huffed out a breath and rolled onto my back. I stared up at the white ceiling, watching the fan above me spin in endless circles.

Closing my eyes, I sank deeper into the mattress and pondered what it would've been like if I'd given in and allowed myself to kiss him.

Would he have kissed me back? Would his hands have drifted down my back and slid below my pants so that he could brush over my bare skin? Would he have let a finger wander lower until it brushed up the middle of my panties?

I sensuously inched my hands from my stomach up to my breast and squeezed, causing that familiar tingling sensation I knew well to spread throughout my body.

Sliding my fingertips across my skin, I mimicked the same motion on the other side, but this time, I pinched my nipple between my thumb and pointer finger. Warmth spread straight to my core as I repeated the motions once again.

With my left hand toying with my nipples, I slowly grazed my right hand down my stomach and beneath the waistband of my slinky shorts. Spreading my legs wider, I teased my middle two fingers up and down my slit until I could feel my arousal.

I dipped both fingers inside my heat before pulling them out to swirl wetness around my clit, excitement dancing beneath my skin. Holding back a moan, I continued to work my fingers in a steady circular motion until I could feel my orgasm beginning to build at the base of my spine.

Bucking my hips against my own hand, I dipped two fingers back down inside me once again, quickening my pace as I shoved them in and out.

I did my best to stifle the moans that threatened to spill out of me, knowing that Abel was just behind the wall next to me, but a small moan escaped my lips unexpectedly. My pussy clenched around my fingers just thinking about Abel, imagining that these were his fingers instead of my own.

I clasped the hand that was playing with my nipples over my mouth to muffle the noise as my orgasm grew closer. Picking up the speed of my fingers, I arched my back and my pussy began pulsing tightly around them.

Oh god, I needed to come.

An orgasm tore through my body so hard that I felt like I was floating. My body thrashed against the sheets until I steadied my rhythm, coming down from the high that relieved me of the ache I'd had since arriving at the beach house.

My chest heaved while I tried to catch my breath. Keeping my eyes closed, I let myself lay there, mindless and sated, for a long while until I eventually drifted off into a deep, deep sleep.

WHEN I WOKE up the next morning, I threw caution to the wind and wandered down the stairs without brushing my hair or teeth first. I'm sure Abel couldn't have cared less what I looked like after waking up anyway. If he thought that I was one of those girls who woke up looking polished and pristine, he was wrong.

Oh so very wrong.

I almost forgot that he'd seen me just after waking up when he spent the night at the pool house a few weeks ago. The realization hit me like a slap to the face. Abel and I had fallen asleep together... twice now.

And both times it was the best sleep I'd gotten in weeks.

That couldn't have been a coincidence, right?

I made myself comfortable around the kitchen nook that overlooked the foggy morning shoreline. Abel made me coffee in the kitchen and handed me the cup before taking a seat across from me. I blew the rising steam from my mug as I read the latest Page Six headline that Lea had sent me late last night.

Abel Abbott, is pink his new obsession? Click here for exclusive pictures of the football player and his favorite travel accessory and all the other pink items he keeps around.

I doubled over in laughter, reading the link to the obnoxious headline while I scrolled through—what appeared to be—every photo of Abel holding something pink to ever exist.

There was one with him at the grocery store buying pink flowers and another where he was obviously holding a little kid's pink purse at one of the team's youth sports camps they put on during the off-season… but all the kids had conveniently been edited out of the photo.

God, the lengths these media outlets would go to for a few website clicks was outrageous. Abel popped a brow at me, and I slid my phone across the kitchen table to him so he could read the article.

The housekeeper, Janice, left us an enormous breakfast fit for a family of five. Which I guessed, when you were feeding a guy Abel's size, made sense. Trust me, I of all people would know.

I immediately dove in, shoveling food onto my plate and downing it all just as quickly—waffles, bacon, eggs, fresh fruit—leaving Abel in the dust to eat my scraps.

Maybe it was just me, but there was a special *something* about eating another chef's food that always made it taste ten times better than anything I could've made myself.

Granted, in this case, it was probably the fact that Janice had fifty years of experience in the kitchen on me, but still.

I made a mental note to remind Abel to ask for some of her recipes before he came back home, so I could try some of them out myself.

I would've liked to ask her myself, but my trip to see Abel was a short one, and she wouldn't be back over tomorrow morning before I left. As much as I wished I could've stayed longer, I knew that he'd be back home in a few days anyway and everything would go back to normal.

Abel picked up my phone from the table and quickly skimmed the article, rolling his eyes before sliding it back down to me.

"Remind me to get you a pink game day suit for your first game."

"Not funny," he huffed, though the edge of his lips budged the tiniest bit. Oh god, and that deep, raspy morning voice. The good news was that if he ever got injured and couldn't play in the league anymore, he'd have a *hell* of a second career making audio porn. "Did you sleep alright?"

"Fantastic. You?" My voice rose an octave when I spoke.

"Same… for the most part, at least."

Uhhh, okay… wasn't entirely sure what that was supposed to mean but alright.

Abel filled his third plate of the morning with another waffle, some eggs, and three pieces of bacon while I twirled my fork around my plate, toying with the few bites I had left.

"So about last night…" he started.

Oh god. Oh god.

We were going there. Right now. At the breakfast table.

It was hardly eight in the morning! I hadn't even had time yet to formulate a reason as to *why* I was sleeping on top of him and, more importantly, *why* I almost kissed him without warning. "About that…" I trailed off but was saved by the bell when Abel's phone started ringing over by the coffee machine.

He wiggled out of the nook and walked over to grab his phone.

And I shoved whatever conversation he thought we were about to have under the rug for another day—or never—by sneaking up the stairs to take a shower.

"I'LL BE BACK in a few hours. You sure you don't want to come?" Abel questioned as he stood in the doorway of my room.

He told me earlier that he needed to leave for a few hours to finish up his commercial for his brand partner. He'd asked me to go with him and meet everyone he'd been working with the last few weeks, but I politely declined.

It wasn't that I didn't want to go with him. Hell, I flew halfway across the country to see him, of course I wanted to spend time with him, but what I couldn't do was pretend we were in a fake relationship anymore.

Especially in front of *dozens* of strangers.

Every touch. Every hug. Every almost kiss.

I couldn't take it.

What was the worst that could happen if I told him how I really felt? He'd say he wasn't interested and we'd have to endure an awkward car ride to the airport tomorrow? I could handle that.

In the meantime, I planned to sit on the couch and watch reruns of cake decorating shows on the Cooking Channel.

But… that didn't last long.

Left up to my own devices, I realized that I had an *awful lot* of free time to wander around the house. It was a gorgeous two-story home with massive floor-to-ceiling windows that looked right onto a private beach.

Unlike Mae and Abel's magazineworthy interior-designed mansions, every piece of furniture or decor in this house appeared to be handpicked. No two things matched perfectly, yet at the same time, everything flowed together in a way that was cohesive enough to make it seem like it was done by a professional.

Making my way up the stairs, I peeked into the other two guest rooms that weren't being occupied before stumbling upon an office at the farthest end of the hall that was tucked away from all the other rooms.

Curiosity got the best of me, and I poked my head through the half-opened doorway to find a gorgeous mahogany desk. The walls had giant vision boards leaned against them that were covered with sketches of dresses with fabric scraps pinned onto them.

Oh my god.

This was *her* house. Abel's doorstep mystery woman.

Not only was *Abel* staying in her house, *we* were staying in her house together.

Okay, obviously she wasn't here with him. That was a good sign, right?

Well, at least she hadn't been since I'd arrived.

There was something weird going on with Abel and this girl—whoever the hell she was. If she was just some fling from Abel's past, then why was she still popping up at every corner?

On second thought, I didn't want to spend my time holed up alone in some random house all day. I had less than forty-eight hours to spend with Abel. Why would I throw away a few of those hours by sitting around and doing nothing?

I backed out of the room and strolled back to my bedroom to get ready and change clothes.

Abel would need lunch, right? And who better to bring it to him than his personal chef?

SEVENTEEN
SCARLETT

I SLAPPED TOGETHER two turkey club sandwiches and sliced them diagonally with a knife before wrapping them in reusable sandwich wrappers I found in the drawer. Snatching a few bags of chips from the pantry and two bottled drinks from the fridge, I shoved them into a tote bag.

Pulling my phone out of my back pocket, I opened up the rideshare app on my phone and plugged in the location of Abel's shoot that he'd texted me "just in case I decided I wanted to come along."

Lucky for him, I did.

Fifteen minutes later, I was en route to the practice field, holding the bag with two lunches in my lap. My driver played the same heavy metal song on repeat for the fourth time and I tried not to choke on the overwhelming lemongrass essential oil that exuded from the air vents, but holding my breath wasn't going to cut it much longer.

Thank *God* the place wasn't much farther down the road.

When I arrived on set, I stood off to the side and

spotted Abel who was standing in place waiting for the scene to begin. His eyes found mine and he shot me a quick wink that made my stomach erupt with butterflies. I gave him a small wave back before someone snapped the clapper board and filming began.

Once they were done, Abel walked over and draped a warm arm over my shoulders. The delicious smell of his sandalwood cologne filled the air around me. Which was much more appealing than that god-awful lemongrass. I'd have to wash my clothes half a dozen times when I got home and I still wasn't convinced that would be enough for the smell to go away.

"Thought you might want lunch." I held up the bag that had our food in it and Abel smiled down at me.

"You're staying to eat with me, yeah?"

"Of course."

"You want to meet everybody?" His left brow shot up and he intertwined my hand with his and led the way before I could even mutter out a reply.

Abel spent the next twenty minutes walking me around the set and explaining the plan for the commercial. If I was being honest, I had absolutely no idea what he was saying, but that was mostly because I still knew nothing about sports. Everything he said went in one ear and directly out the other.

Maybe one day I'd understand, but that day was most definitely not going to be today.

During our tour, he introduced me as his "girlfriend" to all of the crew members and some of the players from other league teams who were doing the shoot with him.

My eyes lit up every time one of the crew members was kind enough to show me behind the scenes of their job. I met Ricardo, the sound guy who assured me that he had never dropped the boom mic on someone's head in his entire career. And Lux, the makeup artist with gorgeous teal-blue hair who inquired all about Abel's skincare routine.

Initially, I wanted to laugh at them for asking his chef such an absurd question, but before I did, it dawned on me that I myself was acting in the role of "longtime girlfriend" still.

I hated lying to them by saying that he only used bar soap, but I couldn't think of anything else on the fly.

After thanking them and waving goodbye, I tucked myself underneath Abel's arm. "Uhh… weird question, but what kind of face soap do you use?" I asked uneasily, and he responded by listing off some brand I'd never heard of that sounded both expensive and not at all like bar soap.

Abel took the tote from my shoulder and shuffled it onto his while we looked for a spot in the grass away from everyone else to eat lunch.

Thankfully, I'd packed a small blanket too, in the hopes that we could have a picnic because it seemed everyone else was eating their lunch crowded around a table that was filled with catered lunch from the burger joint across the street.

I should've assumed they would've had food here, but oh well. It's the thought that counts, right?

Abel and I sat on the ground and he pulled out our food from the bag and placed it in front of us. I popped open a bag of jalapeño-flavored chips and tilted the bag over to him so he could grab a few.

We sat in silence, eating our lunches for a little while. It wasn't awkward at all… if anything, it was actually kind of refreshing not having to force conversation with someone.

"Can I ask you something?" my voice piped up shyly after a few more minutes.

"Anything."

"Will you tell me about the girl who came to your house that day you kicked me out?"

Abel's face fell.

That wasn't what I'd been expecting him to do, yet it was also somehow… worse.

"I can't."

"You can't?"

What the *hell* did that mean? He couldn't or he wouldn't or he didn't want to? My last eye exam said I had twenty-twenty vision and I was pretty confident there wasn't someone holding a gun to his head right now.

He shook his head and slumped his shoulders.

My focus jumped down to the ground beneath me, where I pulled up blades of grass to avoid making eye contact with him. So maybe I was lying about what I said earlier… being in silence with someone suddenly felt excruciating, awkward, painful… just to name a few.

"Hey hey hey, I need you to know that it's not because I don't want to tell you. Right now, I just… can't." Abel sighed deeply. "Please trust me, Red, when I say that, when I can tell people, you'll be the first person to find out."

"I don't understand why you can't tell me. What's the difference between today and a few weeks from now…"

"It's complicated. There's family involved and it's just…"

"Complicated," I finished for him. "I got it."

I didn't say a word for a long while as I plucked more fistfuls of grass.

"You're thinking really loudly over there. Care to share what's going on in that pretty little head of yours?"

"Nothing. It wasn't my place to ask anyway." I brushed it off. "So, what teams do the other guys play for?"

Abel knotted his brows and squinted his eyes at my change of subject. What else did he want me to say?

Thankfully, the director called Abel over to pick shooting back up again. I gave him a smile and a wave goodbye before packing up the blanket into my tote again and calling a car.

I trusted Abel, I really did.

So, if he couldn't give me any answers right now, there was obviously a good reason as to why, right?

Only time would tell, I thought to myself.

I SPENT most of my late afternoon back at the house, working from the comfort of the covers while finalizing the recipe I was posting on the blog this week and sifting through the photos I was going to use for the next one.

The final rays of sunlight retired below the horizon when a light knock at my bedroom door startled me.

I kept the door half-open to hear when Abel came home, but the door creaked open fully and I looked up over the rim of my laptop to find him leaning against the doorframe.

How long had he been there? And when did he come home?

"I have a surprise for you." He beamed, making his way over to me. "Follow me?" He held out his hand, which I willingly accepted, and he helped me out of bed. His grip on my hand stayed firm while he guided me out of the comfort of my suite and down the stairs.

"Where are we going?"

"It's a surprise," he said mockingly, leaning over so his hot breath brushed my ear which sent a shiver down my spine. "Shoes." He looked down to where my sandals lay on the floor next to the bottom step.

"Cover your eyes." I did as he commanded and felt his hands wrap around my waist. He led me forward and I heard a door open and the smell of salty air as I stepped outside.

A cold breeze made goose bumps stand up on my arms., Maybe I should have worn a sweater? I hadn't planned on Malibu being so cold in the evenings and my sleep shorts and oversized lounge shirt weren't exactly going to keep me warm. But then again, I hadn't expected to spend time outside this late in the evening either.

Abel must've noticed my chills because he pulled my back closer to the warmth of his chest. His heat radiated down my back and I sank into him, wanting more.

He tugged at my waist to stop my stride.

Nerves and excitement filled my chest while I uncovered my hands from my eyes.

I gasped.

"Abel…" I croaked out in shock, taking in the display that was in front of me. A projector screen setup, the outdoor coffee table covered with my favorite snacks, and a mound of blankets sitting on the couch to keep us warm. "What is all of this?"

"I wanted us to have another movie night, but this time I came prepared." He pulled a slow smile that melted my insides.

Somewhere in the recesses of my brain, I'd known for a while that I was falling for him, but this solidified it. How could I *not* be in love with someone who put so much thought and effort into everything that he did for me?

When did he have time to do all of this?

My eyelids grew hot thinking about what Mom would think of all this... of him.

"You okay, Red?" Abel's brows knitted together.

"Y-yes, yes." My voice broke, but I cleared my throat to cover it. It was hard to navigate the swirl of emotions in my chest while simultaneously pushing down the tears that pricked the back of my eyes. "I'm more than okay." I sniffled with a pitiful smile, taking in my surroundings once again.

It was moments like this that made me think that the way I felt about Abel wasn't all that one sided after all. How could it be when he planned an entire date for us? I use the term "date" loosely since he hadn't officially asked, but this took too much effort for it not to be.

People who were "just friends" would throw on sweats and sit on the couch, fighting over what movie to watch while shoving three different types of chips into their mouths at once.

So, by that logic, Abel and I most definitely weren't friends in his mind, right?

Dear God, I hoped so because at some point tonight, I was going to confess my feelings for him... when it was the right moment, of course. Maybe after a glass of wine? Or two? Okay, fine. Definitely after three... maybe five. Who knows?

I jumped up into Abel's arms and threw my hands around his neck and wrapped my legs around his waist. My stomach dipped when he held me up by gripping the lowest part of my ass.

That was sort of our thing now—me wrapping my legs around his waist whenever we hugged. Granted, he was an entire foot taller than me, so it made sense. But still, every time, without fail, it made my entire body tingle.

"You like it?" Abel questioned, setting me back on the ground.

"Mhmm."

What's not to like?

I stayed glued to his side while we walked over to the couch. I plopped down, closing my eyes and letting the soft cushions mold against me. Abel got comfortable next to me—sitting so close the outermost parts of our thighs were touching—and placed a blanket over our legs.

He handed me one of the buckets filled with popcorn and candy that was sitting on the coffee table in front of us. "Unfortunately, there's only one blanket... laundry day."

"It's Saturday, not Sunday." I arched a brow, and all he did was shrug with a small smile. "So, what are we watching?"

Abel put on a romantic comedy at my request, although he didn't grumble and groan about it. He could deny it all he wanted, but he loved a good rom-com. Nothing could prove otherwise.

What started as the two of us sitting side by side slowly turned into my back pressed against his front with his arm wrapped around my body.

By the time we were halfway through our second movie, I was dozing in and out of wakefulness while Abel's hand rested steadily on my hip bone. He'd occasionally drag his hands up and down my thigh or across the waistband of my shorts over the course of the movie which prevented me from fully falling asleep.

Every time he ran his hands over me, I held my breath, overwhelmed by his touch. I liked watching how naturally he looked doing it. Like we'd done this a thousand times and would a thousand more.

Did he have any idea how much he was driving me wild?

When the credits of actors and production crew members began to roll down the screen, I turned on my side so that we lay face to face.

Now was the time. I needed to tell Abel how I felt about him or I was going to internally combust.

I could do this. I could totally do this.

"I want to tell you something but I don't want things to get awkward between us…" My words dropped off and my hands began to tremble, but I forced myself to maintain eye contact.

Reading someone's microexpressions, especially the ones they made with their eyes, could tell you a lot about a person and how they were feeling. As much as I wanted to turn my face away from him or focus my gaze behind him, I *needed* to see his eyes when I said the words to him.

"You can tell me anything, Red." He lifted a hand and brushed my hair out of my face and tucked it behind my ear.

I took a deep breath and exhaled slowly.

A twinge of doubt seeded in my brain, telling me to play it off like nothing in case he rejected me, but there was no going back now.

"I don't want to be your fake girlfriend anymore." My voice shook as I gathered my words and Abel's face scrunched together. I took a measured breath and exhaled before more words tumbled out of my mouth. "Mostly because I like you… maybe even more than like you. I don't know. I've been trying to remind myself that everything between us is fake, but I'm sorry it just doesn't feel that way to me. And I totally understand if you don't feel the same—"

I was interrupted by Abel's lips smothering mine.

Oh my god.

He was kissing me. *Abel was kissing me!*

"Then be my real one."

"What?" I muttered, still shocked at the fact that two and a half seconds earlier, his mouth was on mine.

"You said you didn't want to be my fake girlfriend anymore, so be my real one."

"Are you being serious?"

"Dead."

"Okay," I said breathlessly.

Abel tilted my chin upward and intently scanned my face like he was trying to memorize every line and feature before I disappeared forever.

I'd never felt so content in a moment before. I had never felt so content with another person before.

He placed a gentle kiss on the tip of my nose which made my bones turn to goo. Then he grazed his lips mere millimeters over mine before pressing the tiniest peck against the corner of my mouth.

Abel's lips found mine again, but this time his kiss was slower, gentler. He lingered like he was savoring every moment. Then he kissed me again. And again.

I wasn't sure how long we stayed like that, kissing innocently with no desire to push boundaries. Allowing the innocence of love to tangle us together in more ways than one.

Breathless, I gave in to the affection that I'd been craving since he first wrapped his arms around me at the charity gala. Letting him kiss me and kissing him back with reckless abandon.

"We should go to sleep, Red," he said in a tired voice, peppering kisses against my cheeks and across my jaw.

"I'm not even tired," I whispered, trying to cover a yawn. I had no desire to be anywhere else but in his arms.

Abel looked down at me with awe written on his face

while he ran his hands through my hair until the weight of my eyelids grew heavier and heavier.

I shut my eyes for just one *teeny-tiny* second and felt myself being scooped up, my side pressed against a firm body. I managed to flutter an eyelid open just enough to see that Abel was carrying me through the threshold of the house. I nuzzled my face into his neck as he made his way up the steps toward our rooms.

His voice was low and his lips grazed against my ear. "Stay with me?"

Still riding the brink between wakefulness and sleep, I nodded my honest answer. Moments later, my head was resting on a cold pillow and my body tucked perfectly into equally cold sheets. His warm torso molded against my back and his heavy arm wrapped around my waist.

As I drifted, I silently hoped that when we woke up together in the morning that nothing between us would change.

EIGHTEEN

ABEL

I WOKE to someone stirring up the covers at the edge of the bed. Peeling an eyelid open, a sleepy Scarlett lay on her side, back facing me, at the end of the bed, curled into a fuzzy throw blanket.

She yawned, staring out the enormous bedroom windows while watching the sunrise as it made its way over the ocean-kissed skyline.

Mesmerized, I observed for a long while, studying her movements. Occasionally she'd do a tiny yawn and then tug her blanket tighter against her right after. Or she'd tuck her knees into her chest and wiggle her butt until she was situated comfortably.

It was moments like this that I wished I could hear the thoughts that went on in her head. Sometimes I thought I had her figured out completely, but fuck did she catch me off guard yesterday when she told me that she no longer wanted to be friends.

Granted, it worked out in my favor. But I assumed that *I* was going to be the one to make a grand confession to her before she left today, which would then be followed up with a multi-day sulk session after she rejected me.

Damn, was I wrong but in the best fucking way possible.

I wondered how long she'd waited to say that. Or more importantly, how the *fuck* I hadn't picked up on it.

In a sense, it didn't matter anymore because she'd agreed to be my girlfriend last night—seriously, this time —and too bad for her because I wasn't going to let her take it back now.

Not in a million fucking years. And then some.

"Morning, Red," I croaked out with a raspy voice, nudging her shoulder with my foot from underneath the comforter.

Scarlett looked over her shoulder and gave me a groggy smile that made my breath go flat. Fuck, she looked gorgeous right after she woke up, still bleary eyed with sleep crusted on the inner corners of her eyelids.

"Oh sorry, did I wake you?" she asked in a soft whisper like we weren't the only two people in the room.

My mouth turned up into a matching sleepy smile while I combed my eyes over her face. "I don't mind. Come lie with me?" I opened my left arm to make a spot for her.

She gave me another tired half smile and scooted up next to me, nuzzling her head on my chest while she tucked herself into my side and laid a gentle hand against my torso.

Fuck, a few months ago, the idea of having her pulled against my chest after waking up together was a fantasy. If I thought she'd consumed my brain back then, it was a thousand times worse now. Somewhere along the way, she began to consume me entirely, but I wasn't fucking mad about it.

In the back of my mind, I questioned whether or not she knew the extent of my feelings for her. Surely she must've known that everything that I did was all for her and not the stupid ploy that we had played into, right?

I couldn't pinpoint the exact moment it happened—that I knew that I was falling for her. Fuck, I think I fell for her the first time those big brown eyes peered up at mine, but now… now I knew for sure.

Without a shadow of a fucking doubt.

I loved her. So fucking much.

My lips turned up while I reminisced, lightly grazing my fingertips up and down her spine as we watched the sunrise together in silence. After a while, our breaths became synced and I watched with a smile as she absent-mindedly glided her fingers across my bare chest.

God, what I would give to spend every morning like this with her.

Lowering my gaze, I studied her for a few minutes while she stared out at the waves crashing against the shoreline. Both of us still tiptoeing around the looming conversation of last night and replacing it with comfortable silence.

I shifted my body to face her so that we lay parallel on our sides. Her eyes fluttered closed while I carefully brushed the crust from her eyes with my thumb. I ran my fingers through her hair, tucking loose strands behind her ear so I could better see those brown eyes that peered up at me through her lashes.

I paused for a brief moment, knowing that the next words that came off my lips could change our relationship if she didn't feel the same way. Fuck it, if she was going to deny me, I needed to know. I didn't want to draw it out and wait until we were both back home to sort things out.

"Red, you can pretend like nothing happened between

us last night… but it happened," I whispered. Doubt crept through my mind when her face remained neutral. "And I'm not going to pretend like it didn't."

Scarlett stared back at me, her expression shy, but her eyes held mine. The heat that had been building the last few months loomed over us. "Okay," she said in a soft voice, inching her face closer to mine.

"You still wanna be my girl?" My brows shot up in surprise, and she nodded in response. Fuck if my heart didn't soar seeing her head move up and down. "No arguments, oppositions, or objections?" I jokingly mocked one of Lea's trademark phrases, gripping the back of Scarlett's neck while lowering my lips to hover over hers.

"None," she replied against my lips while arching her body into mine.

Fuck.

Her breath grew shallow when I didn't immediately crush my mouth to hers. Instead, I patiently, patiently waited to make contact, drawing out the tension between us. When those big brown eyes flickered up at me eagerly, every ounce of shyness on her face dissipated. Her eyes burned bright with an insatiable hunger.

That's my girl.

"Scarlett, are you sure you want this?" I breathed out in a serious tone. She responded by slowly bridging the gap and pressing her soft, wet lips to mine. I welcomed her mouth as she deepened our kiss, simultaneously pulling me deeper into her orbit.

Breaking our kiss for a split second, I looked down at her with a seductive smile. "Good, because you have no idea how long I've been waiting for this."

I impatiently reclaimed her lips and ardently began exploring the recesses of her mouth. Leisurely moving my hands down her body, I tugged her waist against me, flushing our fronts together completely.

Scarlett wrapped a leg around my hip, making us closer in all the ways that counted. My cock instantly grew hard at the feel of her pussy pressed against my sweatpants.

Rolling her onto her back, I positioned myself on top of her so that we could both better feel as I ground my length against the seam of her shorts.

Those fucking sleep shorts had such little material that I could feel the heat radiating from her cunt. I was going to have to fucking *murder* any man who dared to look at her longingly if she ever decided to wear these in public. Fuck, I was going to murder any man who looked at her, *period*.

I trailed hot kisses down her neck, sucking and licking as I explored her sensitive flesh until she let a small moan pass between her lips. God, that sound was going to be the death of me.

After peeling off her T-shirt and shorts, I sat back for a moment, raking my eyes over her as my hands roamed her fully naked body for the first time. Her breasts just barely spilled over my handful and her curves accentuated her pear-shaped figure. And that pussy… goddamn.

I loved that she didn't shy away from me as I admired her and instead kept her eyes locked on my hands as they explored.

Fuck, she was perfect.

And all fucking mine.

Her nipples grew hard as I palmed the swell of her breasts and the sight of her arousal made my cock twitch. I bent down and pulled one of her taut nipples into my mouth, swirling my tongue around her peak while I pinched the other and rubbed it between my pointer finger and thumb.

Scarlett wriggled beneath me, impatiently bucking her hips for more, but I wasn't going to give in that easily. If she wanted my mouth on her pussy, she was going to have to beg for it.

I flicked my tongue against her other nipple before dragging open-mouth kisses along her collarbone as I moved upward until I reached her mouth. A whimper escaped her as I placed a knee between her thighs, giving her more pressure. She wiggled her hips and ground her center against my leg.

Scarlett and I made eye contact, her chest rising and falling recklessly beneath me.

"I have a confession..." She bit her lip as her words died away.

I arched a brow at her.

"I uhh... played with myself yesterday while thinking of you..."

She what?

I paused, blinking at her slowly. "Yesterday... in this house?"

"Yeah... after I almost fell on your face on the couch..." She gave me a nervous smile, almost like she was embarrassed to admit it. "I wanted to kiss you so badly. So freaking badly, Abel. I couldn't stop thinking about it."

"So instead of kissing me like you wanted to... you came upstairs and played with yourself while thinking of me?"

She nodded.

Fuck. Fuck. Motherfucking, fuck.

As much as I wished she'd kissed me, hearing that she was thinking of me while she got off was the hottest thing I would ever hear in this lifetime. Fuck, probably every lifetime before *and after* this one too.

While I'd lain in my bed trying to wrap my mind

around what the fuck happened—or almost happened—between the two of us on the couch, she was on the other side of the wall rubbing her clit and plunging her fingers inside her pretty little cunt wishing they were mine.

Fuck me.

"Tell me what you thought about," I rasped, desperate to draw as many answers about her little fantasy as I could.

"I-I thought about your mouth…"

"Where?"

"Here." She placed a hand on the back of my head and positioned me so that my lips were against the thin flesh just below her ear.

I ran my tongue across her skin and sucked the hollow of her neck, feeling as her nipples grew even harder against my chest and goose bumps began to erupt across her entire body. "Like this?"

"Mhmm."

"What else?" I whispered against her neck.

"Your hand…"

"Show me where," I insisted, and she grabbed my hand and laid it just below her sternum and slowly dragged it down her stomach. "Are you wet for me, Red?" I taunted in her ear and she nodded back in response. "I want to hear you use your words."

"Yes," she managed breathlessly as my fingers finally made contact with her slit, faintly teasing her with my fingers.

Wanting more, I dipped my middle finger into her wet heat and she instantly clenched around it. Fuck, she was tight. Scarlett groaned at the loss of contact when I pulled out of her and stuck my finger between my lips to get my first taste of her.

"Fuck, you taste so good."

A blush rose to her cheeks, but I wiped it off by thrusting my tongue between her lips.

Every nerve ending in my body tingled as I drank in the sweetness of her kiss for a moment before trailing my mouth down her body, spending extra time flicking her nipples with the tip of my tongue and placing teasing kisses along her stomach to draw out the tension.

I kept a hand cupping her cunt but didn't move my fingers to grant her the indulgence she desired. Scarlett's arousal began to soak my hand as she tried and failed to wiggle her hips to get a taste of release.

I wasn't done teasing her yet. Like I said, if she wanted my touch in her most sensitive spots, she was going to have to beg for it.

Moving lower, I dragged kisses up and down one of her thighs, getting agonizingly close to her pussy before pulling away and moving to her other leg.

"Please, Abel. I need your mouth," she finally begged, spreading her legs wider for me, fully exposing her tight, pink cunt.

Seeing her arousal drip all the way from her pussy to her ass made me smirk against the flesh on her inner thigh. My cock ached, knowing she was begging and desperate for me.

Placing small kisses against her folds, I tantalized her some more by purposefully avoiding her throbbing clit. When she began bucking her hips against my mouth and the room flooded with her desperate moans, I finally decided to give in.

I swirled a few laps around her swollen clit before pulling it between my lips and sucking hard. Scarlett's delicious moans echoed off the walls, making my cock swell against the seam of my sweatpants.

Jesus fuck, I was going to come in my pants just from eating her pussy if she kept making noises like that.

I felt a bead of precum begin to spill from my tip when I lined up two fingers against her opening and slid them deep inside her, curling upward until I found the spot that made her back arch.

Her pussy clamped around my fingers as she cried out my name. If only she knew how many times I'd lain in bed, fisting my cock until ropes of cum spilled out of me while imagining her screaming my name like that.

Scarlett's eyes rolled back while I lapped every drop of arousal that spilled out of her. She began winding her hips up and down, riding my face toward her peak.

"Come on my tongue, Red," I murmured.

"Oh my god." She cried out for release and her pussy convulsed around my fingers, all the while a lusty moan broke free from her throat. I steadied my pace as she pulsed, coming down from her high.

"Such a good girl." I kissed along her thighs while she caught her breath.

Scarlett lay there with her head lolled to the side, lost somewhere between postorgasmic bliss and slumber while I walked into the bathroom and grabbed a rag from the towel rack. I soaked the rag with warm water from the sink and wrung it out before walking back into the bedroom.

Smiling down at her, I swept the rag over Scarlett's skin, helping clean her up.

I couldn't fucking wait to get back home and wake her up with my mouth like this every morning.

We had another hour before we needed to leave for the airport, so she could make her flight. I set the alarm on my phone, crawled back into bed, tugging her against my side, and closed my eyes.

Forty-five minutes later, the alarm sounded from my cell. Reaching over to the nightstand, I turned off the horrible noise and Scarlett roused next to me.

She trailed her fingers along the waistline of my shorts. My cock began stirring, but I did my best to will it down. "I didn't make you finish earlier." She looked up at me with those big brown doe eyes while rubbing her hand on the front of my sweatpants.

"No, Red," I taunted with a hand wrapped around her neck. "As much as I'd love for you to wrap those lips around my cock right now… the first time I come with you, it's going to be deep inside your tight little pussy."

I smashed our lips together and pressed a possessive kiss against her lips. "But right now, you have a flight to catch. Grab your bag. I'll drive you to the airport."

Scarlett rolled her eyes, crawling out of bed, still naked. My hand slapped against her ass playfully while she stumbled away and the sweet taste of her ChapStick lingered on my lips.

The corners of her lips turned upward while she grabbed her clothes from the end of the bed and walked that gorgeous fucking ass back to her room to finish packing.

NINETEEN
SCARLETT

ABEL LEANED sideways against the doorframe with a cocky smile on his face while watching me get dressed.

"Staring is rude, you know," I poked, stepping one foot and then the other into a fresh pair of pale-green underwear and pulling them upward. His eyes stayed glued to them until the string in the back disappeared between my ass cheeks.

"Forgive me, Red, for being so ill-mannered." His smirk never wavered while his husky voice rasped out his words.

Jesus Christ, I needed a new pair of underwear already.

I quickly threw on a pair of shorts and the only other clean T-shirt I had left in my bag, ignoring Abel so I wasn't drawn in by his temptations. Once I was fully dressed and my bag was zipped, he walked into the room and threw it over his shoulder.

I took my time walking down the steps, taking in the gorgeous beach house one last time. Was it too soon to hope that Abel and I would come back here again one day?

Outside, Abel placed my bag into the back seat of his rental car, and we made our way toward the airport. Neither of us said much for the entirety of the car ride, but his hand rested on my inner thigh the entire ride which made my skin buzz.

When we pulled into a parking spot in the short-term lot, my heart instantly sank to my stomach.

"Stay." Abel unbuckled and leaned over the console, kissing me hard. Like he was going to die if our lips parted from each other's.

In that moment, I wanted nothing more than to drive back to the beach house and cuddle up on the couch with him for the rest of the day.

And *maybe* repeat our escapade from earlier another time or two....

But we both had jobs to do and I already promised that I would be at my meeting with Gina later this afternoon. Plus, he'd be home in less than a week, anyway. It wasn't like much could change between now and then.

Unless he didn't want to be together once he got back. Or if he thought this was just a one-time thing. Or, even worse, if he wanted to go back to being just friends.

Oh god, there was no way in hell I'd be able to go back to being *just friend*s with Abel after this weekend. It would hurt too much for my little heart to handle.

Not to mention the fact that I'd have to end our arrangement, quit working for him, *and* find a new job. Hell, I'd probably move to another town and convince Mae to come with me because there was no way I could risk going over to her house knowing I could run into him at any given moment.

Nope. Nada. Not happening.

"Hey." Abel broke our kiss and tilted my chin upward while his other hand fervently gripped the nape of my neck. His stare pinned me in place. "Stop overthinking this, Red. I want you. I want us. For as long as you'll fucking have me. The only way this ends is if you say it does, got it?"

My heart skipped a beat as his words buried themselves into my soul. "Okay."

He kissed me. Again. And again.

"If I kiss you any longer, you're going to miss your flight," Abel teased, pulling away from me.

"I'd be okay with that." I planted my lips against his this time. "Are you sure you don't want to have a quickie in the back seat?" I joked.

A roar of laughter spilled from his chest. "Don't tempt me, Red. I'm a weak man."

My cheeks turned rose colored at the fact that I'd even suggested it. I wasn't a prude, but it'd been a while since I'd been with anyone—well, that wasn't one of my beloved audiobook boyfriends—so I was more than a *little* eager to jump Abel's bones.

And by jumping his bones, I meant screw him into oblivion over and over… and over. Obviously.

Abel grabbed my bag from the back seat and walked me to the entrance. Pausing in front of the doors, he cupped my cheeks between his hands. I snaked my arms around him and tugged him against me, not wanting to let go as he pressed his lips to mine one last time.

I hated that every time something good began to happen with us, we got ripped away from each other immediately after.

"Don't fall in love with anyone else until I get back, got it?" His mouth quirked against my lips. "I don't want to hear about you going on any dates with any fuckers named *John*, you hear me?"

Oh, if only he knew how much I'd fallen for him already.

Nobody, not even the Johns of the world, stood a fighting chance anymore. Not even freaking close.

"See you in a few days?" Hesitation coated my voice as I removed my arms from around him.

He nodded, giving me a quick kiss on the tip of my nose. "Bye, Red."

Trudging my way through the automatic sliding doors, I turned around and gave him a small wave. Emptiness rang deep in my bones with each step that took me farther away from him.

I'd just made it to the front of the security line when all of a sudden I heard a shout from somewhere behind me. "Red, wait!"

Turning over my shoulder to see Abel barreling his giant frame through the crowd, my eyes widened in shock as he grabbed my elbow from behind and turned me around. When his lips found mine, he kissed me passionately for at least a minute, if not more, before pulling back. "I needed another one to hold me over."

I stood there shell-shocked and slightly embarrassed about the fact that I'd just had a public make-out session while Abel turned around like nothing out of the ordinary had just happened. His broad shoulders ambled back toward the exit and my eyes stayed glued to his back until the navy-blue Matrix shirt he wore was no longer visible.

And just like that, he was gone.

I MADE it back to Miami in a tizzy.

After barely making it to the plane on time—which

was Abel's fault, not mine—I crashed to sleep in the comfy seat before the jet began taxiing.

I got great sleep whenever Abel was next to me, but I was so wired the entire time I was visiting him that I'd only slept a few hours total the whole weekend.

It was okay to still be a *little* nervous around him even though we were together, right?

Once the plane touched down in Miami, the sweet flight attendant nudged my shoulder to wake me alongside a stream of apologies. Five hours passed by in a blink when you were dead asleep.

Hell, aside from the wake-up call, the flight attendant didn't have to do a single thing for me. Must've been an easy flight for her.

How much did private flight attendants make anyway?

Hmm, maybe I should've gone to flight school instead of culinary school. I'm sure it would've been a hell of a lot cheaper and the job seemed a thousand times more interesting than quite literally watching bread rise.

Slightly jealous I missed my calling in life, I thanked the crew as I walked down the steps of the plane and settled into the black SUV that Abel said would be waiting to take me to my meeting.

When I opened the giant office doors to the Red Reading Publishing building, I looked around at the sea of empty desks. Aside from Gina's office lit up at the end of the hallway, it didn't look like a single other soul was there.

Granted, it was a Sunday in the middle of June and most sane people were out spending their time off at the beach or day drinking while trying to forget that they'd be glued back to their desks again at nine o'clock the next morning.

One glance at Gina and I thanked God that she was

starting maternity leave tomorrow. By the looks of it, she could've given birth on the carpet any minute.

She stood over her desk rearranging papers when I thumped my knuckles against the glass door with a smile and she waved me in. She had a black pixie cut and always wore these enormous red-framed glasses that were two sizes too large for her head that she somehow made look stylish.

"Scarlett, dear! Lovely of you to come in on the weekend. I hope I wasn't interrupting any fun plans?" she inquired.

I shook my head. "Hi, G. How's the girl?"

"Threatening her entrance into the world with each passing minute." She waved for me to sit in the chair across from her. "Sit. Sit."

"Okay, I'll keep this short. Here are the final photos that the team has chosen for the book. Glorious, aren't they?" I shuffled through some of the pictures in the stack she handed over to me.

They were, in fact, glorious.

A million times better than the measly ones I took on my two-hundred-dollar camera and self-edited.

"They're amazing." I beamed up at her.

"Email Seraphina if you have any questions. Obviously, this process has gone quickly for you, primarily due to the fact that most of the content had already been written and lightly edited for the blog. We will begin the marketing campaign in a month and the public relations team will be in contact with you about some press interviews that they've set up."

"When will it be out?"

"The first Tuesday in February."

Four years ago, when I started that silly little blog, I

never would've imagined I'd have hundreds of thousands of followers or a freaking book deal.

I couldn't wait to video call Abel later to tell him about it, although I was a little disappointed at the fact that this meeting *definitely* could've been an email. Not that Gina knew I flew in from across the country to make it, but either way, it totally could've been an email.

"Alright, dear, skedaddle on out of here and enjoy the rest of your weekend! I'll be sure to send you a photo of the girl once she arrives, but for now, she's dancing on my bladder so I have to run."

I muttered my goodbyes and well wishes as she waddled out of her office in front of me.

To celebrate the good news, I had the driver stop by the grocery store on our way home so that I could grab a few things for a new recipe I was planning to try tonight.

Back at the pool house, just as I was in the middle of gathering together the other ingredients for the recipe, the special ringtone I had set for Lea blared from across the counter. I paused the latest audiobook I was listening to about a broody Mafia boss who fell in love with a girl twenty years younger than him.

"Lea!" I exclaimed, answering her call with a giant smile. Our schedules hadn't overlapped for weeks now and we kept barely missing each other. "I was just about to call you to see what your thoughts were on throwing a surprise birthday party for Mae in a few weeks. Maybe we could do something small, not a lot of people. A nice dinner or some—"

"Scarlett." Lea's curt tone cut me off from blabbering further. "Are you sitting down?"

"I can be…" I dropped down onto the only barstool that wasn't taken over by packages. "What's wrong? Mae's okay, right?"

I saw her car in the driveway when I came home, but all of the lights were off in the house so I assumed she was either asleep or out to dinner with friends.

"I-I don't know how to tell you this…" Lea's voice trembled as the next words spilled from her mouth. "But there's an article coming out about Abel in twenty minutes and you're going to want to read it before it does."

"What do you mean?" I furrowed my brows.

What was so bad about this article that Lea, of all people, was calling me with a shaky voice?

"That girl you told me about. You know the one who showed up to his house that one time?" I nodded, although she couldn't see me on the other end of the line "…they were seen together on a date last night."

What. The. Absolute. Freaking. Hell.

I knew he said that they weren't together and gave me an ominous answer about how he couldn't tell me about her right now, but "*he would when he could.*"

Deep down in my gut, I knew something hadn't been right with me about the whole situation, yet I still jumped into his bed hours later without questioning him further.

God, was I really that big of an idiot?

I trusted him. I really did. But what could he possibly be hiding with her that he not only "couldn't tell me about," but also had him having secret dinners with the girl?

"You know they own the house together, right? The one you just stayed at."

I had a guess, but hearing the words that they owned a freaking house together was a blow to the stomach.

Buying a house with someone wasn't something that you did on a whim with one of your week-long hookups. It was something that a *couple* would do—or at least one who had previously been together. One who *not only* planned to spend the foreseeable future together but was also okay with sharing a huge financial responsibility.

Because a beach house in Malibu… not freaking cheap.

What didn't make sense, though, was the tabloids and Lea mentioning that he hadn't dated anyone in years.

Maybe he'd been hiding a secret girlfriend that entire time?

And if freaking so, why didn't he ask her to be his "*fake girlfriend*" or come out about their relationship to get the PR team off his back, huh?

I tried to gather my thoughts enough to say something back to Lea, but I was too stunned to even formulate words. Instead, I sat there open mouthed, staring at the countertop.

I thought I'd made it perfectly clear on Saturday that I was skeptical about their relationship, yet he didn't have the decency to tell me they were meeting together just a few *hours* after I left the next day?

Maybe they weren't together and he was sorting out whatever crap was going on between the two of them so he could tell me what he wanted to say?

Jesus Christ, why was I making excuses for him?

I was better than this. I *deserved* better than this.

"Can you send me the article? I gotta go," I replied to Lea after a few long moments of silence and quickly ended our call. I placed my phone face down on the counter and inhaled a steadying breath.

I refused to be taken for a fool by this man once again. Eight months I'd felt like an idiot because of him. *Eight months*!

If this article gave me even the slightest indication that he had been unfaithful, he would have to provide some *rich* explanation to dig himself out of the hole that he'd dropped himself into.

Even then, I was doubtful that would be enough to convince me to take him back.

God, I hoped this was some sort of sick freaking joke.

I should've known from the beginning that our "relationship" was doomed.

TWENTY

SCARLETT

SICK.

I was going to be sick.

A notification pinged from my phone and I hovered my finger over the link to the soon-to-be-published Page Six article. A pool of nerves began to stir into the pit of my stomach.

I shut my eyes and expelled the breath in my lungs before peeling one eyelid open to find that the article hadn't loaded yet.

A silent hope slipped from my lips, begging that I would be met with a 404-error message once the arrow on the screen finished spinning in a circle.

I waited a few more seconds before my eyes instantly grew wide as the article came into view.

I read the headline and my heart sank straight through the floorboards.

No, no, no.

Jesus Christ, tell me this was not happening. I reread the headline again to make sure that I'd read it right the first time and much to my dismay, I had.

Mr. Tight End, Abel Abbott, spotted on a private date with Los Angeles's elite fashion designer, Aera Chase! A close source to the league player said that the football star's relationship with Scarlett Sawyer has been "on the rocks" for a few weeks now and the couple mutually agreed to split. Click here to read this Page Six exclusive for more details and exclusive photos from the new couple's fancy beachfront date night.

What. The. Holy. Hell.

Somehow, I managed to keep reading, holding back the tears that welled behind my eyes. My throat tightened as I scrolled through the rest of the article, staring at pictures of Abel and Aera on a dinner date together.

Maybe it was fake? Hell, all of the articles that were posted about Abel and I had been filled with half-truths.

But what I couldn't shake was the feeling that there was something different about these photos compared to Abel's and mine.

I stared at them a bit longer and then it hit me… he loved her. It was that kind of love that transcends photos. The kind that the viewer on the other end couldn't help but feel too.

Bile rose in my throat. I felt like I was going to suffocate.

How did I let this freaking happen?

The stinging in my chest grew, knowing that all of the feelings that I thought were reciprocated, all of the thoughtful gestures, were just a part of the ruse he had planned.

But then again, I couldn't be mad.

I signed up for this.

I was the one who spread my legs for him. I was the one who had broken two of the three rules we had set.

How could I be such a fool?

All of the signs that he was seeing someone else had been right in front of me the entire time and I chose to ignore them.

The dress.

The sneaky text messages.

The beach house.

As much as I wanted to put the blame on him, I couldn't. I was a damn fool and there was no one to blame but myself. I was still the foolish, naive girl I'd always been.

When Mom was on her deathbed, dying from terminal cancer, I held hope that she would make a full recovery. When I walked in on my college boyfriend cheating, I believed him when he said he didn't mean it. I let myself believe that Mae still wanted to live out our childhood dreams of raising our families together, but deep down I knew that her buying this house was proof that she couldn't care less anymore.

Stupid, stupid girl.

I had been disappointed time and time again, so why did I let myself believe that it would be any different with Abel?

News flash, Scarlett: maybe it's time to stop disappointing yourself with the false realities you create in your head.

My self-deprecating thoughts were interrupted by a call flashing on the screen… Lea again.

I sucked in a deep breath and exhaled, quickly pulling myself together and slapping on a fake grin as I pressed my thumb against the green button, accepting the call.

"Scarlett…" Lea's somber expression came into view on the screen and I wanted to slap it off of her. I hated the pity that sounded in her tone. There was nothing more mortifying than publicly finding out that you had been "cheated on."

We'd only officially been together for all of twenty-four hours, but still, we'd agreed that we wouldn't see other people while we were doing our little song and dance. I guessed it was my fault for assuming that he was the kind of person who stuck to his word.

How could I have been so freaking stupid?

"I'm fine. I'll be fine. I promise," I lied through my teeth.

I was not fine. Not even close.

"You sure, Scar? I can come over if you need me to."

"Oh, don't worry about it. I'll be okay. I should've seen it coming."

"Don't say that. I've known Abel for over half a decade and I wouldn't have seen this coming from left field." Which was saying a lot, considering the fact that Lea could read through anyone. It was part of what made her so good at her job.

"You know it wasn't real, don't you?" I questioned. She hadn't outright said it, but part of me always figured she knew.

"I guessed. I might've accidentally been the one who gave him the fake dating idea, but I hoped I was wrong," she admitted and sadness clouded her face. "Scarlett, there's something else you might want to know… I don't know why the article didn't mention it, but if you zoom in closely on the photos… she's wearing an engagement ring."

Jesus Christ.

I couldn't catch a fucking break, could I?

"Oh," I managed. Which was all I really had to say anyway. It wasn't like I could change it, no matter how badly I wanted to. "I'll be okay, I promise. It was all just a publicity stunt anyway, wasn't it?" I smiled cheekily at the screen before ending the call.

The screen went black and my smile fell almost as much as my heart did.

FOR THE FIRST hour after I hung up with Lea, I drank the bottom-shelf tequila from my cabinet without a shot glass or chaser, reread the article at least a dozen times, and printed out the photos so that I could analyze them closer.

She was, in fact, wearing an engagement ring.

There was no denying that.

Once I was good and thoroughly intoxicated, I did what any scorned woman would do... I left my "ex" an overly dramatic voice mail where I spilled my heart out as I paced across the bedroom until the only feeling I was left with was numbness.

The voice mail was something to the tune of, "Hi Abel, it's Scarlett. Your *fake* girlfriend. In case you couldn't tell from my voice, there was a heavy emphasis on the word fake. Because that's what we were, right? Fake. What was this whole thing between us anyway? A fun game called The Fantasy League? Maybe that was your plan all along... trying out different girlfriends until you found one that stuck." I didn't hide the disgust in my voice as I spit out each word. "That's low, really fucking low."

I paused my rant to take a few deep breaths.

"And what's even lower..." I picked back up again. "... aside from your spot in Hell, was that *you* let *me* believe that there was something more to this. *You* took me to your favorite restaurant. You're the one who came to my house during a storm because *you* wanted me to be safe. You even hired me a private chef, goddammit." My voice began to crack as I held back a sob, pain seeped with every word. "*You* invited me to Malibu and planned a movie date under the stars. Yet, I'm the idiot for believing that maybe, *just maybe*, if I let my walls down that you could love me too."

I hung up the phone and threw it across the room, hoping that it would break, unfortunately for me, I had bad aim and it landed on a pile of clothes in the corner instead. Sitting on the edge of the bed, I dropped my face into my hands while Abel's empty words sounded inside my head.

You're mine, you know that?

Please, Red. I want you there.

Every word I said was the truth, Red.

I'm going to kiss you now.

You're fucking stuck with me, Red.

Stay with me?

No, Red. The first time I come with you, my cock is going to be deep inside your pussy.

Stop overthinking this, Red. I want you. I want us. For as long as you'll fucking have me. The only way this ends is if you say it does, got it?

Well, at least one thing was obvious. My new least favorite color was red.

No matter how hard I sucked in big gulps of air and expelled them from my lungs, I felt like my chest was going to collapse. I pushed myself off of the bed and stumbled into the bathroom, picking up my phone on the way, in case my stomach decided to evict the tequila I'd consumed.

Everything hurt.

It hurt because his face was the one I wanted to see sitting across the table every morning at breakfast. It hurt because his hand was the one I wanted resting on my thigh during every car ride. It hurt because his mouth was the one I wanted pressed against mine with every kiss.

It hurt because I wanted him.

So, I gave in. Letting the hot tears flow down my cheeks while I curled into a ball on the cool bathroom tile. Somewhere between sobs, I managed to send Mae one measly text begging her to come to the pool house.

I didn't tell her why or what happened, but it wasn't like I could manage to type much anyway with a phone screen blurred by tears.

She must have run to find me, because not even a minute later I heard the front door slap shut and heavy steps trampling toward the bedroom.

When she opened the bathroom door and found me in a puddle of despair, she didn't say a word or ask a single question. Instead, she just scooped me up into her arms and held me as I cried away every ounce of heartbreak.

I didn't know much in life, but I knew one thing for certain. If soul mates were real, she was unequivocally mine.

"Lea sent me the article. I swear to whatever gods are above that I'm going to chop both of his balls off and force him to watch as I slice them with a mandolin." Rage filled her voice.

"Don't waste your time. It was all a ruse anyway."

"What are you talking about?"

"I lied," I admitted. "Abel didn't actually ask me to be his girlfriend. Well, he did but he asked me to be his *fake* girlfriend to help trick the tabloids into thinking that he was in a relationship to get the team off his back."

"Scarlett, why would you agree to that?"

"He offered me his house." I sighed, suddenly feeling foolish at how all of this sounded saying it out loud. "I knew I could never afford to move into this neighborhood and we both know that I can't live in your backyard forever, so when he offered me his house, I guess it just seemed like the only way for me to still stay close to you."

"Scar…" she said softly, wiping the tearstains on my cheeks with her thumb. "You thought I didn't want to live next to you anymore?"

"Well, yeah…" I slouched my shoulders. "I mean, you bought the most expensive house in the wealthiest neighborhood in town. It seemed like as good of a sign as any."

She let out a ragged breath. "I probably should've told you sooner, but when I bought this house, I *also* bought the house next door that Rita lives in. It wasn't for sale at the time, but I talked her into it and she's been renting it from me for the last few months"—which I knew from experience meant Rita wasn't paying a dime—"I was planning to surprise you with it once the old hag finally kicked the bucket."

"Mae!"

"Oh, give me a break, she's ninety-eight! She can't have that much life left in her. She's the one who said that if she had any say in it, she wouldn't make it to her next birthday!" We both laughed. "I would've told you sooner if I'd known how you felt. You're my sister, Scar… I hate to break it to you but we're stuck together."

We both did our best to hold back the tears that welled in our eyes.

All this time I thought that she'd given up on the idea of us raising our families together. But she bought a house for me. Right next door to hers. Like we'd always dreamed of.

My chin quivered, trying to hold back a sob. "Thank you."

"I'd do anything for you, Scar." She hugged me tightly

and neither of us let go for a long while. "I do have one question though. If this whole thing with you and Abel was all fake… why are we crying on the bathroom floor right now?"

I pulled back from our hug and flickered my gaze to the tile floors. "Because somewhere along the way, I became an idiot, and it stopped being fake for me." I sniffled. "We hooked up in Malibu and he convinced me that he wanted us to be together. Which in my love-drunk state I thought meant together, *together*, but I'm starting to think he just meant as friends with benefits."

"Was his dick big at least? It'd be a shame to waste tears over a man with a small dick."

"Mae!" I squealed with a laugh.

She was the only person who could make me laugh whenever something horrible was going on in my life. The day after Mom passed, instead of focusing on funeral arrangements and listening to detached condolences from distant friends and relatives, she and Dads took turns doing stand-up comedy routines until I peed my pants laughing… twice.

"I didn't see it. We just fooled around."

"That's a damn shame." Mae rolled her eyes, which made me laugh again despite the tears that were rolling down my cheeks. "You'll make it through this, Scar. You always do."

I COULDN'T SLEEP.

Mae passed out in my bed hours ago while I tossed and turned underneath the covers. Exhaustion swept through my body, and my brain worked overtime trying to piece together answers to the questions that I would never get the chance to ask.

I hated that part of heartbreak. That piece of time where you sat in limbo between figuring out your new reality while silently mourning your old one.

In a way, falling out of love is like reading a good book. You become so attached to a character and how they make you feel. You follow alongside part of their story and somewhere along the way, they become a part of you, so you do everything in your power to prolong the ending. No matter how inevitable it may be. And the heartbreak of reality after you've removed yourself from their world is only worsened by the delay.

The only difference between books and real-life heartbreak was that in real life, it happened quickly. In the sixty seconds it took to read an article and see the smile on his face in the photos, the culmination of the love I'd come to have for him over the last three months came to naught.

Sixty seconds. That was it.

It was well past midnight when I moseyed over to my desk and opened my laptop to type out a quick resignation letter. After double-checking that I wrote "effective immediately," I pressed send and closed my laptop before crawling back underneath my covers.

It was over.

Abel and I were over.

And what I hated most was knowing that we never got the chance to try.

It was a special kind of hell to mourn something that never was.

TWENTY-ONE
ABEL

I WOKE TO AN ODD SCENE.

Somehow during the night, I'd twisted and turned out of my sweatpants... which meant I lay *completely naked* with my cock out for anyone to walk in on.

Thankfully, Janet was the only other person in the house this morning and she once told me she'd rather "never walk again" than go upstairs.

She was pushing eighty though, so I couldn't exactly blame her.

The only thing worse than waking up unexpectedly naked was waking up unexpectedly naked with a raging hard-on pressed against my stomach.

Suffice it to say, I think I missed Scarlett.

Fuck, it'd been less than twenty-four hours since I'd last seen her and twice already—well, three times if you counted my current predicament—I found myself jacking off while drawing from the memory of devouring her sweet cunt and how eager she'd been to suck me off before I denied her.

I couldn't get the feeling out of my head of her clit

pulsing against my tongue while she shuddered around my fingers.

Fuck, I could hardly wait to get back to Miami so I could drown my cock in her pussy until kingdom fucking come. I'd even looked into earlier flights last night, thinking of cutting my trip short.

I took a few deep breaths, trying to will my cock down, but it wouldn't budge. Just thinking about Scarlett made a bead of arousal slip from my tip.

Fisting my cock in my right hand, I gave in and began stroking up and down slowly. I picked up my pace, imagining it was Scarlett gripping around me instead of my hand.

Thinking about how she'd probably taunt my tip before sinking all the way down onto me. I wondered whether she liked it deep and hard or fast and rough. My bets were on deep and hard. The thought made a low groan escape me. Fuck, I was seconds away from coming.

Fuck fuck fuck.

With a final thrust into my hand, my cock expelled ropes of cum all over my stomach and the blanket that lay half on top of me.

Jesus fuck, I'd never blown a load that big before.

Bad news was that I was going to have to buy a new throw blanket for the bed before my trip ended. *And* come up with an alternate story as to why I had to buy a new one.

This might've been my room at the beach house, but if anyone would notice a new blanket… it would be Aera. She handpicked everything in this house, after all.

Coffee stain. Yup, that's what I'd tell her. That I was drinking my morning coffee in bed and spilled it on the blanket. That was believable, right?

Fuck if I didn't feel like a teenager again, lying to my

mom about why she could no longer wash my socks. Absolutely no mother in the world would be foolish enough to believe that their son was the only one who would wash his socks because "They smell bad. Like really fucking bad, Mom."

Speaking of smells, freshly cooked bacon filled my nostrils from where Janet was cooking downstairs. Normally, I'd be ecstatic about waking up to a smell like that, but my chest ached knowing Scarlett wouldn't be the one that I found in the kitchen once I walked down the stairs.

I rolled onto my side and reached for my phone on the nightstand to call her, but came up short. *Where the fuck did I leave my phone?* I hadn't seen it since last night.

Last night, I was so exhausted from playing ball with some of the guys from the shoot that after my quick dinner with Aera and Tye, I came home and immediately passed out on the couch.

When I woke up at two in the morning, I drowsily moseyed up the stairs to the bedroom, but not before stopping by Scarlett's room and grabbing the blanket on her bed that still smelled like her.

Which also happened to be the same blanket I'd, well… finished on.

It felt empty without Scarlett here trying to cuddle up underneath me all night long or steal all the fucking covers even though she was half my size and didn't need a California king-size comforter all to herself.

Groaning, I got up out of bed and tossed the blanket in the trash bin and hopped in the shower. I got in with the intention of quickly cleaning myself off and heading down for a big breakfast, but then I started thinking about Scarlett again and what I'd be like if she'd been in the shower with me.

Would those lips be wrapped around my cock while she fingered herself? Or would she want me to fuck her doggy style with her breasts pressed against the glass?

Needless to say, it was twenty minutes later before I found myself dressed for the day and walking down the stairs.

"Morning, Janice," I called over to her as I walked into the kitchen. Sunlight poured into the breakfast nook where she already had a steaming cup of coffee waiting for me at the table.

"Good morning, Mr. Abbot," she singsonged, walking toward me with a breakfast plate so full a piece of bacon threatened to fall off as she handed it to me. "Table for two this morning?"

I met her halfway and grabbed the plate from her before bringing it over to the nook and setting it down next to my mug. "Nope, just me today. Scarlett left yesterday morning to fly back for a meeting. Did I tell you that she's publishing a cookbook?"

Selfishly, I begged Scarlett to stay and ride out the rest of the trip with me, but with her editor going on maternity leave, I knew she wouldn't be able to stay.

Despite the lonely feeling that consumed me with her gone, I was so *fucking* proud of my girl. She'd shown me a few of the recipes she was working on, and even gave me a subtle mention in one of them, which made me smile.

I loved it even more now, knowing that we were together, and it wasn't just for publicity anymore.

She mentioned that it'd still be a few months before it was published, but hey, any attempts at early promotion for my girl couldn't hurt, right?

"Only about five times, sweetie." Her face softened into a smile before a tumble of confusion washed over her expression.

Huh, that was odd.

Janice wobbled back into the kitchen and moved some of the pots and pans she was using over to the sink for me to wash later. "Um, Mr. Abbott?" she started. "I know that we don't know each other all that well... but would you mind if I asked you a personal question?"

"Sure, anything." I shrugged a shoulder as I shoveled an enormous bite of French toast into my mouth. What could an eighty-year-old woman ask that would make me feel uncomfortable?

"Now, I know it isn't my place to judge, especially a handsome fella like yourself. But isn't it a bit... distasteful going steady with two different women at the same time?" Her brows folded down and she bobbed her head to the side. "I mean, I was known to go to a swingers' club or two back in my day when my Donny was still alive, but—"

"What do you mean, two different women?" I cut her off primarily due to confusion but also partly due to the fact that my appetite disappeared the second she started reminiscing about her glory days attending *swingers' clubs.*

Fucking Christ.

I was so nauseated I'd never be able to enjoy pancakes again.

My mind reeled as she slowly, slowly walked back over to the counter by the stove to grab her phone and took what felt like hours to unlock it and search for *something.* What, I wasn't fucking sure yet.

Finally, after the most agonizing few minutes of my life, Janet handed me over her cell, which was about six models outdated, and my eyes were met with a headline from Page Six's rival, The Post:

Mr. Tight End moved on too quickly? Abel Abbott was recently spotted on a private dinner date with Los Angeles elite fashion designer Aera Chase! Click here for full details on the football star's recent breakup with celebrity chef Scarlett Sawyer and exclusive photos of the newest power couple.

Fuck no.

This was bad.

This was really fucking bad.

When was this posted? I glanced down at the screen in my hand… *fourteen* hours ago. Knowing Lea, she'd likely seen the article at least half an hour or so before it came out like usual.

Why the *fuck* hadn't she given me a heads-up about this?

So much for protecting my "precious image."

"Janet, how many news sources posted an article similar to that?" I questioned, standing up from my seat and rubbing a hand down my cheeks.

"Oh sweetie, at least a dozen. But my glasses prescription is a little outdated so it might be less… might be more, not really sure."

"Fuck!" I shouted.

Janet raised an eyebrow at me. "So, I take it you're not dating two women at once?"

"Aera never told you?"

"Told me what?" She shook her head side to side. "She never mentioned anything. I always assumed y'all were secret lovers having an affair or something."

"So does the entire world now, apparently." I groaned. "Fuck!"

Likely not wanting to deal with the aftermath of my world blowing up, I heard Janet slip out the front door as I walked back and forth in the living room. My feet stopped, not even realizing when or how I'd started pacing.

Scarlett had rubbed off on me more than I thought.

Scarlett.

No. Fuck no.

She had to know about this by now, there's no way she hadn't heard about the article. Anger burned in my throat while I flopped down onto the couch. With my elbows rested on my knees, I hung my head in my hands and let out a groan of frustration.

How did I let this happen?

If Scarlett left me, I wouldn't be able to fucking survive it. She'd ingrained every fiber of her being into my soul. And the thought of seeing her move on with someone else all because I wouldn't let Aera come clean about us? It would fucking gut me.

My mind raced with thoughts, knowing that whatever steps I took next would be crucial. Not only for the sake of Scarlett's and my relationship but for the other people who were involved in the situation too. Aera. Our families.

Where the fuck was my phone?

I searched through the couch cushions and found it, hesitantly unlocking the screen to find the only notification I had was one missed call and a voice mail from Scarlett.

Fuck.

I almost pressed play but decided I wouldn't be able to stomach listening to it right now. If I heard even an *ounce* of heartbreak dripping in her tone it would fucking crush me.

Who was I supposed to call first? Aera? My mom? Scarlett? This was a nightmare. And the worst part about it was that it was entirely my fucking fault.

Goddammit.

I slumped down into the couch cushions again, taking

a moment to steady my breaths long enough to formulate a rational thought. After a moment, I opened my contacts list and searched through to find the only person that could help me salvage this situation.

I let out a sigh, and defeat coursed through my veins, weighing me down further with each passing ring in my ear.

How could I have fucked this up so horribly?

Ring. Silence. Ring. Silence. Ring. Silence.

My heart pounded in my throat.

At the last second, when I expected an automatic voice mailbox system message, the dial tone ended and the other person on the end of the line picked up the call with a disgruntled "Hello."

"Lea?" I started. "I need your help."

TWENTY-TWO
SCARLETT

"I'M GOING on a date with October."

Mae's scoff from across the room at my admission was anything but subtle.

Mae and October had absolutely despised each other since we were kids. What was once an academic rivalry in elementary school spilled into a popularity contest in high school.

While they hadn't seen each other in the better half of a decade, I could've sworn they were still playing their little game when it came to their careers. Her being one of the top-paid high fashion models in the world and him being the greatest quarterback in the league. I was doubtful that was a coincidence.

It would be just like the two of them to still be silently competing against each other all these years.

"It's been, what? Seven years since you've seen him? You can't *possibly* still be holding a grudge this long."

"I am not holding a grudge!" Mae shouted.

She was totally holding a grudge.

For what though, I had no freaking idea.

All I knew was that the last time they saw each other was at his high school graduation party, just before he moved away to play for the best college football team in Alabama, and she told him that she hoped someone sacked into him so hard that he broke every bone in his body.

I'd always assumed there was more to their feud than they let on, but if that was the case, I thought Mae would've told me the whole story by now. Anytime I asked, all she said was that he'd "always been rude" and change the subject.

Seriously, what could two elementary schoolers have *possibly* done to each other that would fuel a two-decade-long feud?

Beats me.

It had been four days since the news broke about Abel's date with that Aera girl. I hadn't received a text or call back from him and he hadn't responded to my resignation email either.

Not that I was keeping tabs on the two of them or anything, *but* if I was, then I would've known that they had yet to make any press statements about their outing.

No social media posts. No paparazzi pictures. Nothing.

It was like the two of them had fallen off the face of the earth. Maybe they were too busy clocking hours between the sheets to come up for air.

Just thinking about them made a shiver crawl up my spine.

Abel never seemed like the kind of person who would go AWOL after something as big as that came out. I thought he would, at the very least, have the decency to apologize. Then again, I guess I didn't really know him at all.

Lea came over to see me two days ago once I finally

had the energy to relocate myself from the bed and over to the couch.

Baby steps.

She told me that she'd spoken to him briefly but she didn't give up any information about what he'd said. Not that I cared anyway. All she told me was that everyone would "find out the truth one way or another."

Whatever that meant.

When October called to ask me on a date earlier this morning, I was shocked. Like defibrillator to bare chest, shocked. I mean, I'd always assumed that guy code was different, but asking your teammate's "ex-girlfriend" out on a date *four days* after their breakup had to be a violation of some sort of ethics, right?

If it was, he must not have cared. But if I was telling the truth… I didn't actually want to go on a date with him, and I had my reasons.

For starters, October and I had been friends for a long time and while we didn't hang out with each other often, it did seem a little out of the blue. We'd known each other for going on twenty years. I had a feeling if he had a crush on me, he would've taken some sort of action by now.

Second, Mae hated him more than Satan hated God. I was shocked she hadn't already murdered me for considering the idea for more than a millisecond. Could you imagine if the date actually went well? I'd be as good as dead to her by morning.

Third and most importantly, Abel was going to find out about it. One way or another, whether it was in passing from teammates, from October himself, or someone snapping a picture of us on our date and posting it on Socialgram.

Abel. Would. Find. Out.

It took some heavy convincing from Lea on the phone

earlier, but I liked her logic that Abel finding out about October's and my date *might* not be the worst thing in the world.

I wasn't opposed to him suffering once he found out either. Even the tiniest modicum of suffering on his end would be worth it.

I wanted Abel to think that I was just as unattached as he was from our little charade.

Oh, Scarlett? Didn't you hear? Yeah, she moved on a week after the breakup.

What Abel didn't need to find out was that I'd spent the last two days bouncing between sulking and binge baking. I'd made so many baked goods that I had to drive down to the local food bank this morning to donate them so they didn't go to waste.

According to him, half-truths weren't a crime, so it's not like he'd care anyway.

I looked over at Mae, who sat on the couch sporting a deathly scowl while typing out a text on her phone. Should I have gotten a living will made before bringing the date up to her? Probably.

"Mae, come on. October will be here in two hours. Will you pretty pretty please help me get ready?" I asked with a pouty lip, giving her my best puppy-dog eyes with batted eyelashes. "I could really use my best friend right now."

"Fine. I'll stand in your general vicinity, but I won't be helping," she grumbled, peering up from her phone. "I want you to look awful so he doesn't end up seeing you as more than a friend."

"Mae!"

"What? I'm not trying to subject myself to my own personal hell if you end up liking each other for real," she scoffed, clearly annoyed.

"It's one date." I walked into my bedroom and looked back to see Mae following behind begrudgingly. "I swear on all things holy that I won't let him fall in love with me before the check comes."

"You know, it's probably wrong to swear on all things holy."

"Probably, but oh well." I shrugged. "Pick out my outfit?"

"Where's he taking you anyway?" Mae asked while opening the doors to my tiny closet.

"No idea, he didn't say."

TWENTY MINUTES after he said he'd pick me up, the sound of Mae's doorbell echoed off the walls of the house and nerves instantly pooled in the pit of my stomach.

I was doing this.

I was going to go on a date with October. I'd get Abel out of my system and all would be right with the world.

"Mae, can you grab that?" I shouted down the hallway as I slipped on a short green dress that made my legs look significantly longer than they actually were.

I cracked the bathroom door just enough to get a front-row view of Mae and October seeing each other for the first time in years.

A smile pulled at my lips as I watched him rake his eyes up and down her body.

I'd always secretly hoped that the two of them would get together one day. I was confident that if they stopped hating each other for a few minutes, *maybe* they'd realize they were actually perfect for each other.

These days I was doubtful that would happen though.

Too much time and animosity had passed between them for them to recover from all of the shit they'd put each other through over the years.

"*March*," October snarled at Mae as he waltzed through the doorway and into the entry.

"*Toby*," she fired back at him with her arms crossed tightly against her chest.

"Please don't kill each other! I'll be out in a second, I promise," I shouted down the hall to them. Leaning against the bathroom sink, I put on the final touches of maroon lipstick.

There wasn't a chance in hell that I'd see Abel in person tonight, but I wouldn't put it past the paparazzi to be scoping out October's whereabouts.

He signed on to the Matrix last year for only one season, and the team hadn't given him an extension offer yet. So, any of the other thirty-one teams in the league could extend him an offer, and after winning the League Bowl last year, he was a hot commodity. With the Matrix training camp starting next month, he was becoming more and more of a hot topic in the press with each passing day.

So, I needed to look my best tonight *just in case* the tabloids had caught wind of our date and snapped some pictures of us together. I couldn't look ugly in them if I was going to print out hundreds of copies and tape them on Abel's SUV while he was sleeping, could I?

Staring at my reflection, I inhaled a deep, steadying breath and smoothed down the front of my dress with my palms. "You can do this."

Mustering up every ounce of confidence in my being, I exited the bathroom and strode into the living room with a big smile on my face. But my smile instantly dropped at the sight of Mae and October standing chest to chest with

233

their faces inches apart as they spit vile insults back and forth at each other.

Oh my god.

"How did it feel winning a League Bowl where the second-string quarterback scored the winning touchdown? " Mae gritted out between her teeth. "Your poor little sprained ankle gonna keep you on the sidelines again this season?"

"How did it feel getting kicked out of your modeling agency for being a bitch?" October jabbed, inching forward slowly until Mae's back touched the wall. My eyes bounced back and forth between the two of them.

"I didn't get kicked out, you imbecile. I quit!"

"*Pretty sure* that's something someone who got fired would say."

The tension between the two of them was electric. Hell, even I caught the buzz of it from across the room. The only thing that would make watching them argue better is if I had fresh popcorn in hand.

Maybe if the two of them had a really good hate fuck their issues could be resolved. A lot could be solved with a hate fuck. And with two people as hot as they were and with tension this thick, they could make millions from a sex tape.

"Alright, boys and girls, let's settle down." I butted in between the two of them. Mae's face was cherry red and her brows grew together in an angry frown. Unfortunately for her, I really didn't have the energy to deal with being a murder witness tonight.

October stepped back, finally breaking his stare from Mae and giving me a once-over. "Scar, you look amazing."

"Thank you." A blush rose to my cheeks and I could've sworn I heard Mae mockingly repeating October's compliment under her breath.

"We should get going. Wouldn't want to be late, would we?" Ironic coming from him, being that he was nearly half an hour late picking me up. His hand rested against the small of my back as he opened Mae's enormous front door and led us outside.

There was no spark with his touch. No swirl of emotions in my chest. My skin didn't buzz in anticipation the way it did with Abel. Like I was going to perish if he took his hands off of me.

With October I felt nothing. Absolutely nothing.

"Great seeing you, March. We'll have to do this again sometime soon," he called back to her.

"I'd rather be brutally murdered than have to have another conversation with you," Mae muttered just loud enough for me to pick up on her few choice words. I threw her a scowl over my shoulder.

"You know Mae is cursing you out right now, don't you?" I lifted a brow at him as I followed him down the front porch steps.

"You sure she isn't flipping me off too?"

Peering over my shoulder, I let out a laugh when I looked back to see Mae standing on her front porch with two middle fingers sticking upward, mouthing something to herself before pressing her lips into a tight line.

"Must take three decades to stop a feud," I quipped as October opened the passenger door of his truck for me. He let out a laugh before shutting the door and rounding the hood.

I gazed out the windshield at October while he called out something to Mae that made her storm into the house and slam the front door shut.

Damn.

October slid into the driver's seat and turned the key in the ignition of his seemingly fresh-off-the-lot truck.

"What'd you say to her?"

"I told her that her breath still smelled like the worms she used to eat on the playground."

"Oh my god." I shouldn't have laughed because she was my sister, but biting back my laughter only made it funnier. Before long, a howl of laughter spilled from my lips, sparking October to join in too.

If it came down to choosing between the two of them, I would always choose Mae's side without question. Every time. But she did have a worm-eating phase when we were five, so I didn't exactly have the grounds to defend her.

"I'm glad to see you laughing, Scar." October reached across the console and placed his hand over the top of mine. His face softened and the corner of his lips pulled down.

I hated that look.

Hate, hate, hated that look.

"How you holding up?"

"Been better. Also been a hell of a lot worse, so…" I gave him a weak smile before drawing my gaze out the window. I knew that if I looked over at him again, the tears pricking the back of my eyes would break free.

I hated this.

I shouldn't have been almost crying about a guy I never really dated, let alone almost crying over him on a date with *someone else*. How freaking embarrassing.

Part of me knew that I was going to have to get over him sooner rather than later, but my heart still ached so badly I felt the need to clutch my chest to ease the ache sometimes. The only thing I could do was hope that one day I woke up to the ache easing the slightest bit. And the next day after that, the hope that it would ease even more.

The thing that I feared most though was the day that I

saw him again for the first time. We were still neighbors, so as much as I would do my best to avoid him, it was never a guarantee.

I could almost picture it.

One morning we'd both be walking out to our cars and neither of us would stop to say a word to each other. And there wouldn't be any courtesy waves because his new girlfriend would be standing in the driveway bidding him adieu while wearing one of his T-shirts.

I'd stare at them dumbfounded while my heart tore in two and he wouldn't even spare me a glance.

I allowed one small tear to slip from my eye before pulling myself together. Deciding to steer my thoughts away from Abel, I decided to make some silly chatter with October. Like always, we cackled while reminiscing about the weird antics and hobbies we had as kids.

That's when I confirmed what I already knew deep down. October and I were good together, but only as friends. Hell, he was more like a brother than a friend after all these years. And I was about to go on a *date* with him... revolting.

Just when I was about to admit to October that I wanted us to be just friends, my phone lit up with Lea's rust-colored hair from her contact picture on the screen. Ehh, I guessed October could wait a few minutes before I let him down. With that, I happily answered her call.

"Hi, Lea."

"Hi, Scar. You sitting down, babe?"

"Uhh, yes..." I trailed off nervously. The last time Lea told me to sit down, she was the messenger who broke my heart. I twirled my little green ring, waiting for her to respond.

"So, I should probably start by telling you that I'm sorry for lying to you."

Dizziness washed over me at her words. "You lied to me? About what?"

"Well, when I told you that I only briefly spoke with Abel the other day, I sort of withheld the truth. He and I had talked… a lot."

"Okay…"

I felt like I was going to faint. Why was she talking with Abel? She was supposed to be *my* friend, not his. Work loyalties be damned.

"There's another article coming out about him in about twenty minutes, but Abel wanted you to read the exclusive first before it gets published." She paused. "And he wanted me to tell you that every word of this one is true. He made sure of it."

"Lea, you're being really weird right now. I don't under—"

"Just promise me you'll read it, Scar." I opened my mouth to speak, but words never came out. "I'll take your silence as a yes. Love you, bye." The line went dead, and not even a second later, a text notification came through with a link to a new article that had Abel and Aera on the cover.

Reluctantly, I clicked the message open and waited for what felt like three lifetimes for the article to load. My eyes widened, and I gasped, reading the headline on the screen in front of me.

Breaking News: Abel Abbott and Aera Chase - SIBLINGS!
The pair has announced that they found out last year
through an ancestry test that they are half-sibs. Chase has
announced her engagement to long-term boyfriend and
tech mogul, Tye Jerod, via Socialgram and Abbot has given
a Page Six exclusive statement confirming he is still with
girlfriend Scarlett Sawyer and that he's "madly in love
with her."

My pulse raced and my stomach turned into knots made of stone.

They were siblings? This *whole time* they were siblings? Why did he let me believe that they were together? More importantly, why did he let the world believe they were together?

I popped my head up from the trance I was in, realizing I recognized the street we were turning down. "Um, what restaurant are we going to again?"

"Mafiosa's. Somebody on the team said it's the best Italian place in town, can't remember who said it though."

No no no. This couldn't be happening.

I needed to get out of this truck *immediately*. There was no way I could go on a date with Abel's teammate to the same restaurant that he took me to on our first date. No no no.

"October... I-I can't do this." The words barely made it out of my mouth before I could even process the fact that it was Sunday.

Abel told me Mafiosa's was closed on Sundays.

"I know," he said, bringing the truck to a stop right outside the front doors of the restaurant. October turned to look at me, placing a gentle hand over the ones in my lap, and tears began to swell in my eyes at the earnest look on his face.

He handed me over a piece of paper that he must have hidden in his side door pocket. I scrunched my face and unfolded the paper to find a note written in that now familiar handwriting that I'd know anywhere.

> *Every word you read was true.*
> *I'm sorry, Red.*
> *I love you.*
> *- A*

"Go get your man, Scar." October gave my hand a squeeze and flicked his gaze toward the entrance of the restaurant.

"Thank you." My voice broke as I quickly threw my hand around his neck. I jumped out of October's truck, nearly tripping as I ran toward the entrance.

It was only once I took a step through the heavy wooden doors that I stopped dead in my tracks. There were lights strung across the ceiling and flowers coating the floor. Oh my god, it was beautiful.

That's when a figure of a man, an extremely tall man, came into view from across the room.

My breath hitched.

My lungs constricted.

My knees buckled.

Abel.

TWENTY-THREE
ABEL

MY MOUTH WAS DRY.

Lungs depleted of air.

Scarlett looked fucking beautiful.

She wore a light-green sundress that made her brown eyes pop. Part of me hated that she looked this good with the intention of going on a "date" with October. Subconsciously, I knew that it was all a part of the plan that Lea and I had created to win my girl back, but I hated that she had considered moving on so soon.

Granted, October did have to beg her a handful of times and Lea said she spent well over an hour convincing her that it was a good idea before she agreed, which helped ease the war that was raging inside my chest.

Fuck, why was my suit so tight? Why had I worn a stupid suit anyway?

Carlo teased me when I walked in, reminding me that I was trying to win her back, not propose marriage. Fucker. Scarlett liked when I wore the suit so I was going to wear the fucking suit.

"Hi," I said from across the room, staring as Scarlett glided toward me hesitantly, with her mouth agape.

"Hi." She sniffled, brushing a lone tear that spilled down her cheek. I fucking hated myself for making her cry. "What are you doing here?"

"Winning my girl back."

"I'm still your girl?" she questioned, stopping a foot in front of me.

My chest ached at the distance between us. One foot felt like a thousand when all you wanted was for the girl standing in front of you to be in your arms. "You never stopped, Red. Even when you thought you weren't, you were always mine."

After reading that clusterfuck of an article that Page Six had posted, I knew that I needed to tell the world the truth about Aera and me. However, there were a few *small* problems I had to attend to before I could do that. Like the fact that I hadn't told Mom and Steve that I had a half-sib I'd been keeping from them for a year.

I wanted Scarlett to hear the words from my lips, but after listening to her gut-wrenching voice mail and reading her resignation, I knew that the last thing she wanted to do was take the time to hear me out.

So, with the help of Lea, I concocted a plan. Lea was reluctant to hear me out at first, as she should have been. But as the team's PR manager, she was technically obligated to help me since it made it to the public eye. She did, however, take the opportunity to curse me out seven ways to Sunday. But I couldn't blame her.

"So, it's true?"

"Yeah, Aera is my sister."

Scarlett expelled a pent-up breath and her shoulders relaxed as she took a step forward and closed the distance between us.

"Remember when I told you that my dad left on that business trip to Seoul and didn't come back?" She nodded her head up and down. "Turns out the reason he didn't come back was because he'd met someone there. They got married and moved back to the States just after Aera was born, but he never told his new family about Mom and me."

She gasped. "How'd you find out about each other then?"

"According to Aera, Greg was a serial cheater and an even shittier father. He cheated on Aera's mom when she was ten. They moved out shortly after and they haven't heard from him since." I was proud of my sister and her mom for leaving a man who was never going to prioritize them over his own selfish desires. "Neither of them knew how long it had gone on, but Aera always had a feeling that Greg had been hiding something, so she did one of those family ancestry tests last year to see if she might have any other siblings."

"And you had the same suspicion?" she asked.

I nodded, pulling her closer to me.

"Wait, so if she's your sister, then why didn't you just tell me instead of kicking me out of your house when she came to stay with you?"

"Aera and I had only found out a few months earlier that we were siblings and neither of us had told our parents yet. By that point, we'd only seen each other in person twice, so it was still new for us too. Both of us wanted to tell our parents in person, but it was hard with them living out of the country." I sighed. "I didn't know you well enough then and I couldn't risk you potentially spilling something to the tabloids before we told our parents."

The truth was, my sister wasn't as much of a bitch as she might have seemed.

If anything, I was the dickhead for blowing her off for months because I was too afraid of upsetting my mom with the truth. My sister wanted the world to know so we could stop hiding out in the Malibu house and do things together as a family.

We'd already lost out on twenty-five years together, and because of *my* selfishness, we'd practically lost another one.

When Aera's mom came to visit from Korea last winter, her visit somehow coincided with the team's bye week. So, I flew out for a few days to meet and hang out with her. Aera's mom was so happy for us and deep down, I knew that my mom would be happy for us too, but I also knew that in a way it would hurt her to get the answers as to why he left us in the first place.

And the idea that I might hurt her held me back.

"So, the dress? Your sister sent it to you?" Scarlett's eyes widened and her fingers toyed with the front of my suit jacket.

I nodded. "I called Aera the day before and asked her to overnight me one of her designs. Green because it's your favorite."

"And the recent tabloids?"

"Hugging my sister because she got engaged to her longtime boyfriend? Not exactly a crime." I chuckled.

Running her hands lightly down my back, Scarlett went still. "But... your mom. You haven't seen her in a year?"

"That's part of the reason I haven't spoken to you in six days..." I started. Fuck, I hated not talking to her. I'd picked up the phone countless times, but she blocked my number so it wasn't like I could call her even if I wanted to. Some things were better said in person anyway. "Aera and I flew to Iceland to tell her and Steve in person. Mostly because it was time that they knew, but also partly because I couldn't risk losing you over a fake fucking article."

She was *my sister*, for God's sake.

I'd never forgive that sleazy reporter for only snapping pictures once Aera's now fiancé had left the table.

Fucking idiot.

Just as I'd suspected though, Mom had been happy for me and opened her arms for Aera without a single hesitation. She told me later, over a late-night snack, that she felt relieved to finally know the truth about why my father had left.

In a sense, I felt the same way too. It didn't excuse what he did, but finally getting closure after all these years felt freeing.

"So nothing between us was a lie?" she croaked out with a wobbly voice. "Please tell me this wasn't all a lie."

"Do you remember when I asked you to go on a date with me?" My voice was hushed just low enough for her to hear. "I wasn't kidding when I asked you on a date then. I only played it off because you rejected me... four times."

Her breath hitched. "What?" she whispered-shouted, flashing her big brown eyes up to meet mine. "So you didn't throw out all of my food because you hated me?"

"No, Red." I couldn't help but let out a laugh. "I was so goddamn nervous around you that my appetite disappeared." I brought my hands up to cup her face. The corners of my lips turned up, reminiscing on how nervous I was when Scarlett first started working for me. "You made me so nervous that I was a fucking mess every time I tried to talk to you."

She didn't respond, peeking up at me through her long

black lashes with a smile before nuzzling her head between my pecs.

Exactly where she was meant to be.

I held her gently and rested my chin on the crown of her head. We stayed like that, in the comfort of each other, for long enough that our breaths began to sync.

Tilting her chin up, her big brown doe eyes looked up to meet mine once again. I let out a sigh to compose myself and pressed my forehead gently against hers.

"Scarlett, this was never a lie for me. This, *us*, was never a lie. *Will* never be a lie." I swallowed down the lump in my throat. Her eyes searched mine, trying to find an ounce of doubt in my words.

She wouldn't find any. Not a single fucking drop.

Until this moment, I didn't know it was possible to love someone so much that you felt like you couldn't breathe. Love was suffocating. Yet, somehow in the absence of my breath, she was simultaneously the air that filled my lungs and I'd forever be longing for more.

"I'm so in love with you, Red. How could there ever be anyone else?"

Her mouth curved into a smile, and she pressed a kiss against my lips. It was soft and tender, just like her.

I returned her kiss hungrily and she slipped her tongue between my lips, making me groan. "I love you," I whispered, breaking apart from our kiss briefly before going in for another one.

"Say it again," she breathed out against my lips.

"I love you, Red." Scarlett pressed a soft kiss against my lips. "I'll say it as many times as you want to hear it."

"I love you… so much." Fuck if my heart didn't soar out of my chest at the words I'd waited to hear pass between her lips for eleven months. I lifted her off her feet and spun her around in my arms.

"So…. now is probably the time to tell you that I burned the dress your sister gave me."

"You what?"

"Burned it," she said with a straight face. "To a crisp. Removed from the face of the earth."

"Why?"

"I *kinda* thought she was your ex after you kicked me out of your house that one time. You were an asshole for that, by the way."

I couldn't disagree with her on that.

"You thought I dated *my sister*?"

"Well, in my defense, I didn't know that she was your sister." She had a point, but it was still fucking disgusting. Aera told me she vomited after her fiancé showed her the article about us. Couldn't fucking blame her. "And second, don't look so shocked. The entire world was convinced you guys were dating six days ago, and until twenty minutes ago, neither of you denied it, so it was a valid assumption."

"Fair."

"You should probably tell her about the dress before you introduce me to her. Do you think she'll hate me for it?"

The breath was knocked out of my lungs. "You want to meet her?"

"Yeah, of course. I'd like to meet your mom and Steve too." Her eyes softened as she wound her arms inside my jacket and around my back. "Only if you want me to though."

My girl wanted to meet my family.

I cupped my hands underneath her butt, lifting her up into a hug and she instinctively wrapped her legs around my waist. I was half tempted to carry her out to the car and take her home right then. "You're in luck, because they already fucking love you."

"You told them about me?"

"How could I not?" I crashed my lips to hers again.

"I missed you."

"I missed you so fucking much, Red. I couldn't eat, couldn't sleep. That voice mail you left me broke my fucking heart. Don't ever do that again."

"Don't give me a reason to."

"Deal." I lifted her up just enough so she could unwrap her legs from me and placed her feet back on the ground.

There'd be more time for her to be wrapped around me later. A lot more time.

"Aye, my boy!" Carlo walked out of the kitchen and slapped a hand on my shoulder with an obnoxious wink. "Look at you two lovebirds. *Il vero amore*." Scarlett smiled at him and let out a faint laugh.

"Fuck off." I rolled my eyes.

Carlo chuckled to himself as he walked back to the kitchen.

I laced Scarlett's fingers with mine and led her over to a table that Carlo and I had set up earlier. I wanted us to have our first real date in the same place as our first fake one.

Well, fake for her. As far as I was concerned, that was our first official date and she couldn't convince me otherwise.

I wasn't lying when I said that she was the only person that I'd ever brought here. Even back then, I think I'd held on to the hope that Scarlett and I would end up together.

At least now we wouldn't have to lie whenever we were asked about where our first date was, no matter which time line you looked at.

"Please tell me we're eating dinner here too?"

"If you want to."

"Did you order the risotto?"

"Carlo's in the back making it right now."

I held out a chair for Scarlett and she plopped down into it but immediately scooted her seat closer to mine. She smiled up at me with a seductive grin and rested a hand on the upper part of my thigh, which was incredibly close to my cock.

"If you keep this up, we're going to have to take this food to go," I said in a hoarse voice while peppering kisses along her jaw all the way to that spot she liked just below her ear.

"Carlo!" Scarlett twisted her head, shouting toward the kitchen. "We'll take everything to go, please!"

A chuckle burst from my chest, and I pulled her closer to me. She turned her head back toward me, and I closed the short distance between our lips.

I couldn't get enough of her mouth. Or touching her.

Fuck, I loved this girl.

"Quickly!" I chimed in.

MY FINGERTIPS slowly grazed across her inner thigh as we drove through the busy streets. Scarlett peeled my hand from her thigh, interlocking her fingers with mine, and I brought her hand to my mouth to kiss the back of it.

When we stopped at a red light, I pulled our woven hands into my lap and Scarlett untangled our hands to teasingly run her fingers over my growing length.

For a brief second, I was tempted to pull over to the side of the road and fuck her so hard that the car shook for a passerby to see. But I stopped.

I wanted her all to myself.

And I was much more of a gentleman than to fuck her in the back of my car for our first time together.

"No, Red." I plucked her hand off of my aching cock and placed it back over on her side of the car. "I don't like telling you no, but I want you to finish first... *always*." Scarlett's jaw dropped. "Got it?"

A devilish grin took over her lips, and I moved my hand back over to her clenched thighs, massaging her soft skin.

At another stoplight, I leaned over the console and whispered in a low, husky voice against her ear. "Plus, I already told you the first time I come with you it's going to be so deep inside your pussy your head will spin." My hands primally gripped the upmost point of her thigh and her legs clenched my fingers even tighter than before. "You going to be able to wait until we get home?" I taunted with a smug smirk.

TWENTY-FOUR
SCARLETT

ABEL WHIPPED his blacked-out SUV into the driveway after going ten over the speed limit through the entire neighborhood. He was definitely going to be waking up to a firm email from security patrol reminding him that inching his vehicle closer to the gate will, in fact, not make it open any faster.

He came around the car to open my door, and I barely made it out before our mouths were connected once again. Our tongues desperately glided against each other and our hands desperately grabbed at each other's clothes as we stumbled our way toward the front door.

Abel kept our mouths locked and one hand cemented on my hip as he reached into his front pocket for his house key and unlocked the door. "Inside," he rasped, motioning for me to walk through the doorway ahead of him and slapping my ass as I did.

The second the door closed behind us, he twirled me around at the waist, and before I could blink, his lips crashed down to mine again. Both of his hands slid into my hair sensually and he slowly walked me backward until my back pressed against the wall.

I felt drunk at the taste of him.

Like one more taste would never be enough of him to ease the ache in my core.

Our tongues swept against each other's, fighting for control. His hands slid down my neck and chest until he was caressing both of my breasts. Abel sucked my bottom lip between his teeth and tugged softly, sending a moan from my lips.

An impatient groan tore out of him at the sound and he instinctively dug his hardened length against my stomach, which made heat settle between my legs.

Holy hell, that was hot.

Dragging me back away from the door, he inched me backward into the kitchen, keeping our lips sealed until I felt my butt hit the cool kitchen island.

He wrapped his hands underneath my thighs and hoisted me up to sit on the counter and my dress pooled up around my hips, exposing my panties. Abel looked down at the green lace thong that left little to the imagination with a smug smile before grinding his hard cock up and down my center as he kissed me until my underwear was soaked with arousal.

I was so hot I was surprised that I hadn't left a wet spot on the front of his pants.

Abel's fingers looped the straps of my dress and dragged them down to expose my bare breasts. Never in my life had I been so grateful for dresses with built-in padding until this moment. Abel must not have expected me to be braless under my dress based on the sharp breath he sucked in. I could feel his lips curving into a smile against mine.

He trailed his mouth across my jaw until he reached

my neck. His lips sucked hard against the sensitive skin, which made me gasp.

"Fuck," he whispered against my skin, inching downward and sucking one of my nipples into the warmth of his mouth, flicking and swirling the tight point with his tongue. My back arched instinctively and when his teeth tugged lightly, I couldn't stop the loud moan that passed through me.

Abel immediately pulled me down from the counter and whirled me around, bending me over the island and shoving my dress over my hips. He palmed my ass with one hand and smacked it with the other so hard that the sting lingered. "I fucking love this ass."

I groaned as my nipples hardened against the cool marble countertop while he pressed his bulge against me. I arched to mold into him and wiggled my ass up and down against him. Pulling my hair to one side, he kissed the nape of my neck, which elicited a shiver down my spine. He sucked and licked so vigorously that I was sure I'd have hickeys to cover up tomorrow.

Worth it.

Pretty sure my boss wouldn't mind either.

"You have no idea how many times I've thought about bending you over this counter and fucking you senseless, Red. No idea." A whimper left my lips as he kissed down my back. He continued to move downward while pulling my soaked panties over to the side. I felt the cool air as he spread my ass cheeks apart. "You drove me fucking crazy walking around here in the mornings with those short shorts and tight-ass jeans."

Every nerve ending throughout my entire body felt like it was going to combust. His hot breath ignited my skin with every word he spoke.

I wasn't sure when I became a fan of dirty talk, but

holy shit, was it doing something to me. I could feel my wetness begin to drip down my thighs while I waited for Abel to put his mouth on me.

"So fucking wet for me." I could hear the smirk in his voice as he ran a finger down my slit. His throaty groan sparked a shudder throughout my body that made my core clench. "So fucking perfect."

Holy. Freaking. Hell.

I was panting. God, I felt like I was going to die from pleasure and he hadn't even put his mouth on me yet.

Was it possible to still get into heaven if you died fucking someone out of wedlock? Either way, I was about to find out.

Abel's tongue finally made contact with my pussy, and I moaned loudly when he sucked my clit between his lips.

Stars flooded my vision as he continued to lap at my clit with a steady rhythm. His hands gripped my ass securely the whole time, only removing them long enough to take his suit jacket off.

The sounds he made while he ate me... it was almost as if *he* was the one on the receiving end of the pleasure. Knowing how much he enjoyed it made it that much hotter. "Fuck, I missed this pussy," he rasped.

My heart thumped heavily inside my chest and I could feel myself on the brink of an orgasm. But just when I was about to be sent over the edge... he stopped.

I could feel his lips form a smile against my pussy before he quickly moved back up and wrapped my hair in his hand. He kissed my exposed neck and I tilted my head to the side to give him better access, which he took full advantage of.

"Please," I begged, my voice laced with desire.

Abel grabbed my hips and twirled me so we were face to face again, tension and breathy moans rippling between us. His hands cupped the back of my thighs and he hoisted my legs around his waist yet again—this seemed to be his preferred form of transporting me these days—and clasped me tightly against his chest as he carried me up the stairs with ease.

Holy shit, he was taking me to his bedroom.

I'd never been upstairs before. I'd never had a *reason* to be upstairs before until now.

Oh my god. Oh my god.

Abel stopped in the hallway just outside what I assumed was his bedroom door and pressed my back against the wall. He steadily stroked his length against my center while placing soft, open-mouth kisses along my collarbone. He slowly, slowly traced his lips up my neck and the shallow breaths he left on my skin drove me deeper into oblivion.

"Fuck, Scarlett," Abel rasped, his voice sensual and husky. A tingling warmth ran down my spine at his words, knowing that I made him feel this primal, this turned on, making my pussy pulsate. "Are you on birth control?"

I nodded. "No condom."

"Fuck." Abel let out a throaty groan. Taking my lips once again, he gripped my ass firmly and I immediately felt my back peel away from the wall as he carried me through the doorway before stopping at the foot of his giant bed.

I was too distracted to take in his entire room, but I knew it was nice. And *clean*. Which was a big improvement from the rooms of the other handful of other guys I'd been with.

Abel bent down and slipped my dress over my shoulders, leaving only my green lace underwear. Simultaneously, I began unbuttoning his dress shirt with trembling fingers and ran my hands over his abs, slowly tracing down to his body until I reached his cock.

He groaned at my touch, quickly sucking in one of my nipples and releasing his mouth with a pop sound. His fingers brushed my slit tauntingly for a few moments before he shoved his two middle fingers inside and began working them in and out of me.

A jolt of impatience grew inside me as my orgasm built. I felt like I was going to burst if he were to deny me an orgasm again.

I lifted my hips upward so his fingers hit my G-spot at the most invigorating angle, which gave me the confidence to continue bucking my hips against him as I inched closer to ecstasy.

"You look good when you fuck my fingers like that, Red," he praised in a low voice. The smirk that peeled the corners of his lips as he watched me with such amusement only intensified the pleasure inside me.

If I hadn't already been on the brink of an orgasm, I most definitely would've been now simply at the sight of him watching me. "Look at you being such a good girl for me."

God, those words alone were nearly enough to send me over the edge.

His tongue drew a path from my ribs to my stomach while his thumb circled my clit. He watched under lowered lashes as I squirmed and writhed underneath his perfectly crafted touch.

A wave of warmth swirled in my core as he sucked my clit between his lips and lapped it with his tongue, each circle making it more sensitive.

"I need you inside me," I cried out breathlessly. "Please, I want to come on your cock."

He sucked my clit into his mouth one more time before

standing to slip off his pants. I lay on my back, dipping two fingers inside myself while I stared at his cock as it was released from his boxers.

Holy shit. How big was that thing... nine inches?

Abel sported a smug grin as he shifted his hips to line up with my center. Growing impatient, I wiggled my hips so that I was teasing his tip. He let out a throaty moan that made me shiver.

"Please, Abel. I want you to make me feel good."

With that seductive smile still on his face, his lips found mine instinctively and slowly, oh so slowly, he pushed his entire length inside me on the first thrust.

My breath hitched at the feeling of him stretching me. We both groaned at his second thrust as he filled my warm, wet pussy again.

"That's exactly how I'm going to fuck you. Deep and slow." A man of his word, he pulled back out and pressed into me again. Inch. By. Agonizing. Inch. Sending my mind and body soaring into a state of utter bliss when he reached the hilt.

"Please," I moaned into Abel's mouth. My back arched as he filled my pussy with every inch of his warm cock.

He made me feel completely full in every possible way. Abel had consumed my body and soul and I gave every piece of myself to him willingly.

"Fuck, it's like this pussy was made for me."

He began rocking his hips in short motions on that spongy spot that made my vision go blurry. My head flew back against one of his pillows and ear-piercing moans began pouring out of my mouth.

Abel grabbed my legs and threw them over his shoulders to reach a deeper angle. I did my best to maintain eye contact with him, but his cock filled me with so much completeness I couldn't help but flutter them closed as I took every one of his thrusts.

Abel brushed his thumb across my bottom lip before slipping it inside my mouth. "I want you to look me in the eyes while you come for me." His voice dropped into that low, husky tone that made my skin awaken with desire.

"Harder, please. Harder," I begged as his cock pounded deeper inside me. Pressure built at the base of my spine, eager for release.

"Come on, Red. Come on my cock. Come on my fucking cock." He kept his rhythm steady, grinding his pelvis against my swollen clit with each thrust.

His words pushed me over the edge and an electric shock scorched through my body as I trembled beneath him. My pussy convulsed around his cock as the most intense orgasm of my life ripped through my body.

"That's my girl." A smug smile lit up his face as the pace of his hips slowed while I rode the wave of my orgasm. "God, you look so fucking gorgeous when you come for me."

Abel continued to keep the slow pace and I could feel another orgasm begin to build at the base of my spine. A new wave of warmth and euphoria spread from my stomach and down through my thighs.

"I-I can't… do two in a row." My words came out choppy in between breathy moans. I'd only been able to do it to myself once, but that was a miracle in and of itself. No matter how hard I tried to replicate it, I'd never been able to do it again.

"You can and you will," he demanded in a low voice that was purposefully seductive. I shook my head despite my back arching up from the sheets. "Stop fighting it, Red. Every time you deny it, I'm going to add another one. You're up to three now."

Holy shit.

"Touch my clit… please." I moaned between my words until his thumb found the spot between us. My pussy clenched and tightened around him as he worked my clit, and another orgasm rose to the surface.

Abel rocked into me, making my thighs quiver while my pussy pulsed around his cock. A cry spilled from my mouth and my body shook as I came for him again.

"Give me another one," he growled impatiently, pumping me harder and harder with each thrust.

Oh my god. Oh my god.

Could I even have three orgasms back to back? Hell, I wasn't even sure I'd had three orgasms in *one day* before.

I couldn't do it. I couldn't do it.

"Get out of your head, Red. If you can do two, you can do three." Abel thrust his dick harder against my G-spot and the pressure continued to build toward its peak. "Come with me, Red. Now."

My entire body thrashed around him as my third orgasm exploded and sent my mind into another freaking dimension.

"Fuck." Abel let out a roaring moan alongside me as he filled my pussy with his hot cum.

He kissed me. Again. And again.

Keeping himself inside of me, he held me to his chest and took me with him as he rolled onto his back. Pulling the gray sheet over the top of me, I nestled against his chest, still coming down from the high that consumed me.

"I love you, Red."

"I love you," I murmured back to him, feeling achy and exhausted yet completely content.

I WOKE up from a short nap and slipped out of bed to go to the restroom before sneaking down the stairs—still naked—to grab two glasses and fill them with water from the spout on the fridge. With both glasses in hand, I ever so slowly tiptoed back up the stairs, careful not to slosh any water on the steps.

Walking back into Abel's room, I placed a glass on his nightstand first, then walked over to mine. Once I set it down, his big arm curled around my waist and dragged me back to bed, pressing my back into his front.

He absentmindedly threw a blanket over me in his half-woken state and I melted back into him to bring us closer.

There was something about the way his hands lingered on my skin, even while he was sleeping, that filled my entire being with warmth. And not in a sexual way either. Okay, fine… maybe a little bit. But it was more than that.

It just felt… *right*.

TWENTY-FIVE

ABEL

SUNLIGHT CREPT through the windows and I dragged Scarlett up on top of me and she instinctively curled up against my chest. Our breaths synced together, and I trailed my hands leisurely up and down her back.

She stirred awake above me and began moving her hips so that her bare pussy was rubbing against my hardening length.

Abruptly stopping her movements, she lifted her head up to look at me with a displeased expression. "You lied to me, you know."

"About what?"

"You said that I'd be the first person you'd tell once you were able to tell someone."

That's what she was thinking about while she stroked herself up and down my cock?

Regardless, she was right. Technically, I told Lea before I even told my own mother, which made me feel like a dickhead of a son. Not to mention the fact that I told the fucking tabloids before I ever officially told Scarlett too.

Who knows how many people the article was passed through before she saw it.

October hadn't known anything other than the fact that I fucked up and needed his help, which was a good thing because the guy couldn't keep his damn mouth shut. He would've told her before I ever even got the chance to.

"I hate that I didn't," I told her honestly, slumping my shoulders. "But I tried calling at least a dozen times but it went straight to voice mail."

"You're right because I blocked your number."

"Would you have answered the door if I showed up at the pool house?"

"Nope." She laughed. "If you had, I would've called security patrol and told them you were trespassing."

"I'm sorry, Red." I pressed my lips against hers. "So fucking sorry."

"Just promise me that from here on out I'll always be the first to know."

"Everything." I pressed open-mouth kisses against the side of her neck.

"I should really make you grovel more for this."

"How about I make it up to you by making you come on my tongue?"

"…Deal," she said with a thrilled smile.

I rolled her over onto her back and trailed kisses down her body while she fondled her breasts. My tongue danced against Scarlett's folds until her impatient moans begged for me to extend her mercy and suck her clit between my lips.

In the same motion, I thrust two fingers deep inside her soaked cunt and she slapped a hand against her mouth to stifle a scream. I reached my free arm up and tugged her hand away. A loud moan tore out of her, but I stayed consistent with my movements.

She liked it when I flicked her clit with my tongue and curled my fingers against her G-spot simultaneously, and *I* liked hearing the noises she made while I did it.

Fuck, she looked so gorgeous writhing in pleasure beneath me. And double fuck the fact that I was going to be the only man to ever look at her like this again.

Scarlett bucked her hips upward, racing toward her orgasm, but I pulled away when her moans became rampant. She grumbled a few expletives under her breath at the loss of contact.

"I changed my mind. Want you to come on my cock instead."

"Even better." Her breathing was heavy, but at least she wasn't pissed off now.

Lining up with her center, I plunged my aching cock inside and her already tight pussy instinctively clamped around me in pleasure.

Fuck, I wasn't going to last long if she continued doing that.

I peered down at her whimpering beneath me with eyes that urged for more of my length, which I gave to her with long, hard strokes.

I wrapped my right hand around her neck and pressed firmly against the sides, just enough so that she started to feel light-headed. Based on the carnal look in Scarlett's eyes, she was loving every second of it.

"Open your mouth," I ordered with a smirk on my lips.

Scarlett immediately responded to my request, parting her lips and sticking her tongue out slightly. Spit spilled from my lips and into her mouth, which she swallowed without hesitation.

Fuck, that was hot.

"Come with me, Red."

She nodded, and I pounded into her harder until she

convulsed around me and her pussy milked my cock until every drop of cum was inside of her. I steadied my movements as she pulsed around me, kissing her gently while she caught her breath.

After using my cum as lube and making her orgasm another time on my fingers for good measure, I forced myself out of bed and far enough away from Scarlett that I could put on workout gear for practice without being tempted to climb back into bed with her.

Training camp was officially one month away and my focus was locked in on improving my blocking, not only to make me a better player but also because I wanted nothing to hold back the Matrix from being back-to-back League Bowl champs.

I only fucking hoped the other players on the team gave half a rat's ass while they trained during the off-season or we'd be royally screwed.

After successfully dressing myself, I walked back into the bedroom and grabbed my phone and watch from the nightstand.

"Come back, it's cold." Scarlett's hand reached out from underneath the comforter and tugged at my shirt.

Fuck. I'd spend all day in this bed with her if I could.

"I have to go to practice, Red." I placed a kiss on her forehead.

"Five minutes, please." Her hand wrapped around my wrist. She wore one of my worn-out, oversized T-shirts that I'd thrown her from the closet—well, oversized for her. It fit me just fine—hit her midthigh, one of which was poking out from where she was half covered by the duvet.

She looked so fucking adorable when she was in this delirious half-woken state.

Like any good man would do, I climbed back underneath the covers and tucked her against my side just the way she liked for five more minutes.

Needless to say, I ended up being twenty minutes late to practice.

I'd fallen for her "five more minutes" ruse two more times before Scarlett finally dozed off to sleep, which allowed me to reluctantly wiggle myself out from her grasp.

If I didn't have multiple million-dollar contracts to adhere to, I'd stay in that bed with her for-fucking-ever if that's what she wanted.

Before leaving, I pressed a quick kiss against her cheek and left her a quick note on the nightstand telling her that I loved her.

WHEN I WALKED through the front door later that afternoon, the corner of my mouth lifted at the sight of Scarlett as she lay on my couch, cuddled against a throw pillow with a mound of blankets piled on top of her. She slept calmly, despite the television blaring twenty feet in front of her.

I grabbed the remote off of the coffee table to shut off the noise and admired her for a few minutes, admittedly holding back a tear while I took in her barefaced skin and those impossibly long eyelashes.

Fuck, I was a lucky man.

Crouching down, I peppered kisses along her cheeks, too impatient to wait for her to wake up on her own. "Red, wake up."

She peeled open one eyelid and yawned. "I don't know

what happened. I wasn't even tired," she said with sleepy eyes that fought to stay open.

Fuck, I wanted to watch her wake up every day. Morning, noon, night. Didn't fucking matter.

My heart fucking soared at the thought of her moving in with me. I kissed her hard. I'd give it a week before I asked so I didn't scare her off.

She pulled back. "Want me to make dinner? I'm starving."

"I picked up some groceries on my way home. Can you make that chicken pad thai recipe for me?"

"How do you know about that…" She tilted her head to the side and narrowed her eyes at me. "Have I made that for you before?"

Caught her right where I wanted her.

"No, you haven't." A smug smile played at my lips. "I've been reading your blog for months, hoping and fucking praying for months that you'd make it for me, but you haven't yet."

"You… what?" Her eyes grew wide.

"I read your blog," I admitted. It was never a fucking secret, but I liked poking fun at her by telling her all the things she had no idea I paid attention to. "You've been holding out on me with all the good recipes, Red. I'm a little pissed about it, not going to lie."

"You're joking."

"Oh really? 'Cause I commented on every post." I shot her a look of defiance and her mouth dropped open.

"You didn't." She sucked in a breath. Damn, I wished I had security cameras in the house too, so I could've caught the wave of astonishment that flooded her face on tape.

"Every. Single. One."

"Prove it." She sat up straight. "Prove it right now."

I pulled my phone from my back pocket and thumbed

my way to her blog. "Look, footballguy88, that's my username." Yeah, it was a stupid ass fucking username and most of my comments were bullshit, but I didn't care. "Go on and try to find a post I haven't commented on," I challenged.

Scarlett scrolled through her posts and looked at all of the comments that I'd left the past few months. Some of them she laughed at, like the one where I told her she should make that for her coworkers—knowing that I was her only coworker. And others where I made heartfelt comments on the posts that she talked about her mom, she'd look up at me with a pouty lower lip.

"That is a horrible username." Her chin wobbled and tears welled in her eyes, daring to break at any moment. "I had no idea that was you."

"Even when you didn't know it, I was your biggest fucking fan, Red." She hurled herself into my arms. "Always will be."

I tugged her tighter against my chest and pulled her head back so I could claim her with my lips.

"Up," she ordered, wrapping her hand around my wrist and leading me toward the staircase.

"Where are we going?"

"Bedroom. Stop talking," she demanded.

Red taking the reins? *Fuck. Me.*

She dragged me by the wrist the entire way to the bedroom, but I didn't fucking mind when it meant that I got to watch that sweet little ass poking out from underneath my T-shirt while she bounced up the stairs.

"Clothes off, then bed," she said firmly, peeling off her T-shirt to reveal her underwear.

That was my girl. Always wearing some variation of green lace panties. If they didn't look so fucking good on her, I'd tear each pair off of her in one swift tug.

I shrugged out of my T-shirt and kicked off my shorts, throwing them both in the corner. I lay on my back and watched as Scarlett slipped off her panties.

My cock was already hard for her by the time she positioned herself between my legs. She spat in one of her hands and then wrapped it around my length, gliding it up and down steadily.

Her eyes locked on mine, heated and lusty, as she bent down and flicked my tip with her tongue before wrapping those pretty pink lips around me and taking me as far into her mouth as she could.

Fuuuuck.

I watched as she bobbed her head up and down my cock with hollowed cheeks. Her tongue swirled and flicked against the underside of my dick, and both of her hands twisted in alternating motions.

I fucking hoped she learned all of this shit from those audiobooks she listened to, 'cause if not, I was going to have to fucking kill whoever taught her that.

Scarlett bobbed down onto my cock, attempting to take me in as much as she could until she gagged and popped up, gasping for air before trying again.

Jesus fuck, she was going to ruin me. "Red, I'm not going to last long if you keep doing that."

Scarlett slid her mouth off my cock with a "pop" and shuffled on top of me, turning so her backside was facing me. She inched her wet pussy onto my dick *just enough* that the tip was covered and she moved herself up and down, teasing me with her cunt.

If she thought this was going to make me last longer than her mouth around me... she was dead fucking wrong.

Scarlett let out a loud gasp when I surprised her by plunging my entire length inside her with one thrust.

Moans rang out from both of our lips and her head was thrown back in pleasure as she rotated her hips and found her rhythm bouncing on my cock.

Watching herself in the mirror on the dresser across from us, she circled her clit with her middle two fingers and her tits bounced up and down as her moans grew louder and louder.

"Fuck me harder, Red." I smacked her ass so hard her flesh started turning pink and looked in the mirror to find a smile breaking across her lips.

Scarlett took a page from my book and denied my request. Instead, she worked my cock slowly, taking her time to draw out the pleasure for both of us.

That's my girl.

She kept her eyes on the mirror, glued to the place where our bodies met until it became too much for her to handle and her eyes began to roll backward.

That's when I pounded my cock into her pussy from underneath her. She leaned forward and grasped my upper thighs to steady herself.

"Keep playing with your clit, Red," I ordered, and she obliged.

"Holy shit," she screamed, slamming her eyes shut as an orgasm ripped through her that made her whole body shake. I reached around and circled my fingers around her clit, knowing she could come again quickly if I kept the pace because she was too content to think herself out of it.

"Oh my god! Oh my god, Abel!" She let out a breathy moan while her pussy convulsed around my cock as she came for me yet again. I continued pumping hard and deep inside her, just the way she liked, as she pulsed through her second orgasm. Her pleasure triggered my own release, and I filled her pussy with ropes of cum.

Once Scarlett finally caught her breath, she slowly

lifted herself off of my length but not before pausing with her ass in the air to let me watch as my cum dripped from her cunt onto my dick.

The smirk on Scarlett's lips as she turned around was intoxicating. She used my cum to stroke up and down my cock before bending down to lick up every ounce of it, sucking and moaning as she did.

"Such a good girl," I murmured, pulling her up so she lay against my chest. I pressed a kiss against her lips and she opened her mouth, allowing my tongue inside. My dick grew stiff at the taste of us on her tongue.

I could've taken her again, back to back, but I willed my cock to stay down. As much as I wanted to drown in her pussy for eternity, right now, what I needed most was my girl on top of me while I drifted off into an orgasm-induced haze.

Later that night, after a delicious meal and an ample amount of quality time lounging around with my girl, I gave her my cock again, soft and slow this time, whispering honeyed words in her ear until we came together in a newfound kind of ecstasy.

TWENTY-SIX
SCARLETT

"SO, what are your intentions with my sister?" Mae glowered at Abel from where she sat on one of the accent chairs in his living room that looked like it had never been touched. She had her arms crossed over her chest and her lips pressed into a tight line in an attempt to look stern— which she most definitely was not. "And how do we know you're not lying about Aera being your sibling?"

"To marry her," he said matter-of-factly. I smiled giddily, looking over at him.

Jesus Christ. I kept having to remind myself that we'd literally only been back together for *six days*. Clinging to the hope that he was going to propose soon was *sorta kinda maybe* a lot freaking insane, but excitement hummed through me, knowing that's where he saw our relationship going.

Abel peered over at me from across the couch with a wink. He chose to put not only an *entire* cushion of distance between us but two pillows stacked on top of each other as well.

It was more for him than it was for me. The guy literally couldn't keep his hands off me these days... not that I was complaining. Not at all.

I applauded him for trying to be respectful, but Mae *genuinely* couldn't have cared less. Hell, I'd walked in on her having a threesome once in college and she hadn't even been fazed, just lifted a hand and waved.

"And I've got a handful of DNA tests from different labs, copies of both our birth certificates, which have identical signatures next to 'Father' and the paperwork from when she changed her last name from Abbott to her middle name, which conveniently also happens to be my middle name as well," Abel began again, keeping his eyes locked confidently on hers while he spoke. "But if you want more proof, I'm sure I could get it. Maybe track down my father and interrogate a confession out of him?" Abel said, raising an eyebrow.

Mae had been *ruthlessly* interrogating him since the moment she'd walked in his front door fifteen minutes ago. My eyes were going to fall out of my head from bouncing back and forth between the two of them as they bantered aggressively.

Abel had yet to crack under her pressure, but what Mae forgot was that he'd endured hours of Lea's relentless PR training which had prepared him for far worse than whatever antics she was up to.

But one thing Abel didn't know about Mae was that she was ruthless. I *knew* without question that she wasn't going to give up until she saw him squirm in his seat, even if it took hours.

"And you're aware of her obsession with romance audiobooks and are okay with her lusting over fictional men's penises?"

Oh my god, that was only slightly mortifying.

"Very." He shot me a smug smile.

Correct answer.

After coming home to me listening to one of them while I was making dinner one night, he had zero objections to me listening to them, as long as I promised to practice my favorite scenes with him. Which I *happily* agreed to.

Mae paused, shaking her head up and down with narrowed eyes, assumedly trying to think of her next move. In the meantime, she instigated a stare-off between the two of them to keep tensions high.

Abel leaned back in his seat while keeping his stare locked on Mae's, but it was the smug smile that crawled over her face that let me know she had him exactly where she wanted him.

"So, Abel…" She started off innocently to catch him off guard. "Have the two of you fucked yet?" she questioned with a popped brow.

The blood from Abel's face instantly rushed away at her words. He turned to look at me with widened eyes that pleaded for me to save him. I kept my face impassive and shrugged my shoulders.

Mae shot me a wink from across the room that made me laugh under my breath. "Go on… answer her."

Okay, fine. Maybe it was a *little mean* to leave him squirming high and dry, but watching him crack for a few minutes was a small price to pay after I endured eight months of him being a pain in the ass.

Reparations of this stature might be cruel, but they were necessary.

"We… uhh…" he sputtered, rubbing his palms down his shorts uneasily. A few beats of silence passed between the three of us, but Mae didn't budge her eyes away from him or allow her arched brows to drop a millimeter until he found his words.

Abel turned to look at me pleadingly once again, but I remained firm in keeping my face neutral. He let out a measured breath and his shoulders deflated before he answered with an eye roll. "Fine, yes."

"Thank God! That was exhausting." Mae flailed her hands in the air, dropping back into her seat. "So, Scarlett, how big is his dick? I've been dying to know." She placed her hands parallel in front of her and slowly began inching them away from each other, dropping her jaw farther as the space between her hands got bigger.

"Mae!" I shouted, appalled she actually said that in front of him. Abel, being the good sport he was, threw his head back and chuckled beside me.

"Okay, okay… got it. We'll talk about it later when he's not around." She winked at me, which only made Abel laugh harder. "Anyway, I have to get going now. Just came to say hi and drop off some clothes for Scarlett, so the two of you can remove your… purity barricade now." She waved a hand at the pillows between Abel and me.

I laughed as Abel unstacked the barrier between us.

"Abel… if you hurt my sister again, I'll stick skewers in both of your ball sacs and drain every drop of the sperm from your body so you won't be able to ejaculate ever again."

Abel winced but nodded understandingly.

I popped up from my seat and gave her a long squeeze before we made our way to the front door, keeping our arms linked the entire way. Abel trailed a few feet behind us, and the two of us waved Mae off from the front door. We watched until she made it across the street before Abel shut the front door and locked it behind us.

I was heading for the kitchen, hoping to make a midafternoon snack, when Abel's arms wrapped around me from behind and I was lifted off the ground.

"What are you—"

Abel spun me around and hauled me over his shoulder, holding me in place with one hand on the back of my thigh and the other firmly grasping one of my ass cheeks. He carried me up the stairs and into his bedroom without saying a word and slung me on his bed.

I peered up at him from where I lay on the bed while he stood there staring at me with ragged breath. "You're going to pay for not helping me back there."

"Asshole. Eight months," I responded back firmly.

Tugging my legs to the edge of the bed, he pulled off my shorts and underwear in the same movement. "Fingers, tongue, or cock?" he asked with an arched brow.

"All of the above."

"That's my fucking girl." The corners of his lips curled up into a cocky smile that made a flood of arousal drip out of me.

Abel dropped down and began kissing and licking my inner thighs, making warmth dance throughout my entire body. Growing impatient, I grasped the top of his head and guided his mouth to my pussy.

He smiled against it before granting me my wish. He thrust his tongue inside of me and my eyes shut instantly, overwhelmed by the feeling. His groans, paired with the sound of my wetness, drove me wild.

I didn't know how much more I could take before I was going to burst.

"Move in with me." Abel popped up, removing his tongue from where it was lapping my throbbing clit in circles.

Was he really trying to have this conversation right now... approximately three point five seconds before I came?

"What? Are you crazy?" I lifted my head so he could

see my widened eyes. "We just got together six days ago. We can't move in together."

"Says who?" he challenged.

"For starters, the big man upstairs would probably be disappointed if we moved in together out of wedlock."

"I'm sure he'd be a lot more disappointed about the other *activities* we've done in the last six days." He stared down at my pussy, which was mere inches from his mouth, and smirked. "He probably wouldn't like knowing I stuck my thumb in your a—"

"Don't finish that!" I laughed so hard my head flew back and hit the pillow.

"It's true." He chuckled, pressing two fingers inside of me and working them in and out agonizingly slow, making sure he swept my G-spot with each curled stroke. "I mean it. Move in with me. You only live a thousand yards away and you've spent every second here for the last week anyway."

He had a point. I hadn't seen the inside of the pool house since last Sunday when October picked me up. That was part of the reason I'd asked Mae to bring over some of my clothes earlier.

As much as I wanted to live in Abel's T-shirts day in and day out, I realized that I should *probably* put on pants at some point… and some underwear. Definitely underwear. I'd been using his boxers as an alternative, but they acted more like shorts because of how large they were on me.

"When would I move in?" I asked, trying to pretend like I was capable of having a conversation of this caliber with his fingers inside me.

"Right after our vacation."

"We're going on vacation now too?" I lifted my head up to meet his gaze again, but he curled against that spongy spot again and sucked my clit between his lips. I immediately threw my head back against the pillow with a loud set of moans.

I heard him chuckle again from down below.

He slowed just enough that I could gather my bearings and respond. "Vacation. Moving in. Don't you think we're moving a little too fast?"

"I've been waiting nearly an entire fucking year to have you." His tongue flicked my clit once again, and a rush of breathy moans spilled from my lips. "Forgive me if I want to take my girl on vacation and fuck her mindless for a week straight and come home knowing she'll be waking up next to me in bed every morning."

Well, when he put it that way...

"Technically, this is my house now, according to our agreement," I reminded him.

"Then ask me to move in with you instead," he argued.

"I don't want the house if it means you leaving."

"So, move in and it will be *our* house."

"You're serious about this?" I lifted my head once again to look down at him, watching as his two middle fingers disappeared inside me.

"Dead." He stared up at me, seriousness coating his eyes. "And I'm not letting you come until you say yes."

"You're cra—" He swirled my arousal around my clit with his thumb, making my vision spotted. "Oh my god. Keep doing that."

"Say it," he demanded with an arrogant smile, denying me pleasure as he slowed the strokes of his fingers inside me.

"Please, please, please, please, please. Abel, I need to come." I was practically screaming. My hips were bucked completely off of the bed and my thighs were closing tightly around Abel's head.

"Say it, Red," he demanded.

"Yes," I cried out. "Yes, I'll move in with you."

He paused. "I'll have my lawyer fill out the paperwork to put your name on the deed tomorrow. Now come for me."

Seconds later, I shuddered around his fingers in an orgasm so powerful I swear to God I thought I could reach out and touch the stars. Before I was even finished, Abel had lined up his cock with my center.

Oh god, he was going for multiples again.

I had a feeling that was going to be the new norm, and if it was, I would never be leaving this bedroom again.

Good thing I agreed to move in with him, right?

Abel taunted me with just his tip while I recovered from my first. Only this time, when he plunged into me, instead of fucking me like I'd expected, he kept a steady pace that made his pelvis brush against my clit with every thrust. Bliss seared through my veins as our eyes locked and we came together.

"We can start packing today," I whispered against his lips with a smile.

I WOKE up a few hours later from a post-sex-induced nap and I moseyed down the stairs to figure out where Abel went. Much to my surprise, I walked into the kitchen to find him standing over the pan on the stove with a spatula in hand, wearing nothing but gray sweatpants.

Holy shit, this was a chef's literal wet dream. I nearly came at the sight of him. The only thing that stopped me from doing so was the fact that it felt entirely unsafe for him to be shirtless, standing six inches away from a stove.

I dragged my hand across his back as I walked past him and hopped up to sit on the open counter space near where he was finishing up... hanger steak topped with garlic butter based on the look of it. My favorite.

He took the pan off of the heat and moved it over to a trivet on the island to let it cool before turning his attention over to me. He tilted his head over to the living room, where everything I owned was in boxes waiting to be unpacked.

"When did you have time to do that?" I arched a brow at him.

"You were asleep for *six hours*, Red... and I hired a moving crew," he quipped with a smirk.

Of course he hired movers. I should've known.

"I ALWAYS ASSUMED you could cook, but it's nice to know for sure." I held back a small laugh.

With the corners of his lips turned up, Abel nudged his hips between my thighs and placed a hand on each side of me, pinning me against the counter. "I never wanted a chef."

"Never?" I pulled away from him with wide eyes.

I guessed he didn't *need* a chef, but it was a bit of a surprise to hear him say he didn't want one. He had a way of surprising me with new information about himself whenever I least expected it. What was next... him telling me he had a ring picked out since the day we officially got together?

"I only offered you the job because I wanted to see you every day until I worked up the courage to ask you out," he whispered against my neck.

"You were going to ask me out?"

"Eventually." Abel sucked lightly on that hollow spot

where my shoulder and neck met, causing me to let out a small moan. "In a backward fucking way, I guess my plan worked, didn't it?"

I laughed because it was true. As much as I would've loved to have had him from the beginning, I think we needed to go about it in our own way for us to have gotten to where we are now. Funny how things worked out like that, wasn't it?

"You holding out any more secrets on me, Abbott?"

"None. I was always in it for the long haul, Red." He smirked down at me before pressing his lips against mine. "Welcome home."

EPILOGUE

Two years later

Abel

"YOU KNOW... the last time you dragged me outside with your hands covering my eyes was the night you asked me to be your girlfriend..." Scarlett trailed off with a giant grin on her face as I guided her to the back door.

Of course she was onto me.

For the last few months, any time we went on a date or did something out of the norm, she thought I was going to propose. One night, she even convinced herself I was going to drop on one knee in the middle of the checkout line at the grocery store. How she had come up with that idea, I had no fucking clue.

She was right in thinking that it would happen soon,

but every time she thought it was going to happen, she was dead wrong. Until right fucking now.

"What are you getting at, Red?" I quipped, willing down a smile I knew she couldn't see.

"Ohhh, nothing," she replied in a singsong voice.

I opened the door and a chilly spring breeze swirled around us as I walked her out to the middle of the deck. Much like a two years earlier, I had a full setup for a movie night similar to the first one where I asked her to be my girlfriend. The projector was ready with a few romantic comedies—her favorite, not mine—and those twinkle lights she liked were strung all over the place.

This spot was the start of it all for us and there wasn't anywhere else in the world I wanted to propose to her. *Especially* not the fucking grocery store.

"Stand right here and keep your eyes closed," I said, uncupping my hands from her face. "I'll tell you when to open them."

I took a steadying breath and pulled out the ring that I'd had hidden in my nightstand for months. Last fall, during a bye week, we drove up to the cemetery in Sarasota, where her mom was buried with a picnic basket, homemade lasagna, and fresh flowers. Scarlett spent the afternoon talking to her mom and telling her about the two of us and giving her life updates on Mae and their dads.

Before we left, Scarlett showed me around the town she grew up in and the houses on Pine Street where she spent the first eighteen years of her life that I'd heard so much about. It was surreal seeing the place that shaped so much of the woman I loved.

While she was visiting with a friend at a diner we stopped at before heading back home, I popped into the secondhand jewelry store next door. Initially, I was just trying to get ideas, but the moment I laid eyes on an emerald-green diamond in one of the display boxes, I didn't need to look any further. The ring was so inherently Scarlett that I knew there was nothing else I'd find that would compare.

Dropping down to one knee, I took another deep breath. My heart thumped so recklessly in my chest I felt like I was going to faint. "Open your eyes."

Scarlett gasped as she opened her eyes and both of her hands flew up to cover her mouth.

"Yes," she blurted out before I got the chance to say a word.

"I haven't even asked you yet." The corners of my lips tugged upward at her eagerness. "Scarlett, will you—"

"Yes! Yes!" she interrupted me again.

"Red, I'm pretty sure it doesn't count if you don't let me finish."

She threw her head back, and a laugh spilled from her lips before she looked back down at me with tears welling in her eyes.

"Scarlett," I started. "I'm so in love with you it physically hurts to think about a life without you in it. And I don't want to spend another day without taking the next step toward making you my wife. So... will you marry me?"

It was the longest millisecond of my life before Scarlett jumped into my arms. "Yes, I'll fucking marry you!" She crashed her lips to mine before I had the chance to register what she said.

"Did you just say fuck?" I looked at her with widened eyes as I pulled back. Scarlett had her own preferred strand of expletives, but I'd never heard her use that one before.

"I think so? Maybe?" She laughed. "Honestly, I blacked out."

A chuckle roared through my chest and I held her tightly against me. Scarlett parted her lips and dipped to meet mine. The taste of her cupcake lip balm lingered in my mouth as she pulled away.

Fuck, I couldn't wait to have that taste on my lips for the rest of my life.

FOG CLOUDED the view out the main bedroom window and my now fiancée lay curled between the sheets of the California king bed. I spent the last hour attempting to watch the sunrise through the clouds with her tucked against my side, like usual, before getting up to make coffee for the group.

Aera drove over this morning and picked up Mae and October on the way. They'd booked last-minute red-eyes after Scarlett video called them with the news.

Lea was thirty-eight weeks pregnant and wasn't cleared to fly, so she and Fortune were back in Miami, moving their things into Rita's old house. Once she passed, there was no one else Mae could've envisioned giving the house to, especially with the first baby of their trio on the way.

Scarlett had a small pregnancy scare a few weeks after we got back from our first vacation together, which terrified her. I knew she hadn't wanted a baby so early in our relationship, which was understandable. She'd never admitted it but I always had a gut feeling she was waiting to time it up with Mae so that they could experience it together.

Shortly after, Scarlett suggested that I see a therapist to talk more about my childhood and Aera unexpectedly coming into my life. Being able to finally heal from some of the hurt I'd carried since childhood was liberating.

Not only was I a better person because of it, but when the time came, I knew I'd be a better father because of it too.

So, until Scarlett was ready, we'd just keep practicing.

I shifted on my feet, leaning against the corner where floor-to-ceiling windows met the wall with a cup of freshly brewed coffee pressed to my lips as I watched my now fiancée while she slept.

Scarlett stirred in the bed, wriggling herself halfway out of the covers like usual. "Morning, Red."

"Morning," she replied with half-opened eyes and a groggy smile. "Anyone ever tell you it's rude to stare?"

"Just admiring the view." A smirk pulled at my lips. "Come on, everyone's already awake downstairs," I said, setting my mug on the nightstand before placing a steadying hand on her hip and crouching down to kiss her.

"It's also rude to walk around the house half naked when you have guests." She eyed my bare chest, dragging her eyes down to my sweatpants.

I kissed her again, lingering a bit longer this time. "I knew I should've gone fully nude."

Scarlett rolled her eyes and grasped the nape of my neck to draw me closer. My hand slowly slid underneath her T-shirt, dragging up her torso to rest just underneath her breasts.

"We shouldn't keep them waiting," I taunted against her lips.

"I have ways of keeping you here, you know," she said defiantly.

Scarlett had a way of making us late for nearly everything the last year. Not that I was complaining, but my tardiness at morning practices had earned me a reputation with some of my teammates.

"Prove it."

Scarlett ran a hand over my sweatpants, and my cock grew hard at her touch. I ducked down to kiss her, but she turned her head away at the last second. "Not until you're inside me."

Fuck, I'd taught her well. These days she did more of the teasing than I did and every time, she drove me fucking wild.

I lifted up her shirt and palmed one of her breasts. A small moan slipped from her lips and my cock instantly twitched at the sound. I pulled down her shorts and teased up and down her slit, arousal soaking my fingers as I plunged two of them inside her.

"Oh my god, Abel." She kept her lips locked on mine as she pulled down my sweatpants to release my cock. She broke away from my lips briefly to spit in her hand and then locked our lips again as she began stroking my cock with a tight grip.

I flicked my fingers against her clit until she was wiggling her hips against them. Kicking off the sweatpants that were now at my ankles, I shuffled until I was lined up with her center. Instead of thrusting my cock into her like she expected, I ran my dick up and down between her folds so that the tip of my cock was teasing her clit.

Finding the pace we both liked, I bent down to take her mouth again. She welcomed me between her lips and circled her tongue around mine with a familiar ease.

"I was thinking that when we get home, I should stop taking birth control," she whispered against my lips, knocking the fucking breath out of my lungs.

My mouth covered hers hungrily. "You should stop taking it today."

"Really?" Her eyes widened.

I nodded a response.

"Come inside me," she begged.

I filled her with every thrust until we finished at the same time, and my hot cum spilled from her pretty little cunt.

AS THE TWO of us ambled down the stairs for our walk of shame, I smoothed down Scarlett's sex hair as she walked in front of me. She shot me back a sweet smile that made my lungs tighten.

God, she was so fucking beautiful.

"Congrats on the sex," October chided, tipping his mug at me with a wink.

"As much as I'd love to be an aunt, I'd prefer not to hear the process of becoming one," Aera added in. "When are you guys planning on getting married anyway?"

I'd marry her any day, any hour. Fuck, if it had been up to me, we would've gone to the courthouse five minutes after I proposed last night.

But I was willing to be patient.

She was going to be mine forever either way, so I wasn't going to pressure her on it, no matter how much I wanted to call her my wife or see my last name attached to her first.

"We just got engaged last night," I reminded her.

"You guys should get married here... like today!" Mae jumped up from her seat. "It's perfect. The three of us are here and we can even video call Lea, Dads, and Abel's parents too."

Hmmm, wasn't a bad fucking idea.

It'd take a lot of stress off both of us with Scarlett's next cookbook coming out this fall and the preseason practices starting back up next month. Plus, we wouldn't have to dish out thousands of dollars to impress people we didn't care about with an extravagant wedding.

And let's not fucking forget the fact that half an hour earlier she begged me to put a baby in her.

Needless to say, I had no opposition.

I looked down at Scarlett, who was already looking up at me with those big brown eyes and an adorable smile. "I think we should do it," she whispered after a minute.

"Yeah?"

She nodded, and I placed a kiss against the tip of her nose. We turned to the others who were all quite literally sitting on the edges of their seats watching us and gave them all a nod.

Mae jumped out of her seat with a squeal and pulled Scarlett away from me to wrap her in a giant hug.

"I know a two-hour wedding certificate service!" Aera piped up from her spot on the couch, pulling out her phone and typing away.

"And why exactly do you have that on hand?" I raised a brow.

"I found it when Tye and I were together." She shrunk back in her seat the tiniest bit. If I didn't know her well, I probably wouldn't have noticed, but I knew how much she was hurting from her recent breakup.

"I'm an ordained minister," October cut in, breaking into my thoughts.

"*You're* a minister?" the rest of us exclaimed in unison.

What the fuck…

"Don't act so surprised. I was a priest one year for Halloween, seemed like the right thing to do." He shrugged. "Lying is a sin and all."

"How is that even legal?" Scarlett turned around to whisper to me.

"I heard that," October grumbled.

Scarlett and Mae ran upstairs and Aera quickly followed, shouting up to them to tell them she had an extra spool of white silk in her office and needed to take Scarlett's measurements.

A few hours later, at the house where I fell in love with her, we got married.

When Scarlett walked out onto the back deck, she took my fucking breath away. Wearing a dress my sister had finished making twenty minutes earlier, she'd never looked more stunning.

A small tear slipped from my eye when I saw her and I quickly brushed it away with my thumb.

Mae acted as Scarlett's maid of honor and Aera was my best woman and our parents and Lea joined in via video while October officiated. Still not sure if it was legal, but I made a mental note to check the next morning.

We might not have planned on getting married that day, but it was small and intimate and perfect for us.

Sealing our vows with a kiss, my girl became Scarlett Abbott.

My wife.

"Sooo… I think now it's probably safe to tell you that there was never actually a PR mandate for you to get a girlfriend…" Lea piped in after we toasted champagne glasses through the computer screen and our parents left the video call. "Dad and I may have completely made it up…"

"Lea!" all six of us, including Fortune, shouted in unison.

I should've known Coach Sterling was fucking lying to me. *"I'm more of a traditionalist when it comes to dating,"* my ass.

No matter what Lea and Coach's fucked-up reasoning may have been, it didn't matter because I got the girl.

The five of us waved at the screen before it went black and the others slowly made their way into the house.

High on wedding night bliss, Scarlett and I cuddled outside on the sofa underneath a twinkle-light-covered deck as we whispered sweet nothings in each other's ears until the early hours of the morning.

Our story might not have been conventional, but it was all we could ever ask for.

The End.

Christmas in Comets Valley

MEG READING

CHRISTMAS IN COMETS VALLEY SNEAK PEAK

Chapter One
Aera

I'd come to learn that people handle breakups in one of two ways. One, it broke their heart and thrust them into a spiraling pit of despair. Or two, it shaped and molded them into a better version of themself.

And ten months after finding out my ex-fiancé, Tye, had been cheating on me for the *entirety* of our decade long relationship, I could confidently say our breakup had simultaneously done both.

To the eyes of the world, I was accomplishing the goals I'd dreamed of since the day Ben and I started our fashion brand, Inamra, eleven years ago. While in reality, I was sitting at home alone, holed up in the darkness of my bedroom. Much like I had been for the past three hundred days since the breakup.

I knew my relationship with Tye hadn't been picture perfect, but then again, whose relationship was? So what if we didn't have sex every day or even every week? Okay, maybe it was more like once a month… if that.

In my defense, we both owned two of the fastest growing companies in the country, so forgive me if it was a little hard to find the time. Between days chock-full of meetings, which were immediately followed by late nights at the office finalizing last-minute projects, sex was the last thing on either of our minds.

Or so I thought until ten months ago when I stepped foot into Tye's office for a surprise lunch date after one of my meetings got canceled and quickly learned I was the only one in our relationship who couldn't find time for sex.

Much to my surprise, when I opened the door to his corner office, I found Tye's secretary bent over his mahogany desk while he jackhammered in and out of her like a madman.

She must've been an out-of-work actress based on how piercing and animated her moans were. She and I both knew he wasn't that good, no matter how hard she tried to convince herself otherwise.

I couldn't help but feel bad for the people in the offices next to him who had to listen to her shrill voice yelling, "Fuck me, daddy." Over and over again.

The two of them were too enamored with their impending orgasms to notice I was standing in the door-way, staring back at them wide eyed with my breath caught in my lungs.

In a fit of rage, I stormed out of the building and left the door wide open, hoping it would ruin the high of their orgasms when they came back to earth and realized one of their coworkers could've stopped by to watch the show.

A quick word to the wise: if you're planning on banging

your secretary during your lunch hour, at least have the brains to lock the door first.

Fucking idiot.

Heat flushed through my body as I stomped to my condo a few blocks away with bunched fists balled at my sides. A blaze of fury engulfed me so fully that I was certain passersby on the street could see steam smoking from my ears.

Back at the condo, it didn't take long before I was gathering Tye's things and throwing them into trash bags. Only stopping to toss the bags into the hallway for a courier service to pick up and deliver to his office.

Approximately forty-five minutes later, I'd successfully removed any semblance that Tye Smithgerald Jerod III had been in my life and it was only then that I allowed my fury to melt into embarrassment.

Ten years I'd been with him and *that* was how our relationship ended? At noon on a random Tuesday in February, a decade long chapter of my life came to a close within the span of an hour.

Unbelievable.

A suffocating sensation tightened in my throat, but I managed to push it down long enough to call the building's maintenance team and ask them to come change the locks right away. And I made damn sure they billed the rush charge to Tye's credit card.

It had been ten months since that fateful day, yet it still felt like a fresh blow to the stomach every time I flashed back to the grueling memory.

And while I hated to admit it, instead of coping with the breakup like a normal person, I'd become a recluse. The kind of person who locked herself in her office and threw herself into the thick of work twenty hours out of the day… every day.

My friendships faded months ago. And if it weren't for my half brother and his family coming to stay at our vacation house in Malibu a few times this past year, the likelihood that I would've had social interaction with anyone outside of the office was slim to none.

I'd clocked more hours in the last ten months than I had in the eleven years since Ben and I started the company. While I wasn't exactly proud of my lack of a social life, I had the accomplishments to make up for it. Like finally landing a coveted spot at Paris Week of Fashion this past winter and showcasing two collections of our most detailed haute couture pieces to date.

We'd made it into Miami Week of Fashion a few years back and even headlined the New York shows for the last three, but becoming a key show in Paris... that's when a designer knew they'd reached the peak of their success.

I should've been riding the high of being named one of the "top up-and-coming fashion designers in the world" by nearly every major media outlet in the world — rightfully so, might I add—but with the holidays approaching, all I could feel was a ripple of emptiness settling into the depths of my bones.

No matter how tirelessly I worked day in and day out, I knew when I shut my laptop at the end of the night and laid my head down against my pillowcase, the hollowness inside would consume me whole.

It always did.

So, like any rational person who wanted to avoid their own personal purgatory, I laid in bed tucked snugly beneath a cloud cotton duvet while mindlessly scrolling Socialgram at two in the morning.

There was something about living vicariously through the highlight reels of the friends and acquaintances I used to hang out with that made me feel like we were still connected in a way.

Oh look, Barrett acquired another business. *Scroll.* Stella was moving to Chicago. *Scroll.* Samira won another golf tournament. *Scroll.* Tye was engaged. *Sc—*

Tye was *what*?

I thumbed my way through the carousel of images half a dozen times to ensure I wasn't hallucinating—spoiler alert; I wasn't—before re-reading the caption a second time.

Proposed to my beautiful fiancée, Candace, on our one-year anniversary. Wedding next summer. You're all invited! #TyeingTheKnot

Tye was engaged.

En—fucking—gaged.

Ten months after we ended our *ten-year* relationship? Based on that fact alone, I guessed it took him—what?— half a business day to grieve our relationship before moving on.

It took the guy eight years to propose to me and another two of avoiding the topic of wedding planning and now he was engaged to this—this whore!

Before I could fully process what was happening, I was out of bed and pacing back and forth on an endless loop in front of the footboard. I racked my brain trying to come up with a scenario to explain the monstrosity that was my life.

Shit, I really needed to stop hanging out with my sister-in-law. Her pacing problem was really starting to rub off on me.

I took a deep breath to gather my composure.

Tye was engaged. With a wedding date set. While I, on the other hand, couldn't spend five minutes alone with my thoughts before seeking a distraction. And this entire time he'd been out there happily moved on for... how long? I reread the caption again and my jaw dropped open.

How were they celebrating their one-year anniversary? We broke up *ten* months ago!

Obviously, I knew the guy was a cheater, but getting into a new relationship two months before ours ended... that was low, even for him. And to add an extra splash of drama to the pot, his new fiancée wasn't even the secretary I found him fucking in his office.

How many other women had there been before I caught him?

Nope, nope. I quickly retracted the thought as bile rose in my throat.

"Fuck, fuck, fuckity, fucking, fuck!" I screamed to no one and the sound of my rage echoed off the walls of my room.

Shit, I guessed I needed to stop hanging out with my brother, too. The guy used the word "fuck" like it was the only one in the dictionary and apparently I'd adopted his nasty habit.

I let out a pent-up breath and slumped down onto the edge of the bed, hanging my head in my hands.

I hated myself for not figuring out his lies sooner. And even worse, for still caring about him all these months later. But when you already wasted a third of your life on someone, what was another year of heartbreak added to the mix?

"Ughhh," I groaned, flopping back onto the mattress.

I needed a break. A big fat break.

From work. From life. From everything.

Turning over to the nightstand, I let out a sigh as I reached to grab the purple-colored pill bottle I'd come to know well and twisted off the top. Shaking the bottle, I watched as two giant sleeping pills plopped into the palm of my hand.

There was no way I was getting to sleep on my own, and drowning myself in a bottle of tequila at this hour wasn't an option. I could *not* be hungover for our quarterly investor's meeting tomorrow afternoon.

I grabbed the mostly empty glass of water from my nightstand to assist with chasing down the pill before slipping the silk eye mask over my eyes. Nuzzling underneath the duvet comforter, I waited until the sleeping pills worked their magic, eliciting a warm buzz of tranquility beneath my skin.

Using every thought-blocking technique in the book, I slowly, slowly began drifting to sleep. On the brink of slumber, I silently prayed to whatever gods may be that when I woke up in the morning, all of this would be a horrible dream.

*

BEEP. BEEP. BEEP.

Seething, I threw a hand out of the warmth of my covers, desperate to end the source of my agony. What time was it anyway?

I peeled an eyelid out from my sleep mask and winced at the stream of sunlight pouring through the curtains and straight into my eyeballs. Well, the sun was already up, so it had to be at least six.

BEEP. BEEP. BEEP.

"Shut up!" I grumbled at the deafening noise, flailing a hand over the nightstand until I grasped my phone. I answered the call flashing across my screen and the megaphone-worthy beeps ceased, finally putting an end to my suffering.

"Get your ass up, Aera! Why did *today* of all days have to be the one you picked to be late?" Ben's hushed voice sounded through the speaker. While I might've been half asleep, I didn't miss the bridled anger laced in his tone.

My business partner must've taken up post as the village idiot if he thought calling to yell at me this early in the morning was going to work out in his favor.

Plus, I wasn't even late yet. I still had a full hour to get to the office for our leadership team's morning debrief, and even then, I'd still be two hours early compared to our nine to fivers. If Ben was going to be pissed at me for sleeping in an hour later than normal, so be it.

I pressed the red button in the middle of the screen and hung up on him without an ounce of remorse.

My eyelids fluttered closed, calling me back to my delicious slumber. But right as I got myself tucked perfectly into the warmth of the comforter, the beeping returned.

I could see it now. Today's newspaper headlines would read:

World-renowned fashion designer, Aera Chase, murdered her longtime business partner, Benjamin Fletcher, in a brutal display of vengeance. Click here to read the grueling details about how she chopped off each of his extremities one by one—penis included.

Feeling my body temperature rise, I snatched my phone and slammed it against my ear. "Ben, if Christ himself isn't coming back at this very moment, I swear to fucking god I'm going to murder you," I grumbled into the receiver with a scowl plastered on my face, which he, unfortunately, wasn't able to witness.

"Christ, swearing, and murder in the same sentence? How becoming of you, Aer."

"Get to the point of your call before I hang up on you a second time."

"You're late to our meeting with the investors," he spit venomously. Ben had always been an ass, but he wasn't one to take a vicious tone with me, especially when he was joking around. "I've been stalling for the last half hour, telling people you're having car troubles, but it appears you've taken it upon yourself to sleep in until noon instead. What the fuck, Aera!" he whisper-yelled.

"It's not noon, you imbecile. Our board meeting isn't for another…" I trailed off, twisting my head to get a better view of the clock on my nightstand—12:32 p.m.

I shot up straight in the bed. "Start the meeting. I'll be there in twenty." I hung up the call before he had the chance to respond with another snide remark.

Eighteen minutes later, I strode through the conference room door with a lug wrench in hand and an ashy-colored stain smeared on the front of my shirt.

It was moments like this that made having a condo within walking distance of the office worth the outrageous price I paid for it. I tried not to imagine how much worse this situation would have been if I'd stayed at the Malibu house last night like I'd originally planned to until I got swept up at the office.

"Sorry, boys. I got a nasty flat on the freeway and not a single one of those pesky East Coast transplants were willing to stop and help a girl out." I shook my head and waved the lug wrench around in a circle.

The investors, most of which unfortunately happened to all be middle-aged white men, stared at me with bug eyes, like they hired me to recreate a scene from their favorite porno.

Their wives must be so proud.

"Color me impressed, Miss Chase," Todd, one of our

biggest investors, piped up from the furthest end of the conference table after a beat. "I don't even know how to change a tire myself. How honorable of your parents to teach you how to change one."

Of course Todd didn't know how to change a tire. The guy came out of the womb a billionaire. I'd be shocked if he'd ever set foot behind the wheel of a car before for anything more than a picture. If I was a betting woman, I'd say he had, hmm... five drivers on standby at all times? If not more.

"Oh, enough about silly old me." I gave them all a sweet smile and turned my attention to Ben, who stood at the front of the room in his perfectly tailored navy-blue suit with a scowl on his face as usual. Basking in the magnificence of my power, I shot him a knowing wink, "Ben, where were you?"

*

"Nice save." The corners of Ben's lips twitched upward the slightest hair once we were alone in the conference room. "The lug wrench really sold it." A deep laugh he let few people hear bellowed out of his chest as he grabbed the wrench off the table and waved it above his head like a rodeo clown.

"What? I had to make it seem believable! *And* it got Todd to put up another half a million on his initial investment, which I consider a success." I lifted a hand to high-five Ben, but he left me hanging.

Typical.

"True." He relaxed down onto the edge of the long, rectangular table. "Hey, if shit hits the fan for us in the future, you could make a killing as a car salesperson." His elbow nudged into my side as I took a seat next to him.

"If Inamra went down in flames tomorrow, the luxury car dealerships in Beverly Hills would be my first stop," I quipped with a small smile splayed across my lips.

Ben and I met freshman year when we got paired together for a group project for one of our general electives. From the start, there was no denying the instant draw we felt toward one another's opposing skill set. By the end of that year, Inamara was born out of pure ambition, and Ben had become a permanent fixture in every aspect of my life.

He also happened to be the one who set up Tye and me on a blind date. And if he weren't so damn good at running the behind-the-scenes of the business, that reminder might've given me more motive to follow through with the murder charge I threatened him with earlier.

"You good, Aer?" His brows drew together as he twisted to meet my gaze.

"Not really, B." I slouched forward and let out an uneven sigh, swallowing back the tears that pricked the back of my throat. "I'm sure you've heard the news by now…" I trailed off, alluding to Tye's engagement announcement.

"Yeah…" His voice grew quiet while he crossed and uncrossed his arms, struggling to remain still.

I'd known Ben and Tye remained friends after our breakup, and I'd be lying if I said it didn't hurt. But I also knew that if Ben ever had to choose between the two of us, he'd pick me. Every single time. Though I'd never make him do it.

Ben swore he hadn't known about Tye's infidelity, and I believed him. I knew he still felt guilty about setting us up in the first place, although he never could've predicted how it'd end.

He might've been a bit of a grump sometimes, but I knew he always had my best interest at heart. One day he'd make some girl out there really happy, but that girl sure as hell wouldn't be me.

I cringed at the thought of having to kiss him. *Disgusting.* Or worse, have sex with him. I shuddered inwardly at the thought. *Revolting.*

"I think I need a break." A huff expelled from my lungs after I took a minute to breathe through the dull ache knotting in my chest. "I'm just... a shell of the person I used to be. Outside of work, the only people I talk to are my brother and sister-in-law. I hardly sleep anymore. And I think creativity is taking a hit because of it."

"A break?" Ben replied quizzically, faint amusement flickering in his eyes.

Aside from flying to Florida to visit my brother and sister-in-law every so often, I hadn't been on a *real* vacation since spring break my senior year of college.

When my brother talked me into buying the Malibu house together for family gatherings, I told myself it would be a peaceful escape from work life. Yet, more often than not, when I visited, I'd spent more time in the office upstairs than relaxing on the beach.

I loved my job. I truly did. But last night's wake-up call made me realize that continuing to throw myself into an endless downward spiral over a man who couldn't care less about me was keeping me from living.

Not to mention, the creative lull I was in could've easily killed Inamra's chances of headlining New York Week of Fashion next year. If I kept it up, we'd be out of the running before the officials even began debating which fashion houses to invite.

I needed to get away from this place—my life—and

break free from the gloom-filled cocoon I'd been living in the past few months.

"Yup, I think I need to get out of town and do a factory reset on myself, you know?" I babbled, springing to my feet. "I could go on vacation for the holidays… see some snow. Ohhh, maybe I'll go to a place that has a Christmas festival!" I flailed my arms at my sides, and Ben stared back at me with both brows raised as if I'd abandoned every drop of sanity within myself. "Everyone will be out of office for the next few weeks anyway, so I won't even have to think about work!"

A ripple of uncertainty washed over me for a moment as I observed Ben tossing my words through his brain, astonishment spread over every millimeter of his expression. I only stopped myself when he tilted his head to the side and a wide grin pulled up the corners of his lips.

I knew he'd come around eventually… even if it was only for the benefit of getting me out of his hair for a few days.

Rising to his feet, Ben waltzed over toward the doorway and paused to look back at me before crossing the threshold to the corridor, which led to his office. "Not a bad idea, Aer." He shrugged. "Who knows, maybe it'll be the best damn thing that's ever happened to you."

His words sent a wave of relief flooding over me.

I sure as hell hoped he was right.

MORE FROM MEG

The League

Scarlett & Abel - The Fantasy League

Mae & October - The Red Zone

Lea & Fortune - The Silent Count

Christmas Vacation Novellas

Aera & Elliot - Christmas in Comets Valley

Juliet & Peter - Merry in Malibu

Banks Brothers

Lyla & Barrett - The Physical Attraction Seminar

ACKNOWLEDGMENTS

To the readers, I am forever and eternally grateful to each of you for taking a chance on me and reading my debut novel (Ahhh, that still doesn't feel real to say). I hope you loved Scarlett and Abel's story as much as I do and that you stick around for many, many more books to come.

Natalie, my very best friend. If you would have responded anything other than "omg yes!!!" when I asked if I should write a book, I probably wouldn't be writing these acknowledgments right now. To this day there is no one else I would rather cry over boys on the bathroom floor with. I love you a million ways around the sun, my platonic soulmate.

To my beta reader, Gen, sending you this manuscript was one of the scariest moments of my life. Despite the fear that plagued me of someone reading my writing for the first time, it was also one of the best things I have ever done. Your passion, detail, and wealth of insight not only made this book the best version of itself but in turn, made me a better writer. Without your help, this book would still be an atrocious rough draft buried in the darkest depths of my documents folder.

My Brother's Editor, for being top-notch editing and proofreading extraordinaires. Your attention to detail is unmatched. Thank you for correcting all of my stupid mistakes and not shaming me for my excessive em dash and ellipsis usage. Let's do this a million more times, yeah?

Lucy, for making my cover dreams come true. I'm obsessed in every sense of the word. You're fantastic!

Maddie, my sister, and biggest cheerleader. Thanks for always being my biggest supporter and never letting me doubt I can't be whatever I want to be in this world. (P.S. maybe don't tell mom and dad about the last few chapters).

To The Eastern Peak, who fueled my two week spicy pad thai stint when I was so consumed in finishing this book and couldn't be bothered with going to the grocery store. You're the greatest. Love ya, mean it.

To myself — you did it, bitch!!

Thank you. Thank you. Thank you. To every person who has helped make this crazy dream that has swirled in my brain for years become a reality. There aren't enough thank you's in the world to express my gratitude.

ABOUT THE AUTHOR

Meg Reading is a contemporary romance author whose family knew she was destined to become a writer long before she did. Although, her imaginary friends and the stack of fictional stories she wrote about her middle school crushes made it kind of obvious. However, Meg was too engulfed in reading books to notice her calling, and it took her another decade to finally put down the books and start writing her own instead.

She is a self-proclaimed homebody who has two cats named Gomez and Fester. When she's not reading, writing, or procrastinating, you can find her incessantly re-watching Gilmore Girls and surviving off of copious amounts of hazelnut coffee.

Printed in Great Britain
by Amazon